THE GIRLS LEFT BEHIND

J P TOWNLEY

Copyright © J P Townley 2021

Excerpt of two verses (edited) (pages 286-287) from 'Black Swans' by "Banjo" Patterson, first published in The Sunday Mail, 22 July 1893.

First paperback edition October 2021

Typeset in Buenard

Cover design by J P Townley and Daniel Townley with stock images from:

Background photo © Gwendal Cottin / Unsplash

Little girl photo © ART_Photo_DN / Shutterstock

Stuffed rabbit photo © Marie C Fields / Shutterstock

ISBN 978-0-646-84424-4

www.jptownleyauthor.com

This story is dedicated to my beautiful girls, Ember and Jade. My inspiration, not only for this story, but for everything I do in life.

April 8

Mummy hadn't moved for two days.

Zoey stood in the bedroom doorway, peering into the darkness. Hopkins dangled beside her, one long floppy ear squeezed tight in her fist. Her shadow crept across the carpet, braver than her, up the side of the bed to where a lumpy shape lay, covered from head to toe by a thin sheet. A bruised arm dangled over the edge. Chalky grey. On the bedside table, bright green numbers on the digital clock blinked on and off, on and off, but Zoey didn't know what the numbers meant. The only sound in the house was Spongebob's cackling laugh coming from the room at the other end of the hall. Once, a long time ago, that had been one of her favourite sounds, but now she just wanted to cry. The DVD had been looping through the same four episodes for so long now.

'Mummy,' she whispered. 'Mummy, I'm hungry.'

Silence.

Zoey took a couple of wobbly steps into the room but had to stop when the smell pushed back on her. So strong it scraped the roof of her mouth. Tears tickled her cheeks.

'Mummy,' she sobbed. 'Where's Daddy?'

Silence.

Zoey backed out of the room and scampered down the hallway. She hurried past the lounge room where Spongebob was chasing a jellyfish with a net and went into the dining room. From the big window behind the table, she had the best view of the street. Every day she would stand there and look out, waiting for Daddy's little red car to come around the corner while Mummy set the table behind her. Every day he would flash his headlights at her and she would shout 'Daddy's home!' and run giggling to hide under a blanket or the kitchen table.

But Daddy hadn't come home.

Now when she looked out the big window, all she could see was the big, black car, its front end crumpled against the telephone pole outside, its door wide open, just as it had been for days.

Zoey stood there, waiting with her hands and nose pressed against the glass, until the Spongebob DVD returned to the title menu and then eventually began to play through again. The world on the other side of the glass was silent and cold. She sat down on the carpet and took a handful of Froot Loops from the box that lay beside her. There wasn't much left now, just the broken bits and sugary powder that came out in the last bowl. That had always been her favourite part. She'd already eaten all the biscuits and chips from the pantry, Daddy's Weet-Bix, a carrot and even some raw spaghetti. By dragging a chair from the dining room, she could reach the second shelf that had the chocolates and nuts. Those were all gone now, not that there had been much left to begin with, and although she'd pulled and pulled on the fridge door, it wouldn't let her in. When she was thirsty, she pushed the chair over to the sink and drank from the thin stream that trickled out of the tap.

Licking the coloured powder from her fingers, she lay her head down on Hopkins' soft body and soon fell asleep.

A sound from outside pulled Zoey from her dreams. She sat up and rubbed her eyes. Three Froot Loops that clung to her face fell silently, one after the other, to the carpet leaving red imprints in her cheek. Daddy? The sound was some sort of engine, but it was too loud to be Daddy's car. Too deep and angry, like a lion's growl.

It was dark now, inside and out, but there was a light moving in the street, making long shadows of the trees and telephone poles. The sound grew louder until a single, dazzling headlight burst around the corner. Zoey was blinded by the light and clamped her eyes tightly shut. The growl stopped outside the window and died down to a stuttering purr. Then a rush of footsteps, a loud voice.

'Lisa!'

Someone was hammering on the door.

'Lisa! If you're in there, open the door!'

The noise stopped for a moment while the voice talked to itself quietly.

'Please, tell me you got out of here. Got far away. Please. Please. Please...'

Zoey clutched the curtain with one hand and tried to see the man at the door, but the light from the thing on the lawn was still shining straight at her and she could only make out the big dark shape of him.

'Lisa! Mark?' The hammering began again, and the man said some angry-sounding words that Zoey didn't understand. 'I'm coming in, okay?'

There was silence for a moment, then the smash of breaking glass. Zoey knew that was a bad sound. Once, when he was putting away the dishes, Daddy had dropped one of Mummy's favourite glasses and it sounded just like that. Mummy had shouted at Daddy and then Daddy shouted back at Mummy and then they didn't talk to each other for a long time. She had been very frightened then, too, but this time it was worse.

The front door clicked, flew open with a bang, then heavy boots were stomping through the house. Zoey hid behind the curtain.

'Lisa!'

The footsteps went down to Mummy's room and stopped. It was quiet for a while. Then a long scream, starting out like a howl and becoming a roar, came thundering down the hallway. Zoey drew the curtain tightly around her as her insides trembled.

Something crashed. It sounded like the man had picked up a chair and was slamming it again and again into the walls and floor, shouting with each crash. 'Son. Of. A...' The last word was drowned out by a terrible smash, as he threw something through the big window in Mummy's room.

Zoey scrunched her eyes closed and pressed her hands to her ears. For a while it was quiet again, but when she lowered her hands, she could hear an occasional loud sniff or a sob.

The man shouted, taking to himself again. 'I won't do it! Not again! Not Lisa...'

The bedroom door clicked gently shut, and the footsteps came back down the hall towards her. She was only partly hidden by the curtain when the man entered the room, but he still didn't see her. His steps were slow and his eyes dark and wet.

Zoey thought he looked like a dirty Santa Claus, dressed in

black. He wore a leather vest over a stained, white t-shirt that had a picture of a skull on it and was stretched to its limit over his bulging belly. His arms were thick, hairy, and covered with drawings, and while Santa's beard was fluffy and white, this man's was a greyish brown and looked as scratchy as steel wool.

The man leaned his back against the wall and slid heavily down to the floor where he bowed his head.

Zoey stood and watched him for a long time. She still didn't know who he was, but somehow he didn't seem as scary anymore. His body shook silently as he cried.

Slowly, she stepped out from behind the curtain and felt around for Hopkins, while keeping her eyes on the dirty Santa. She took a few steps toward him, but he didn't look up. It was only when she was right beside him that he seemed to notice her. When he raised his head to look at her, his face was blank. Slowly, slowly, a look of confusion washed over him. After a moment it became a look of understanding and his body collapsed a little further.

Zoey held Hopkins out to the man. When she was feeling sad, Hopkins could always help to cheer her up. The man took the bunny and turned his puffy, bloodshot eyes from Hopkins to her and back again. Then he said another word that Zoey didn't understand.

'You must be Zoey,' he said. 'You've grown a bit since I saw you last. Heck, you were only a few days old then.'

Zoey stared back at him.

'I'm your uncle Barry, but everyone calls me Bear.'

He held out a giant, brown hand for her to shake, but she just continued to stare at him until he lowered it again.

'Guess your mum told you not to talk to strangers. Good girl.

Here, let me show you something.'

He leaned to one side and pulled his wallet out of his back pocket. From the space in the middle, he took a small, folded photo.

'See, that's me, and your mum, and your uncle Jay.' He tapped the photo a few times.

'Mummy...' Zoey said, recognising her. She recognised the dirty Santa man too, even though his beard and his tummy were much smaller in the photo. Standing between them with an arm draped around each of their necks was another man. He was even bigger than this man, but his face was mostly hidden by the white, crumbling fold down the middle.

She looked up at Bear. She didn't know what 'uncle' meant, but he knew her Mummy and somehow he wasn't scary anymore.

'Mummy won't wake up,' she said.

He nodded, opened his mouth to say something, looked away instead.

'I'm hungry,' she said.

Bear smiled and handed Hopkins back to her.

'Are ya? Me too. Let's see what we can find, eh?'

With one last great sniff and a tired groan, he stood up. As he started to walk to the kitchen, Zoey spoke up again.

'Mummy said...someone would be coming. We have to go soon, don't we? Mummy said we would.'

Bear stopped in his tracks and his head drooped again. He shook it, sadly.

'You're a smart cookie, just like Lisa. That's right, little miss. We'll go soon, but let's eat something first, okay?'

Zoey nodded and followed him into the kitchen.

* * *

'Sorry, I haven't got a kiddie seat or anything,' Bear said as he stuffed her pink backpack full of clothes into one of the pouches on the side of the motorbikyle. He hoisted her onto the seat. Shiny handlebars stretched over her head like the tusks of a silver elephant. The plastic clip of her pink bike helmet pressed uncomfortably into her chin.

The bike dipped as he lowered his weight onto it. He placed a sofa cushion between them for her to lean against. 'Comfy?' he asked her.

She nodded and squeezed Hopkins tightly against her chest.

'Let's see... seat belt...' He squirmed behind her, removed his belt, wrapped it around her waist and threaded back through the loops on the front of his jeans. Zoey was pulled back a little into the cushion as he secured the buckle.

'This'll have to do for now,' Bear mumbled. 'Stevo's Road King has a side car...not too far...should make it if we take it slow. Would've been better to stay here until morning, but by then Lisa might be...'

He sniffed again as he looked up at the house. Then he switched something on the side of the bike and turned the key. The engine roared to life.

Zoey had forgotten how loud it was, and the shock almost sent her tumbling off onto the lawn, but the belt and one of Bear's big, hairy arms held onto her.

The bike rolled slowly backwards as he walked it down the driveway and into the road. Zoey's eyes never left her house. Fragments of glass on the ground outside her parents' bedroom twinkled like little stars as the headlight swept across the lawn.

Mummy came to the window and watched them go. She seemed to be smiling, clicking her teeth together slowly, and

7

jerking her head up now and then. She swayed from side to side.

Zoey wanted to jump down and run to her side, but she knew she couldn't do that. Mummy was always cranky when she woke up from her naps, so instead Zoey just raised her hand and waved. Mummy didn't wave back.

Bear swung the bike slowly out into the road, pointed them down the hill and began threading his way through the abandoned cars, as they broke their way, rumbling and growling, through the silent streets.

March 1
(5 weeks earlier)

There was someone outside her window.

Merry glanced at the clock. 3:47am. Whoever it was had been out there for almost half an hour. Taking little shuffling steps across the lawn, stopping for a minute or two to cough and gasp, then shuffling around some more.

At first she'd thought it was just the quiet rustling of a mouse or rabbit through the flowers. Then, perhaps a possum scampering across the lawn. One time a few years ago Mr Harrison's sheep had escaped and made a midnight snack of Mum's geraniums, and freaked her right out, but even that hadn't sounded anything like this.

She'd been in bed with a fever for a few days, and while her pounding head struggled to follow a logical train of thought, it had no trouble parading a cast of hoodlums through her mind. An escaped lunatic, pacing back and forth with a rusty knife in hand, ready to snap at any second. Escaped from where? Unimportant. Or maybe a drug addict with a used syringe, stoned off his face. Shivers. She'd hardly taken a breath in the last thirty minutes. She wanted desperately to dash down the hall and jump into Mum's bed, but she was thirteen now, she wasn't a baby, so instead she just drew the covers tighter under her chin and stared at the ceiling. What was that saying? The only thing to fear was fear itself? Maybe fear and murderers...

She looked over at her sister's empty bed, wishing Claire were here. Claire would have no problem opening up the window and telling whoever was out there to 'eff right off'. But she was spending the night at a friend's house.

The quiet electric buzz from the clock radio seemed to grow louder and louder, but now there was nothing from outside. Had they gone? Had she imagined it all? A nightmare, maybe, brought on by her fever? That had to be it. Just last night she'd dreamt she was a jellybean farmer from Peru and woke up demanding to know who'd taken her watering-can full of Fanta.

Sure, another fever dream, that's all this was. There was nobody outside. She swallowed, suddenly dry in the throat, and sweating all over. With a surge of courage, she sat up and listened. Nothing. She pushed the covers down to her ankles in one quick movement. Her muscles tensed as she peered over she edge of the bed, then she leaped to the rug in the middle of the room—she knew it was completely illogical that there'd be someone under her bed waiting to grab her exposed ankle, but it was better to be safe than sorry. She fought a wave of dizziness, then spun and faced the window, part of her expecting to see the curtains part, and a hand enter, waving a knife or syringe at her. But of course there was nothing there.

Merry's feet padded softly on the carpet as she crept down the hall, keeping to the right to avoid the creaky floorboards. The kitchen was just as silent as the rest of the house. She flipped on the light and took a glass from the cupboard, filled it with water from the tap. As she stood by the sink sipping her water, she tried to slow her thumping heart.

The latch on the glass sliding door clicked, and the door slid open just enough for a hand to slip in around the doorframe. Merry squeaked and dropped the glass into the sink where it shattered. Another hand appeared and prised the heavy door open.

'Taxi!' Came a voice from the just outside, followed by a burst of sputtering laughter. Her sister's frizzy blonde head appeared. 'Go home, Merry, you're drunk.'

'Claire! Shivers. What are you doing here?'

Claire laughed again as she tried to close the door behind her. 'Shivers,' she mocked. 'I think you mean...shiiiit. Was that one of the good glasses?'

Her words tripped over each other, like she couldn't be bothered opening her mouth all the way.

'Are you...drunk?'

Claire grinned and held a finger to her lips.

'No, you shush,' Merry whispered, hugging her elbows. 'You're going to wake everyone up.' She should have known it was Claire. That must have been her out on the lawn, drinking with Rachel, trying to scare her.

'Pshaw, I won't make a sound. I'm a fuckin' ninja—' As she came toward Merry, her foot caught the edge of the rubbish bin, toppling it to the floor, and sending a cascade of rubbish across the kitchen. Claire snorted a laugh, then shrugged and took one extra-long step over it, holding onto the counter for balance.

'You can't just leave that there. Mum'll kill you.'

'I'll do it in the morning, before she wakes up.'

'As if. You won't be up before noon.' With a sigh, Merry walked around the counter, righted the bin, and started picking up the rubbish. 'And just so you know, I wasn't scared.'

She heard the clink of a glass, then the running tap and Claire gulping down huge mouthfuls of water. 'As if you weren't scared. No, you dropped that glass to test its durability.'

'I mean before. I knew all along it was just you and Rachel outside my window.'

'Haha, the frig you talking about? Have you been having more of your trippy dreams?'

Merry glanced sideways at her, trying to read her sister's expression to tell if she was still messing with her. It wasn't easy because with one eye half-closed, Claire's expression was something like a drunk baby trying to pass wind. 'You and Rachel...you were walking around outside my window.'

'I'm not retarded. It's like pitch black and freezing out there. And...' She squinted and looked down her nose at Merry, swaying a little, '...if you must know, the slut, formerly known as Rachel, is also now formerly my friend, since she ditched me to hang out with Douchebag Darren...'

Merry stopped listening as a chill ran through her. If it wasn't Claire, then she must have dreamed it, right? She glanced at the window—wait!—did something just move by it? It was too dark to tell.

'...and I was the one that got the drinks. Two whole bags of goon, man. Had to let Mike O'Neil's pervy brother touch my boob and everything. I tell you, you can't buy good friends these days—'

'Shh. Shut up, will you?'

'Geez, everyone's a bitch tonight...'

The hairs stood up on her arm as she heard a soft scrape on the concrete step outside. It was followed by a dreadful bang, as someone crashed into the glass door, rattling it in its frame.

'Holy shit!' Claire cried.

The body rested against the doorframe for a moment, filling the kitchen with its short, haggard breaths. Then one small, strained word. 'Help...'

Slowly, the door slid open, and a man in a blood-stained singlet stepped in, his head drooping low against his chest. As he lifted his head and turned it towards them, Merry gasped.

'Mr Harrison...'

Their elderly neighbour tried to speak again, but was overcome by a coughing fit. Hacking, he clutched at his stomach, and Merry noticed speckles of blood spraying from his mouth onto the linoleum. He looked up at them and she saw blood filling the whites of his eyes. One side of his neck had ballooned out in some sort of bruised growth, netted with blue veins. He took another step towards them, reaching a hand out.

'Oh, Christ,' Claire muttered. She staggered around the counter and pulled Merry back, holding a hand protectively across her chest.

'Wa...ter.' Mr Harrison took several more lunging steps towards them before tipping forward, raking his fingernails down Claire's bare legs. The man's nails peeled back like they'd been held there with nothing more than bubble gum, exposing the blackened, macerated flesh beneath. Claire tripped over the pile of rubbish that still littered much of the floor and they both watched in wide-eyed terror as the old man clawed at his throat, heaved his last few breaths, then lay still.

March 2

She didn't remember much after Mr Harrison dropped dead in their kitchen. Mum was in there pretty quick, dragging them out of the room, checking Mr Harrison for signs of life, asking them over and over what had happened. Merry must have fallen asleep eventually because the next thing she remembered was waking up on the couch with her head on Claire's lap, listening to muffled voices talking in the kitchen.

'The police have already been. That's someone from the hospital, I think,' Claire whispered to her. 'Said they wanted to talk to us both as soon as you woke up.'

'Where are Kate and Dana?'

'Mum told the lil' turds to stay in the back room. They're too young to understand any of this. They're fine, though. She put Spongebob on, so the world could crumble around them and they wouldn't notice.'

Merry tucked her knees into her chest. 'Don't tell Mum I'm awake just yet,' she said. 'Let's pretend it was a bad dream. Just for a bit.'

That poor old man, begging her for water. It was all too horrible to think about.

'Sure.'

Merry closed her eyes while Claire stroked her hair. Her sister's stomach grumbled loudly, and Merry looked up at her. 'How are you feeling, anyway?'

Claire chortled. 'Eh, like a bear sat on my head and took a crap in my mouth. Here, taste...' She burped under her breath and blew it into Merry's face, and Merry could smell the cheap alcohol mixed with corn chips and sick.

She gagged and covered her face with her hands. 'You're disgusting. How does all this not bother you?'

Claire shifted on the couch. 'Who says it doesn't? But crying about something doesn't change it. You know what you need to do? Just smile—'

'Don't say it—'

Claire grinned. 'Just smile and be Merry.'

'I hate you. Let's get this over with.'

The woman sitting with their mother was wearing a face mask that covered her nose and mouth, and was awkwardly nursing a mug of tea. As Merry and Claire entered, she raised the mug halfway to her mouth, seemed to suddenly remember she was wearing a mask, and quickly lowered it again, spilling some tea on the plastic-covered tablecloth. Her hair, which had been drawn back in a tight ponytail, was being undone by the March heat.

'Meredith, precious, how are you feeling?' Her mum almost knocked her chair over as she jumped up.

'Fine.' Merry managed a weak smile as her mum held her by

the sides of the head and examined her, kissing her twice on the forehead once she was satisfied there were no injuries. 'I'm fine, Mum.' Her smile quickly faded as she turned to study the other woman. She was watching Merry and Claire with an almost fearful look in her eyes—eyes which kept darting to the scratches on Claire's legs. Mum had clearly washed them and dabbed on some iodine cream, making them look much worse than they were.

'This is Miss, uh…sorry,' Mum started.

'Please, call me Joan.' Her voice was muffled by the mask. She made no attempt to shake their hands. 'I'm from the Health Service. I'm so sorry to hear what happened,' she said in a voice that sounded sorry only to be trapped in their tiny, sweltering kitchen.

When nobody else said anything, she continued. 'It must have been traumatising. I know you'd probably like to forget the whole thing, but I'm afraid I need to ask you some questions.'

Claire shrugged and leaned against the counter, still looking very pale. Merry chose a seat at the table next to Mum.

'Can you describe his symptoms?'

'Sure,' Claire said. 'He looked like a zombie.'

'Claire,' Mum warned. 'This is serious.'

'What do you want me to say? He staggered in here, spit blood all over the place, and fell down. Oh, and he scratched me with his gimpy fingernails.'

The woman from the Health Service jotted something down on her notepad.

'Make sure you get that part,' Claire said. 'Fingernails. Gimpy.'

'Do you know what was wrong with him?' Mum asked. 'Was it that new virus they're talking about, is that why you're here?'

'We're still looking into that. It'll take some time to run the tests.'

'I thought that was only happening in Asia. They stopped all the flights.'

Joan, clearly uncomfortable with the new direction of the conversation, cleared her throat. 'And did any of you see or talk to Mr Harrison recently?'

'He doesn't socialise much...uh, didn't socialise much,' Mum corrected herself. 'Kept to himself since his wife passed a few years ago. We see him out in his garden sometimes, or at the store. Occasionally we'd buy eggs from him if he had them, but I hadn't seen him in town for, oh, some weeks. Girls?'

'Nope.' Claire's answer was blunt, making it clear that she wanted to be done with this as soon as possible. But Merry remembered something.

'I saw him...' Even to herself she sounded timid, almost apologetic. 'He was in the Milk Bar, looking at cans of dog food. He wasn't wearing a shirt, either. I remember thinking it was weird, because he only keeps a few chickens. No dog...I think, anyway...'

'And how did he seem?'

'Confused...I asked him if he was alright, but he just stared at me for a bit, then he walked off.'

Joan didn't look up from her notepad. 'When did you say this was?'

'Um...a few weeks ago. Right before...I got sick...'

The scratching pen stopped dead, and the woman adjusted her mask. 'You're sick, did you say?'

'Just the flu...I'm feeling better.' She had been feeling better, hadn't she? But what if that was part of it? What if she was about to die the same way Mr Harrison did? She looked to her mum for reassurance.

Her mother put a hand on her arm and glared at the woman. 'Meredith has been in bed for a few days, but like she said, it was the flu.'

'I'm sure you're right,' Joan said, but her eyes, and the way her hands wrung tighter around the mug, told a different story. 'But...'

She tapped her fingertips together and Merry had the impression she was choosing her next words carefully. 'Would you be willing to bring Meredith to the Royal Adelaide for observation? They've got a dedicated quarantine ward set up to monitor suspicious cases...'

'Quarantine?' Mum's voice, which was usually so calming, had taken an edge, like a swordsman from one of Claire's samurai movies thumbing his sword out just an inch—a warning that heads were about to roll. 'You want me to take my perfectly healthy daughter, who just witnessed a man die, to a hospital almost three hours away and lock her up with a bunch of people you think might be infected with this unknown, but fatal, disease?'

The woman tried to laugh it off. 'Well, I wouldn't put it that way.' She mumbled something about taking every possible precaution and the best available medical care as she studied the pattern on the tablecloth and twisted her pen almost in half.

Mum let her squirm.

'Do you have children, Joan?'

The woman shook her head.

'Well, I was trained as a nurse. And as a mother, my children will receive the best possible care right here, at home. So you can write in your little notebook that we will self-quarantine in this house to prevent any possible community transmission, but I will not subject them to any more traumatic experiences today.

'So, if you've finished frightening my girls, and if you're quite done with your tea, I think it's time for you to leave.'

She stood up abruptly, and snatched the still-full mug of tea from Joan's hands, dousing the woman's notebook in the process.

Joan took the hint. She scrambled from her chair, dabbing her notebook with a handkerchief. 'Well then, uh...I'm very sorry to have upset you. Someone will be in touch over the next few days to check up on you...'

Claire hopped off the counter, edged past Mum—who gripped the back of her chair so tightly her knuckles were white—and addressed Joan with a wide grin. 'I'll show you out.'

It took just over a week for the world to realise how underprepared it was. International flights were suspended only after the virus had already spread to every corner of the globe. Anyone with symptoms was ordered to stay at home, though the virus was most contagious before symptoms developed. Social distancing and face masks did little slow the spread of what was being called the splinter virus—so called because in the beginning it seemed appropriate to name a mutated rodent flu strain after a fictional mutant rat; because, in the beginning, it was just another warning that everyone would forget about when the next emergency came along to knock it off the front page; because most people thought it was as fictional as its namesake.

The trickle of new details quickly became a flood of paranoia and misinformation, but while many still denied its existence, and others were panic-buying half the grocery store, the splinter virus quietly spread. Being airborne, with a long incubation period and a mortality rate estimated at more than 99%, there was no stopping it.

A week after the Government declared a state of emergency, Mum and Claire got sick. Along with half the country.

Efforts to contain the illness hadn't been successful, the news said. Hospitals were overwhelmed and the death toll soared. The reports got so bad that Mum told them all to leave the TV and radio off. In the space of just a few weeks, everything changed.

Merry folded the wet washcloth and laid it across Claire's forehead, pressing it slightly so that little rivers trickled over her temples. Even without touching her, she could feel the heat radiating off her sister's head. Claire moaned softly and opened her eyes.

'Can I get you anything else?' Merry whispered.

'How's Mum?'

'She's okay,' Merry lied. 'Getting better.'

'And the lil' turds?'

'Mmhmm.' She couldn't bear to tell her Kate and Dana had both taken fevers too. At only seven years old, the twins had gone downhill quickly. The antibiotics the doctor gave her on his last visit had done nothing, and now she couldn't even reach him on the phone. The only thing that helped were the anti-anxiety tablets, which put them to sleep. Her eyes blurred, but she fought back the tears.

'I don't want to die, Merry,' Claire whispered. 'Not like he did. Not all covered in blood and shit like that. I was supposed to go out in a blaze of glory...' She licked her cracked lips. 'I'm so goddamn thirsty.'

'Nobody's going to die,' Merry said, as she held a bottle of water to her sister's mouth. The lie came out as a reflex, some foreign script of optimism that had long since lost any meaning. Because her mind screamed the opposite. Everyone is going to die.

April 5

Merry's shoes scuffed through the red dirt along the road that led
to town. Over one shoulder she carried her empty school bag.

The north wind that had scorched the town and pelted the
houses with dust for the last few days was beginning to break,
and on the horizon she could see a deep blue mass of storm
clouds gathering. Already she could smell the cool scent of
approaching rain. Though she tried to suppress the thought, she
wondered if the real reason she was out here wasn't just to
scrounge supplies—maybe, more than anything, she needed to
escape that house. Escape the suffering and the smell of sickness.
And the moaning. And the nightmares. And all of it. She wanted
so badly just to keep walking and never go back. Mum. Dana.
Kate. Claire. She didn't want to see them as they were now—at
the end. She didn't want this to be the way she remembered
them. Yellowed and sunken with disease. What difference would
it make if she went back or not? They would die, just like Mr
Harrison had, no matter what she did, no matter who was there
to watch them do it.

Guilt gripped her by the throat and for a moment she thought she was going to throw up right there on the side of the road. She doubled over and held her knees, gasping. It doesn't matter that there's nothing you can do, she told herself. You just need to be there with them.

After a few deep breaths, she found that she could go on, and so she straightened and continued walking.

It was amazing how quickly the world had emptied. She walked by the turf farm, where huge rolls of still-green grass, all set to become someone's lawn, sat abandoned in the empty field.

On Wigun road, she passed house after empty house, all with their front shades drawn, the only sounds the creaks and twangs of corrugated tin verandahs as they relaxed in the cooling air, and the blare of cicadas. On the corner a postbox, filled with letters that would go forever unread. Perhaps only a few days ago some of them had been important.

Even McKinnon Street, which marked the centre of town and contained the milk bar, supermarket, butcher, bakery, bottle shop, the pharmacy and the post office, and which was usually full of familiar faces, was all but deserted. A few cars had been left, presumably abandoned, on the grassy median strip between the eucalypts that divided the east and west facing lanes. The traffic lights at the middle intersection blinked amber.

A rusty Holden Commodore idled out the front of the bottle shop, one back wheel mounted on the curb. There was no mistaking the large yellow bumper sticker on the back that read: "Caution, this vehicle stops frequently (at your mum's house)."

Douchebag Darren.

She could see three figures in the back seat. Normally, she'd cross the street to avoid Darren and his stupid mates, and their stupid jokes about whether she'd "gotten her tits yet", but she was just too exhausted to care. She kept her head down and tried to hurry past, but as she did, two people burst through the bottle shop's plastic fly curtain and almost collided with her.

'Merry?'

Rachel was carrying a huge carton of cigarettes under each arm. Darren, wearing his trademark blue beanie that Merry thought his parents must have glued to his head as a child, hung to the side, shifting awkwardly with a slab of beer resting on one shoulder.

As she looked closer, she noticed Rachel's puffy eyes, and the streaks of mascara down her cheeks.

'Shit, Merry…how are you? How's Claire? Is she…?'

Merry stared at her for a moment. How could she answer? She's fine? She's been better? There's a good chance she'll be dead by time I get home? 'She's…uh…not good…'

'…Yeah,' Rachel said, as though she could read it all on her face, and thankfully didn't press her any more on the subject. 'So listen, me and the guys are getting the hell out of here. Shit's crazy. Everyone's fucken dying.' She shook her head and lowered her voice. 'Not just that. They reckon some of them what got sick go insane. Like, seriously aggro. Their brains get fried or some shit, and they just start attacking anyone around them.'

Merry had heard rumours like this. At first, she hadn't put much stock in them, but just last night, during a quiet moment between the moans and delirious cries of her mum and sisters, she'd heard someone walking past their property, making the strangest sound. It was almost like a laugh, but there was no humour in it. A high-pitched, dry cackle was the best way she could describe it. Like someone had filled a cane toad with helium. She'd spent two terrifying hours before dawn by the window in the dining room, peering through a slit in the curtains, with a cricket bat gripped tight in her hands, waiting, but whoever it was hadn't returned.

'We're getting out of this town while we can. Shannon knows this abandoned place out near Franklyn. We could squeeze you in if you want, right Daz?'

Darren re-positioned the slab of beer, holding it against his chest. 'Um…car's pretty full, babe…'

Rachel shot him an icy stare.

'Whatever, sure, I guess. The more the merrier…uh, no pun intended…'

Merry shook her head quickly. The thought of climbing into a car with Darren and his friends made her want to throw up. 'No,' she said, pushing past them. 'No thank-you. I have to go.'

'Merry, you can't stay here…'

But Merry didn't look back.

The pharmacy looked like it had been hit by a hurricane. Panic buying had seen the shelves quickly emptied of all the essentials, but items which were of little interest to those desperately seeking some sort of cure or relief now lay strewn across the aisles. A couple of the shelves had been toppled, gouging holes in the plaster walls, and Merry had to wade through a river of perfumes, sunscreens, insect repellents, head-lice treatments and birth control to reach the dispensary at the back. She took the empty medicine carton from her pocket and carefully studied the name of the active ingredient: Chlorpromazine.

During her last visit, just a few days ago, the place had been crowded, with a line out the door, people shouting, shoving, coughing. Desperation turned neighbour against neighbour as they demanded to be given something, anything, that would help. Poor Mr Lu, the pharmacist, had retreated out the back as the boldest among them hopped the counter and started helping themselves to the prescription medicines. Since then, however, it seemed that practically everyone had either left town, or fallen too ill to venture out of the house.

As she squeezed behind the counter and saw that it had been all but stripped bare, her hopes of finding anything quickly deflated. She crouched, picking through the mess of scattered papers, broken glass and empty pill bottles. The handful that remained gave no indication of what they were for, and none of the drug names meant anything to her. She shoved them into her bag, anyway. Her mother had some old medical books from when she'd worked as a nurse. Maybe if she could figure out what these drugs were for, there was a slim chance...

Slow footsteps on the pavement outside turned her rigid. Keeping low, she inched closer to the counter until her back was pressed against it. The footsteps dampened as they entered the pharmacy and she heard a long sigh. Someone began picking through the items scattered on the floor, now and then stopping to stuff something into a zippered bag.

She wasn't sure why she felt the need to hide, exactly. The place was abandoned, the whole town was pretty much deserted, all laws and boundaries of society forgotten, but still, being discovered here, in the pharmacy, looting... It was impossible to shake the years of lectures from her mother about right and wrong, and how important it was to follow the rules. Not for the first time, she wished she could be more like Claire. Claire wouldn't be hiding here like a scared little mouse. She'd just sling her backpack over her shoulder and stroll out, bold as brass, probably pausing only to flip them the bird.

Merry smiled at the thought, but the smile quickly faded as she remembered how she'd left her sister—wrapped in a sweat-stained sheet with a sick bucket by her head. Claire and the others needed her. She didn't have time to hide. Before she could talk herself out of it, she stood up and turned to face whoever had come to judge her.

He was standing by the door carrying a blue duffel bag in one hand, surveying the pharmacy. When Merry stood up, she saw a flash of surprise on his face, but it was gone in an instant. Mr Blake, manager of Campbell's Foodmart across the street.

'Meredith. Hello. I didn't know you were in here.' He looked away briefly, as though he'd walked in on her in the bathroom.

'I...Mum and my sisters aren't well. I was just looking for something to help them,' she mumbled.

He fixed her with a long stare, bringing one finger slowly to his lips. Being under his gaze—those small, piercing eyes and his expression that gave nothing away—made her uncomfortable. Absently, he stroked his moustache with the back of his thumb.

'I'm very sorry to hear that.'

Merry shrugged. 'Well...' She rounded the counter and started picking her way back down the aisle. 'I need to get back—'

'Wait.'

She froze as he unzipped the bag and began searching inside.

'Here. It won't make them better, but it will help them sleep. That may be all you can do for them.'

In a few steps, he closed the distance between them and handed her a bottle of pills. Triazolam.

'Th-thank you.'

'I would do more if I could. Much more. You know I've always admired your mother. Such a strong woman. Raising four girls alone...' He glanced backward across the street. 'I've moved into the Foodmart. It's more secure there. If there's anything else you need, you can find me there.' He gave her a concerned nod, then quickly exited.

Merry let out the breath she didn't realise she'd been holding, looped both arms through the straps of her bag, and hurried back into the street.

The house appeared just as she'd left it, dark and silent, but as Merry reached for her keys to unlock the door there was the soft thud of something heavy falling onto the carpet.

'What the...'

She flung open the door and started down the hall. It took a few moments for her eyes to adjust to the darkness, and as she steadied herself with an arm against the wall, she listened intently.

'Mum?'

She checked on Claire first, since theirs was the first room she passed. The door was closed, and there was no sound from within. When she nudged the door open wide enough to peer around, she saw her sister lying in bed, fast asleep, her chest rising and falling sharply. Was it her imagination, or had some of the colour returned to her face? Not wanting to wake her, she slipped her backpack off her shoulders and set it gently just inside the room, then pulled the door closed and headed down the hall to the twins' room.

She stopped short. The door was ajar. She could have sworn she'd closed all the bedroom doors before she went out. She had, hadn't she? But surely Kate and Dana were too sick to get up and go walking around. She must have been mistaken about closing it. Or perhaps a draft had blown it open? A sense of dread crept through her body, a voice that would not be ignored, screaming that something was dreadfully wrong. With a sense of foreboding she couldn't shake, Merry pushed open the door.

April 8

They rode slowly through the streets, but even then the cold wind hurt Zoey's eyes and so she kept them closed most of the time. That wasn't the only reason she kept them closed, though. There were lots of crashed cars or cars just parked in the middle of the road and some of them still had people in them, but the people weren't moving or trying to get out. She wished she could close her ears, too. The sound of Uncle Bear's bike made it difficult to hear anything else, but sometimes when he had to slow down or go up onto the footpath because there was a telephone pole in the road she could hear other sounds. Loud bangs, people shouting, or worst of all, people laughing. She couldn't think why anyone would be laughing like that, in the dark, when everything else was so silent.

It wasn't long before she saw one of them. A laugher. He was standing in the front yard of one of the houses they passed, his legs pressed up against the wire fence, watching them with wide eyes. His head was tilted a little to the side, and he was grinning, clicking his teeth together. His laugh was like some sort of animal sound. It reminded her of her cousin's dog. She was a tiny thing covered in yellow fluff that was turning white as she got older. Her cousin Russell called her Cujo and laughed every time he said her name, but Zoey didn't understand the joke. Her daddy called it a purse rat. Once, Russell had taken her into their basement and said he wanted to show her something funny the dog could do. Cujo had just finished eating, and Russell picked her up and squeezed her really hard in the tummy three times. Cujo yelped at first, then started making a wheezing noise. First one long wheeze, then lots of small gasps, then another long wheeze. Russell said she was laughing. He thought it was very funny, but Zoey hated him for it. Eventually, Cujo waddled into the corner and threw up, then ate it again. Russell found that even funnier. Zoey was glad when, a few weeks later, Cujo bit Russell on the chin after he'd been pulling faces at her and he had to get stitches, but she didn't see Cujo anymore after that.

The wheezing, gasping sound this man was making was just like Cujo. Like someone was squeezing the laugh out of him. Uncle Bear put a hand around her and rubbed her shoulder and said, 'Just look away, sweetie.'

Eventually, they stopped. Zoey had been starting to doze, but she woke to the sudden silence as the bike's engine shut off. They had parked across the street from a house with lots of other motorbikyles in the front yard. In the dark they looked like a sleeping herd of sheep but Zoey thought that if they were sheep, they would probably go somewhere else because there wasn't much grass on the lawn and what little there was was full of broken bottles and take-away wrappers. Not far from them, in the middle of the street, two cars hugged each other, surrounded by tiny pieces of glass that glittered like diamonds in the moonlight. There was something else glittering on the road, too. Something red and dark, like wet paint, making a trail from one of the cars, past the bikes and into the house.

Uncle Bear pulled off his helmet, wiped his eyes on the back of his arm and ran a hand through his tangled beard. He sat for a long time just staring at the house across the street. At last, he turned to Zoey.

'Time for a new set of wheels, little miss. First class from here on out. Get you your own seat and everything.'

He unfastened the belt that held them together and hefted her off the seat. Zoey felt his chest swell with a huge sigh, then he carried her towards the house. Glass crunched and squeaked under his heavy boots with each slow step and he turned his head constantly, looking up and down the dark street, bending to glance under the smashed cars, peering around each of the bikes on the lawn. He stopped next to a bike that looked like it had a little boat coming out its side. Still holding Zoey with one hand, he reached into the little boat and pulled out a jacket, some cans of drink and some small plastic baggies. He tossed these behind him, along with something that looked like a long, burnt lightbulb that exploded across the concrete driveway and made Zoey jump.

Next he popped open a small compartment in the front and tossed more things to the ground. Some papers, a cracked pair of sunglasses, candy wrappers and a packet of Tic Tacs. When it was empty, he slammed it closed with a growl.

'Dammit, Stevo,' he muttered. 'Since when did you start taking your keys with you. Son of a b—' He glanced at Zoey. '...Bucket.'

Bear squeezed the bike's handlebar several times, looking from the house to the bike and back across the road to his own bike.

'Dammit,' he said again. He set Zoey down, standing her on the side of the bike so they were eye to eye. 'I need to…go inside for a bit. Find a friend of mine.'

Zoey's eyes widened, and she suddenly realised she had to go to the bathroom.

'I can't take you in with me, so you'll have to…' he thought for a moment. 'What we're gonna do is play hide and seek, okay? You ever play hide and seek with your mum and dad?'

Zoey nodded. But she didn't want to play hide and seek. It frightened her, being alone. When Mummy and Daddy told her to go and hide, it usually meant they wanted to fight. They would shout and scream at each other for a while and then she would hear them bouncing on the bed and usually after that they forgot to look for her and she would sit in her dark closet for hours.

'Well, you can hide in here, I'll put this jacket over you, and you stay quiet as a mouse so that nobody will be able to find you.'

Zoey tucked her legs in as he lowered her into the little boat. 'But you'll bemember where I am, won't you?' she asked in a tiny voice.

''Course I will,' he said. 'I'll come find you just as soon as I can. I promise. Can you and bunny stay just as quiet and still as two little mice until I get back?'

Zoey nodded, looking at her knees.

Bear rested one of his hands on her head. It was rough and heavy, but also warm, and she felt safe for a very small moment. Then he took off his jacket and tucked it carefully over her head, and Zoey was left alone in the dark.

The air in her tiny boat smelled like burnt caramel and sick cats. Her finger found a hole in the padded seat beneath her and she started picking out the fluff. Her other hand was pressed between her legs so that she wouldn't have an accident. She really had to go potty. Uncle Bear had been gone a long time. She'd heard the front door creak open, and his heavy footsteps on the wooden floors inside. A little while ago there'd been a loud scraping followed by a bang, as if something really big had been pushed over, but she hadn't heard anything since then. Just someone laughing and gasping a few streets away.

She started to fidget, bouncing her knees up and down and humming quietly to herself to keep her mind off the laughter and the stinging pain that was growing just below her tummy. She hummed twinkle twinkle little star, then the itchy bitsy spider, and she was just about to ask Hopkins what to sing next when she heard something else. A noise from very close by.

It started with a sprinkling of glass. Then the creak of a car door. The creak became a metallic groan, and she heard more glass raining down as the jammed door was forced open. There was a deep thud, crunching, scraping as someone fell into the road and started dragging themselves across the street towards her. Zoey held her breath and squeezed her legs together as tightly as she could. She could hear the person gasping and grunting now. She tried to hope that somehow it was Uncle Bear, that somehow she hadn't heard him coming back out of the house, but she knew these sounds—the rasping breaths, the muttering voice, the stumbling footsteps—couldn't be his sounds.

In the darkness, her mind showed her the laughing man pressed against the fence. It showed her her mother, whose lips, normally so full and bright red, were gone, chewed away, leaving only her chattering teeth. Zoey stuck out her tongue and pinched it hard, a trick she'd taught herself when she was trying not to cry. Her hiding place shook, and something squeaked like wet hands on a bathtub. The sound was right on top of her as the person coughed and spat into the grass several times. Started to hum in a throaty, half-drowned voice.

'Hmm hmm hmm...hmm hmm hmm. Dig a hole. Take my soul. Another name down on the Devil's roll.'

Keys jingled, fell to the ground.

'Drag me down. Not a sound. Through earth and fire my life's unwound.'

There was more gasping and coughing before she heard the key finally slide home.

'Chains of stone. Cage of bone...ahhh—'

The bike choked once, twice, then rumbled to life. The man's voice mixed into the sound of the engine.

'Uncounted...unbroken...awoken...we are Legion.'

Zoey pulled the jacket tight over her head and squeezed Hopkins hard. A warm, wet patch spread down her legs. Then they bumped down the curb and swerved into the street.

April 5

A few days earlier Merry had drawn all the outdoor blinds to try to shield them from the relentless heat. Not that it made much difference. It did, however, block out most of the sunlight, which was a blessing, since it helped her mum and sisters sleep a little easier during the day. As a result, the room was in darkness, aside from the green glow that bloomed around the edges of the thick blinds. The sound of cicadas, though muffled, was still deafening in the otherwise silent house.

'Girls?' she whispered, as she stood in the doorway waiting for her eyes to adjust. 'Are you alright?'

There was no reply. Merry frowned and stepped into the room. The smell came as a surprise—it always did after she'd been outside—but she resisted the urge to cover her nose. Her foot caught on Dana's sheets, which had been flung to the floor, and she stumbled. The bed was empty.

'Dana?' She spun to check Kate's bed behind her—sometimes the twins would sleep together in the one bed, especially when one of them was ill—and found it empty as well. 'How?...' Her heart rose for a moment. If they were strong enough to get out of bed by themselves, surely they'd fought off the fever, just as she had. Thank goodness. But where had they gone? The kitchen most likely, she told herself. They'd hardly eaten in days and had to be starving—

Then she noticed the dark stains covering Kate's pillow. Big smudged splotches with stringy globs trailing between them. She knew even before she touched it and felt the sticky wetness between her fingers that it was blood.

'Oh, God. Kate? Dana?' Her voice rose in a quivering panic. Shivers. Someone's broken in. They've taken the girls. Mum. Wake Mum. She'll know what to do.

Merry staggered from the room and bounded down the corridor to her mum's room. The door was wide open and inside was as dark as all the others.

'Mum! Dana and Kate are gone! Someone's—'

The sight in her mother's bedroom struck the words from her like a slap to the face. Something came loose between her brain and the rest of her body. She couldn't comprehend what her eyes were showing her. Couldn't move a muscle, either to step into the room, or to turn and run. All she could do was stare at the two small shapes perched on the bed over her mother's body and absorb the moist snapping sounds and clicking teeth. Her mother had been opened up from the middle. Ribs protruded outward like giant, grisly fingers cupping a bowl of purple meat.

One of the creatures turned to her, a shred of skin dangling from between its grinning teeth, its eyes two dark orbs with glints of white. Clumps of hair, wet with blood, concealed much of its face, but that grin was unmistakable.

Before they got sick, the twins competed at everything, even down to who lost each tooth first. Kate was older by a few minutes, but Dana always seemed to lose hers first. They'd start to wobble around the same time, but Dana would always come home from school grinning and proudly poking her tongue through the newly vacant space, while Kate spent the next few days sulking. The symmetrical gaps on either side of the creature's mouth told her at once that this thing, somehow, was her little sister Dana.

The world was frozen. Merry's eyes lost focus, her stomach lurched, and all she heard were her own irregular breaths rushing in and out. This was impossible. Impossible. Impossible. One of the fuzzy silhouettes slid from the bed with a guttural moan, and its bare feet padded quickly across the floorboards towards her.

Impossible...

Dana's face appeared out of the haze of tears, wide-eyed, grinning, not Dana anymore. The silver seahorse pendant she always wore flashed white in the light from the open door. Fingers that were far too strong for any seven-year-old closed around her arms, and Merry was forced over onto her back, thumping her head on the floorboards. A wave of acrid breath swept over her face, almost causing her to pass out. Another set of bare feet shuffled down the hall. The connection that had come loose in her brain snapped back into place, giving her control of her body once more. She writhed, attempted to roll to one side, but the thing was too strong, impossibly strong, so that all she could do was stare up into its gaping, snapping mouth as it first reared back, then went for her throat.

A foot came out of the side of her vision and connected with the creature's head—she couldn't bring herself to think of it as

Dana anymore—and clumsy hands were pulling and dragging at her shoulder, dragging her back down the corridor. Claire. Merry scrambled for safety, kicking herself along the floor, too panicked to coordinate her arms and legs enough to stand, but somehow the two of them retreated into Claire's room and slammed the door behind them. No sooner had the latch clicked, when a force crashed against it, shaking the entire wall.

Claire had collapsed against the wardrobe, so Merry grabbed a corner of one of the heavy beds and tugged at it. Inch by inch she moved it until she had it firmly wedged against the door, trying to ignore the croaking sighs and sounds of tiny scratching fingers. The Nirvana poster on the back of the door rippled with each blow.

'Claire!' Merry breathed. 'What is going on? How...can this be happening? My God, Mum was...and the girls...it's not...oh—' Her legs gave way and she sank to the floor. She'd thought nothing could shock her anymore after what she'd been through the last few days. She thought she'd prepared herself for the worst. What could be worse than watching your family die slowly around you? But this was worse than anything she could have imagined.

Claire shifted onto her side, reaching for the wardrobe handle to pull herself up. Merry crawled to her and threw her arms around her sister, clinging to her like she was a life preserver in shark-infested waters. Each time one of the creatures in the corridor struck the door, she would flinch and let out a soft whimper, squeezing tighter. Claire was saying something. Her voice was barely a scratch of a whisper.

'...off Merry...can't stay...help me...up...'

Reluctantly, Merry loosened her grip and helped Claire stand. Her sister was breathing heavily, resting all her weight on Merry.

'Get your bag...pack clothes...'

At first she didn't understand what Claire was saying, but another crash against the door jolted her out of her daze. She helped Claire open the wardrobe doors and started tearing clothes from the hangers and stuffing them into the backpack she'd left by the door. Her heart was thumping in double time, following the beat of a mad drummer, and she felt sure it must be about to burst; part of her hoped it would. She tried to focus on her sister, to push everything else out of her mind.

'Food. What about food?' she asked.

Claire shook her head. 'Can't...go back. We'll find some...' She gestured to something in the back of the wardrobe. 'But we need...weapon.'

Merry followed her sister's gaze and saw Claire's hockey stick propped up behind her coat. She grabbed it and the coat with trembling hands.

Claire took the hockey stick, clung to it with both hands, and using it like a crutch, shuffled to the window. The banging at the door didn't relent—four hammers attacking it in a frenzy. Merry was sure she could hear bones snapping with some of the blows.

'Oh, my God,' she cried, unable to stop the tears. 'We can't just leave. That's Kate and Dana out there. We can't leave them...'

Claire turned to her, her chest heaving with exhaustion. She sniffed, wiped the tears from her own eyes and shook her head. 'No, they're gone. It's just us now.'

They walked slowly, stopping often so that Claire could catch her breath. They didn't speak. What could they possibly say? Merry just let the song of the cicadas fill her mind, focusing only on helping Claire take one step after another. She didn't have a clear idea where they were going, just away from the house. Perhaps they should make for the town. Mr Blake had said he was staying at the Foodmart and had offered to help in any way he could. The guy gave her the creeps in a major way, but until she could figure something else out, it seemed like their only option.

The sky was dark with rainclouds now, and the vague thought occurred to Merry that they would need to find shelter soon. At the rate they were going, they wouldn't make it to town before nightfall, much less before the storm hit. She looked up and saw that they were approaching Mr Harrison's house. She shuddered at the thought of breaking into a dead man's house, but Mr Harrison had lived alone, and they knew he wasn't there any more, so it should be empty. She nudged Claire and pointed up the long dirt driveway to their old neighbour's dilapidated house. Claire nodded weakly and the two of them turned off the road.

The door was locked, but Claire's hockey stick worked just as well as a key by knocking out one of the loose glass panels by the handle. Inside was silent and still, and the air smelled of tobacco and cat urine—still a few notches better than the stench she'd grown used to at home. A quick search confirmed that it was deserted, so she helped herself to some stale biscuits and boiled some water on the stove to make tea. When she returned to the living room, she found Claire slouched in a threadbare recliner, her eyelids drooping.

'Here,' she said, holding a biscuit near her mouth. 'Eat something.'

Claire took a bite and chewed slowly. Her pupils were dilated and she seemed miles away. 'It's a joke, Merry,' she whispered, rolling her head to the side. 'I get it now. They kept talking about this virus and how they were going to find a cure. Gotta find a cure. Hurry, 'fore it's too late. But they got it all backwards. The virus is the cure. We're the virus, and it's the cure. Get it? We're the disease and it's the fucken cure. It's the plague. It's the flood. God sure is a funny fucker.' She let out a weak chuckle. 'Smile. Be Merry. It's all just one...big...laugh...'

Merry set the biscuits and tea on the coffee table and crawled into the chair with Claire, slipping her arms around her and resting her cheek on Claire's shoulder. The storm clouds had darkened the sky to near night, and as the first fat drops of rain fell noisily on the tin verandah, she slipped into a death-like slumber.

April 6

Merry awoke with a jolt to the rumbling echoes of thunder. It seemed to reverberate in the air around her. For a moment, she looked about her in shock, unable to recognise anything in the room. The walls were covered in unfamiliar wallpaper, darkened by spots of shadow and water stains. Peculiar paintings hung crooked on the walls, though it was too dark to make them out clearly, and against one wall stood a cast-iron stove. By the window across the room the sheer drapes billowed slightly, as though reaching out to her. Instead of her bed, she appeared to have been sleeping in an old, musty armchair. She struggled to remember how she got there, then immediately wished she hadn't as the horror and grief coursed through her all over again.

Rain was rolling over the roof in overlapping waves, filling her with a sense of claustrophobia. The room lit up briefly in a flash of lightning, and a fraction of a second later a deep rumbling boom struck overhead. She screamed and drew her knees to her chest.

'Shhh.'

Emerging from the grey light by the window across the room

was the silhouette of her sister. Claire was still carrying the hockey stick, and although she moved with a painful slowness, she seemed to have regained some of her strength. She leaned over the arm of the chair and put her lips to Merry's ear.

'Don't make a sound. They're outside.'

Merry's eyes widened with fear, her chest tightened its grip on her heart. She didn't need to ask who "they" were. As they sat together in silence, she started noticing other sounds beneath the storm: the irregular slaps of bare feet on hard, muddy ground; the splintering cracks of weatherboards breaking; the furious beating of wings, and the strangled cries of birds.

Merry gasped and squeezed her eyes closed. 'Mr Harrison's chickens—'

Claire silenced her with a clammy hand over her mouth. She didn't need to see outside for her mind to show her the carnage as the poor, starving birds were chased down one by one and ripped apart. Thankfully, the slaughter didn't last long. Soon the only sound was the thrashing rain, trying futilely to wash away the horror. Without a clock it was impossible to tell how long they waited in the dark, listening. Merry felt pins and needles creeping into her folded legs. She was about to risk moving them, when the rain subsided briefly, and she heard a long, rasping sigh by the window across the room. Another bolt of lightning flashed, illuminating the window, and a silhouette leapt against the drapes—thin arms splayed out, its head cocked to the side. There were no footsteps or crashes against the glass. It was just...standing there. As still as a corpse. Listening. Waiting.

Merry shuddered. Claire leaned closer, her lips actually touching Merry's ear, and when she spoke it was barely more than a breath.

'You're going to be okay, Merry,' she whispered. 'I won't let anything happen to you.'

For a long time she sat with her eyes closed, listening to Claire's breath on her ear, taking comfort from its warmth as it tickled the tiny hairs on her neck.

'Do you remember Damien Martin?' Claire whispered.

Merry started. Had she heard Claire correctly? Why would she be asking about some boy who'd bullied her in grade three?

'The little shit that stole your recorder after music class, remember? The teachers had all gone home. All his mates were egging him on. You just stood there. Couldn't understand why he was doing it. I remember it. He took it into the boy's toilets, stuck it in a urinal, and pissed on it.'

Merry nodded. She would never forget that day. Their dad had died earlier that year, and she was floundering at school. Even simple things like walking or breathing were a struggle. Then Damien transferred into her class from another school and seemed to have it out for her since day one. It was the first truly cruel thing that anyone had ever done to her. But why was Claire bringing it up now?

'He bought you a new one, though, right? A few days later?'

Merry swallowed and tried to concentrate on what Claire was saying. 'Mhm. He said his parents made him...'

'Bullshit. The next day after school, I was waiting for him by the bike shed. After his friends had all taken off, I went over to him and kicked his bike over. Told him who I was. Told him that he was going to buy you a new recorder right now. You know what he said to that? Must have thought he was so tough. He said those two little words that made me the happiest girl in the world. He said: "Make me."'

45

Merry brought her thumb to her mouth and bit at the skin on her knuckle. 'What did you do?'

'He tried pulling my hair and hitting me, but he hit like a little boy, and I was too pissed to feel it, anyway. I dragged him to the toilets. The recorder was still there. Nobody wanted to touch it, but I made him pick it up. He cried when I made him put it in his mouth and play Hot Cross Buns. I felt a little bad about that part, but he goddamn had it coming. I was like one of those ronin samurai from the movies. Dishing out fucking justice, man.'

There was a rustling outside the window and they froze. Somewhere in the distance a dog howled, causing a burst of excited gasping from the thing outside, then they heard its footsteps rapidly disappear into the storm. Merry scarcely breathed for another ten minutes.

'Why didn't you ever tell me?'

Claire shrugged.

'Why did you do it?'

'He deserved it, didn't he?'

'I guess. But why are you telling me now?'

Claire sat slowly up, wincing as the blood rushed back into her extremities. Dawn was almost upon them. The rain had eased, and a soft grey light was filtering through the windows. 'Because...I dunno. Just forget it, okay?'

Merry smiled weakly and stretched out her legs. She didn't know whether to be grateful or resentful. For so long she'd been relying on her mum or Claire to fight her battles for her, but in her mind, Damien Martin had been one of her personal victories, or so she'd thought. The part of the story Claire didn't know was that she'd gone to speak to Damien at lunch the day after the incident, when none of his friends were around. With a stomach

46

full of butterflies, she'd marched up to him and told him, all in one breath, that she was sorry if she did something to upset him, but it wasn't okay to do what he did, and he shouldn't do mean things to impress his friends, but she would forgive him if he said he was sorry and got her a new recorder because their recital was coming up next Thursday and she had to practice, and maybe they could be friends one day but right now she had to go to the bathroom. She'd turned and run the other way before he could say a word, her pigtails bouncing confidently behind her. When he presented her with a muttered apology and a new recorder the following day, she'd been so proud of herself. Only now she knew it had all been Claire's doing.

'Stay here, I'll go check it out,' Claire said, using the hockey stick to stand up. She shuffled over to the window and peered through the drapes. 'Jesus Christ, what a mess. I can't see any sign of them, though.'

Merry slid off the chair with a sigh, stretched, and joined Claire by the window. The chicken coop had been demolished, leaving mangled wire, splintered wood and countless feathers trampled into the mud. She craned her neck to see beyond it, to where the swollen river coursed angrily behind a row of trees, looking for any trace of "them", but there was nothing.

'Let's see if Mr Harrison has any breakfast for us. He's got to at least have oatmeal, right? Old people can't get enough oatmeal...'

'Shouldn't you sit down for a bit?' Merry asked, as Claire bounded into the kitchen. 'You're still sick.' Though, she had to admit, aside from the occasional unsteadiness, her sister seemed almost completely recovered.

'Nah, actually I feel great...all things considered. Gotta keep rolling.'

In the kitchen they found a bowl of rotten fruit, a fridge they didn't dare open, a pantry crammed with dog food and—drawing a celebratory cheer from Claire—oatmeal.

'Ha, called it! You can always count on the oldies for oats.'

After scoffing down two bowls each, and the rest of the biscuits from the night before, they gathered their bags and stepped out onto the porch. Puddles on the road shone gold in the morning sun, and magpies were already feasting on earthworms that had been drawn up by the rain.

Claire rested the hockey stick over one shoulder and sucked in a deep breath. 'Alright, little sis, where to?'

They passed four dead bodies on the road to town.

Death, which had until now kept itself hidden behind shuttered window and bolted door, had broken free of its shackles and stepped out into the light to walk the world with them.

Two were lying face down in the flooded ditch that ran along the side of the road, presumably where they'd dragged themselves in the final stages of the illness, as the fever burned away their survival instinct, and dehydration drove them to find any source of water. Although Merry tried not to look, a morbid curiosity compelled her head to turn. Like Mr Harrison, they were bruised all over and swollen, especially around the neck, and the yellowed skin on their hands and backs had already begun to peel and blister in the sun. She'd thought such a sight would make her physically ill, but all she felt was oddly distant. She knew she should be repulsed, nauseated, terrified, but those feelings she detected only very deep inside her, as though the old Merry had been locked away, and the Merry that was left, the Merry that walked this new world, was someone else.

The third and fourth bodies were inside a car that had tipped on its side and now leaned against a power pole. As they walked by it, they heard a tapping sound, and noticed the vehicle rocking slightly.

'Let's cross,' Claire said, moving away from the car.

'But there's someone in there.'

'Yeah, that's what worries me.'

'We can't just leave them. What if they need help?'

Claire stopped and stared at her for a moment. 'Have you forgotten everything that happened yesterday? Cos I was pretty out of it, but I sure as shit haven't. Now you want to go and stick your dick in a hornet's nest?'

'No, I don't want to stick my...anything in a... It's just...there must be others like us. It could be someone we know.'

Claire shook her head slowly, looking from the overturned car to Merry and back again. She let out a sigh. 'Alright. But I want it to go on record that I think it's a bad idea. So...just remember that when we're being digested.'

Merry swallowed hard and bit at her thumbnail as they turned back to the car. They walked cautiously around to the front and leaned close to peer through the cracked, blood-spattered windscreen. The car lay on its left side, and the driver, still held in by his seat-belt, dangled awkwardly over the centre console. The passenger, a short middle-aged woman, sat hunched on the smashed passenger door, reaching up to gnaw on the driver's left hand, while blood dripped from the hanging corpse onto her face. She had chewed off her own lips, making it look like she was grinning maniacally. When she saw Merry and Claire watching her, she leapt for them, crashing against the windscreen, and sending several more cracks spider-webbing through the glass.

'Sssshhit!' Claire cried, jumping back and bringing the hockey stick up over one shoulder. They both retreated a few steps, out of sight of the woman, but she seemed to lose interest in them, and returned to sucking the flesh off the finger bones of the man that had probably once been her husband.

'Goddammit. So there are more of them. Bloody grinners. Maybe next time you'll listen to me, yeah? Let's get out of here.'

'You said he's living at the Foodmart now? That's pretty weird, right? Why go there, of all places? Doesn't he have a home?'

Merry shrugged. 'I think a lot of those shops have apartments built above them. Makes sense to move in there, I guess. That's where all the food is right now. What's left of it, anyway.

'Geez, I didn't think of that. So when the food runs out we're gonna have to learn to grow vegetables, and raise chickens, or some shit? God, I couldn't even keep my sea monkeys alive.'

Merry didn't answer. As the events of the last few days continued to sink in, her thoughts turned to darker and darker places. She couldn't contemplate growing vegetables or raising animals, or any other long term survival plans because in her heart she couldn't picture herself surviving. She felt like she was clinging to the rail of a ship that had just struck rocks. She hadn't been thrown overboard from the impact, but the ship was still sinking. And all she had over those already drowned was more time staring into the void.

'And he's not sick? It'd suck to walk in there and find another grinner waiting for us.'

'He seemed okay yesterday,' Merry replied, absently.

'Yeah, well, a lot can change in a day. I still think he's a weird dude. You know he had a thing for Mum?'

The trill of cicadas from the trees and all around seemed to laugh at them.

They passed the sawmill with its red earth and piles of logs and white metal sheds. Something moving along the tracks behind the mill caught her eye. A large yellow and brown blur between the trees. She gripped Claire's arm.

'There's something...'

'Hmm?'

'Something moving in the trees. By the tracks. Over there.'

'Yeah, I saw it. Don't worry, it's a kangaroo. It's been following us for the last fifteen minutes.'

'A...are you sure?' As she paused and looked closer, she saw that Claire was right. A large red kangaroo was loping through the brush. It stopped and stood on its hind legs, watching the two sisters watching it. 'Oh, right.'

'Do you think he knows anything's changed? Like, I wonder if he's out here celebrating because there won't be any more dickheads chasing after him in four-wheel-drives at night trying to shoot him in the head. He can watch the hunters hunted. Look at those beady eyes. I bet he's laughing at us.'

'No,' Merry said, staring into the kangaroo's eyes. They glinted in the sunlight. 'I think today's just like any other day to him. To him nothing's wrong.'

'Yeah, except everything's wrong.'

There was a shriek in the road behind them, and the roo flinched and bounded away. They both spun at once. A woman was sprinting up the road towards them, her arms swinging wildly about her. Every step forced an animal grunt from her grinning mouth. Her body was a bloody mess. Ribbons of clothing flew out behind her like streamers, and streaks of red lined her face and arms. The woman from the car. She must have had enough of her husband, and dug her way through the cracked windscreen, slicing her clothes and skin open.

'Oh, fuck me. Run.'

Claire didn't need to say it, Merry was already running. The wind whistled past her ears and her long hair flew out behind her, yet her body seemed to drag. Her feet felt weighted, plodding sluggishly along. Claire dashed ahead easily, athletic and powerful despite her recent illness, used to hours running the length of the hockey field. She was made to run. The extent of Merry's exercise, on the other hand, consisted of walking the length of the library, searching the shelves for something she hadn't read. Although she was slender and long-legged like her sister, her body seemed to move with all the grace and fluidity of a newborn foal.

Behind her, the woman's erratic footsteps grew nearer, her rasping breaths trembling with excitement.

'Claire!' Merry was certain she felt the woman's hands grasping for her hair. Any second she would be yanked backwards into the dirt.

Claire looked back and her eyes widened. She turned, sliding on the dirt road, and readied the hockey stick. As Merry passed her, she swung. There was a crack like one log striking another, then Merry heard a heavy thud and the stick clattered to the ground.

Claire was holding her forearms, shaking, and staggering away from the woman who was writhing on the ground.

'Shitballs...that hurt...'

She grabbed Merry's sleeve and turned her, gradually finding her stride again, and pulling Merry along. But the grinner didn't stay down for long. The sounds of scrambling in the dirt faded briefly, but soon the irregular footsteps returned, slowly at first, then faster. Claire was clutching one wrist to her body as she ran and winced with pain every few steps.

Merry glanced over her shoulder and saw that the woman, though she had dropped back, was keeping pace with them. The sound of an engine pulled her attention back to the road ahead. A car was tearing towards them. She raised her hand to signal for help, but it was already upon them.

The gear shifted. The engine revved high. Tyres slid through the dirt. A sharp thud, followed by two more as the body rolled over the bonnet and onto the road. By the time she looked, it was over. The car had come to rest twenty or thirty metres down the road. A man in a neat button-up shirt stepped out, swept a palm over his forehead and walked towards the twitching body. As he neared it, he calmly pulled a revolver from the holster on his belt and fired twice into her head.

Merry felt as though she might pass out.

Mr Blake kicked the woman's foot, re-holstered his gun. He looked up at them. The cuff of his crisp grey trousers was spattered with blood.

'Hello girls.'

April 9

Zoey and Hopkins tumbled around the tiny boat like clothes in a dryer, sliding off the slippery seat into the space below. She banged her head and knees on the hard metal. The bike swerved from side to side and changed speed all the time, making her tummy turn. It went slowly at first, then faster and faster until Zoey thought the bike would fall apart. The sound of the engine deafened her, and it shook so much that she couldn't feel her arms and legs anymore. At one point it bumped over something on the road and she felt like she was floating in the air for a moment.

She found the seatbelt and held onto it. Looking up, she saw the stars and the moon, big and round, and realised the jacket she'd had over her head was gone. In a way, she was glad. She couldn't bring herself to look at the rider, and so she kept her eyes on the sky. No matter how fast the bike went, or how much it swerved, the moon kept up with her, followed every turn, watched over her.

They went on like that for such a long time—her, Hopkins, the man, and the moon. Zoey felt sure the road had to run out soon.

But maybe it wouldn't run out. Maybe this was what Forever really was. She'd once thought she understood Forever. Sometimes, on a good day, her mummy would tell her that she loved her Forever, and she'd never hurt her as long as there were stars shining in the sky. She thought that meant it would never stop. But the next day when she caught Zoey wearing her favourite red shoes with the tall heels, she screamed at her and pushed her over and then threw one of the shoes at Zoey when she tried to run away. Zoey realised that during the day there were no stars and Forever was sometimes not long after all.

By the time the bike started slowing down, Zoey had forgotten where she was. The stars and the moon were all she could see, and they seemed to dance and shake around before her eyes. She was pressed hard against the side as the bike turned, then they hit another bump and Zoey was knocked down again. The bike came to a sudden, jolting stop, and a tree branch crashed down on top of the bike, blocking her view of the sky. There was a groan, and the man threw up loudly. More coughing, rustling of leaves, then there was a shuddering crash and snapping twigs as something came through the branches towards her. It was a hand, covered in cuts, dripping blood, the fingers twitching and grasping. Zoey pressed herself back as far as she could into the corner, out of its reach.

Gradually, the twitches became weaker and weaker until the fingers drooped and began to curl up slightly. The only sound was the slow pat, pat, pat of blood dripping onto the seat. Zoey closed her eyes. With her eyes closed she could almost believe it was just rain dripping from the gutters, or milk spilling off the counter from a knocked over carton. As the sound of her own pounding heart faded away in her ears, she started to hear birds singing. Some of them she recognised. There was the coo coo of Mr Pigeon talking to his friend in the next tree. And the silly song of Mr Magpie. They were the same sounds she heard outside her window every morning as she lay in bed listening to the world wake up.

Zoey hugged her legs. Maybe if she kept her eyes closed, she could go back to her own bed. Soon she would hear the water running as Daddy took his shower. The coffee pot would start hissing and gurgling, and then there'd be the toaster pop and the scrape of the knife as Mummy made her breakfast. She could already smell the smells of coffee and burnt toast. But when she opened her eyes, the hand was still there, pale and covered in dark streaks like a piece of blue cheese, with black fingernails. Still dripping. Pat, pat, pat.

Then she heard a sound forty hundred times worse. It was the sound she'd been dreading. The slow click, click, click of teeth. It was followed by a rattling breath, and then a soft, gravelly haaaaaa. It was too much. As the hand opened and the swollen knuckles cracked back to life, Zoey screamed.

She knew she was supposed to stay quiet. Uncle Bear had told her to stay just as quiet as a mouse and she'd said she could do it, but now she just couldn't help it. She cried as hard as she could, pulled at her hair, hit the floor with her fists and kicked her feet. Her eyes were blurry and stinging from crying. The gasps from outside grew shorter and faster. She could hear the breaths rushing in and out of its throat, and its teeth clicking hard. In, out, out, click, in, in, out, out, out, click, click. Now and then a little cry of excitement would escape with the breaths. The branches that protected her shook and broke as the hand reached and reached and reached. Fingernails scraped at the seat, so Zoey screamed louder to drown it out.

Hopkins, who sat protectively in front of her, tucked under her chin, gave a sudden twitch as the hand found his ear. A second later, he was gone.

Zoey's head was spinning. She didn't hear the other engine at first. Not until Uncle Bear shouted the first time.

'Stevo!'

She stopped fighting, but she couldn't stop the tears. Her chest and throat hurt as they sucked in one deep breath after another.

The man snarled, and there was a loud bang, like a balloon bursting. She heard the monster beside her gasp and click its teeth excitedly, then the scuffing of its feet as it ran. The sound of its footsteps changed from grass to dirt to gravel so quickly. Two more balloons burst, and Uncle Bear shouted again.

'Basta—' Bang.

It was quiet for a moment. Even the birds had stopped to listen.

One final bang.

The footsteps that came back to her were much slower.

'Please be okay, little Zoey, please,' his voice whispered. 'Please. I can't be too late again.'

Uncle Bear pulled the branch off the bike with a grunt, flooding the little boat with sunlight, and she stared up at him, her chest still heaving. He rested one hand on the bike and rubbed at his eyes with the palm of the other. Then he reached in and pulled her out.

Zoey sat down on the grass because her legs wouldn't hold her up. She felt like she was going to be sick, but nothing came up when she tried. Uncle Bear came down on one knee beside her and brushed some of her tangled hair out of her face.

'Ah, look at you, little mite. Look how banged up—'

Zoey made a fist and hit him in the soft part between his legs, because she knew that's where it hurt boys the most. Her daddy told her that after she hit him there accidentally with a tennis ball and he had to go lie down. But now she didn't care because she wanted to hurt him.

'Leave me alone! I don't want you!' she shouted. 'You said you would come back, and you left. I want Mummy and Daddy! I want to go home, and help Mummy set the table, because Daddy is coming home soon in his red car and I need to hide under my blanket so he can find me. And Daddy said we could go to the zoo next time and I could see the monkeys and have an ice cream with chocolate on top and I want Mummy and Daddy not you!'

Uncle Bear cupped himself with one hand and sat back on the grass and let her finish. He had tears in his eyes. When he reached out and pulled her into a bear-hug she squirmed at first, but he just held her there. His arms were warm and trembling.

'I'm sorry, Zoey,' he said. 'You're right. I shouldn't have left you. I'm so sorry.'

Over his shoulder she could see the other man lying in the road on his tummy, with his legs spread out wide. She couldn't see his head. It looked like most of it was missing. What was left of Hopkins was scattered by his feet. When she couldn't look any more, she put her arms around Uncle Bear's neck and buried her face in his beard. It was softer than it looked. The birds were singing again.

The sun warmed her hair until it was almost too hot to touch, and it dried the tears on her cheeks. Uncle Bear stood up slowly and walked over to the bike that was crashed against the tree.

'I don't want to go in there again,' Zoey said, not moving.

'Front wheel's busted up. Springs are shot.' He rubbed his hand over the bike. 'Gas tank took a bash, too. Nope, don't worry, this old girl's going out to pasture.'

'Out to pasta?' Zoey asked with a sniff.

Bear chuckled. 'Sure, why not. I could go for some spaghetti. You like spaghetti?'

Zoey nodded.

He walked back to his own bike and took her pink butterfly helmet from the bag behind the seat. He held it out to her. 'I'm really sorry about Mr Bunny. I promise I won't leave you alone ever again.'

She didn't say anything, but trotted over and took the helmet.

He shook his head and stroked his beard. 'Fair dinkum, your mum and dad must have been proud of you. You're a heckuva' lot braver than me. Come on, let's get you into some clean clothes and find something to eat. Ready to get out of here?'

She raised her arms, and he lifted her back onto the bike.

They rode until the sound of the wind rushing past blew away the memories of laughter and clicking teeth. When Zoey's bottom went to sleep, Bear pulled the bike over to the side of the road under the shade of some baby gum trees. He unfastened the belt and helped her down, then stretched out his back and rubbed his 'saddle sores'. While Zoey tried to shake the floaty feeling out of her legs, Bear pulled a handful of gum leaves from the tree and started looking at them closely, scratching some of them with his fingernail, then tossing them away. When he found one he liked, he folded it over and held it up to his lips.

The sound was a bit like someone pinching the air out of a balloon—a high-pitched squeak, and Zoey giggled.

'No laughing,' Bear said with a grin. 'This here's a high-tech instrument. It won't work unless we're both completely serious.' He tried to give her a stern look, but he was still smiling under his beard.

Zoey nodded and clapped a hand over her mouth.

Bear bowed and started to play. It was a slow song, a beautiful tune, but still silly because of its squeaky sound. Bear was very good at it. He only missed some of the really high notes, which turned his face red with effort, but Zoey loved every second of it. When he'd finished, he gave her a wink, then squeaked out a fast version of Mary Had a Little Lamb, shaking his hips from side to side with each note. Zoey giggled and jumped with excitement. When he'd finished, he took another bow and she clapped.

'Can I try?'

'Sure.' Bear handed her the leaf. Zoey blew as hard as she could until she ran out of breath. Spit flew out the sides, and then she blew the leaf right out of her hands. Bear laughed and took another off the tree.

He knelt next to her. 'See, the trick is to come at it gently. Put your lips on it like this...that's right. Keep 'em tight together. When you blow, start off with an ant's fart, and work your way up. Always try the soft touch first. Life's easier that way.'

Zoey tried again, and after a while she got a little squeak.

'There ya go!' Bear said, hugging her against his leg.

As they walked back to the bike, she asked, 'What was the song? The first one?'

'It's called Amazing Grace. Or at least, it was supposed to be. Stevo told me once, long time ago...he wanted that played at his funeral.' Bear shrugged. 'Best I could do for him.'

'Did he teach you to play leafs?'

Bear chuckled. 'Nah. He taught me plenty of other stuff, but not that. Some of it got us into trouble more than once. But he taught me some good stuff, too. I owed him a lot.' He had a sad smile on his face. Then he brightened. 'Now, how 'bout a duet?'

Each time they stopped to go to the bathroom, or just to take a break, Zoey would practice a little with her leaf. She could only make the one note so far, but it was fun making Uncle Bear try to guess what song she was playing. Even though he played along, she thought he was worried about something. He kept checking one of the clocks on the bike and tapping it with his finger. He seemed relieved when they saw a small petrol station up ahead. Before they stopped, he did a slow lap of the buildings.

There were only two pumps with a little shop next to them, and a larger building attached that looked like a big, rusty shed. There was also a phone box with a bright orange roof, and a wheelie bin that had been knocked over. There was nothing else around it but more dirt and trees. It might have just fallen out of the sky. Zoey tried looking in the windows. The shop's windows were mostly cracked and too grimy to see through clearly, and the ones in the shed had tins piled up behind them, and spider webs and old tools hanging down.

Bear stopped by one of the pumps and tested it. Nothing came out. 'Figures,' he said, sounding grumpy. He shut off the engine and they walked over to the shop. Zoey thought it would be locked, but Bear gave it a soft push and it swung in a little way.

'See?' he said, 'Always try a gentle touch firs—' The door jammed against something and he walked straight into it. Zoey laughed.

'Of course,' he added, taking a step back and rubbing his nose, 'When that doesn't work...' He gave the door a boot and it flew open, crashing against something and bouncing back. The metal frame was dented and the glass panels had new cracks running through them.

Bugs flew through the dusty sunlight inside the shop, and there was a bad smell, like ham that wasn't good to eat anymore. Zoey covered her nose with her sleeve. There were two short rows of shelves in front of them that were mostly bare. Just some empty boxes that once held chocolate bars, some maps, old newspapers, scattered rubbish. The fizzy drink fridge at the back was dark and empty, too.

'Right, let's see what we've got,' Bear said, stepping inside. 'Stay close to me.'

Behind the door was a sunglasses stand which had toppled over. Bear kicked it out of the way and took a map from the shelf behind it. A quick walk around the store turned up nothing to eat, so Bear got down on his hands and knees and started looking under the shelves.

'Jackpot!'

He pulled out a dented can of Heinz spaghetti. 'Didn't I say we'd go out for spaghetti? This almost counts.'

They didn't find anything else to eat, but Zoey was excited. Mummy sometimes forgot to give her breakfast, so she was used to being hungry, but she couldn't even remember the last thing she'd eaten.

Bear tried the door behind the counter, but it didn't know the gentle touch rule either, so he kicked that one down, too. It led into the shed, which was actually a garage, and it was much darker than the shop. The bad ham smell was worse in here. They stood in the doorway for a moment, listening for any clicking teeth or laughter, but there was nothing except the distant sound of screeching cockatoos outside.

There was a big, red car that had thrown up some of its parts onto the floor, a pile of tyres, rusty metal drums, benches with tools scattered around them.

Bear whistled, walking up to the car. 'Look at that. 1950s Ford Custom. Looks like someone was restoring it. Look at that chrome. White wall tyres, too. Now that would be riding in style. I wonder if she runs...'

As he reached for the handle, a pale face slammed against the window. Its mouth opened and closed, snapping at them, but there were no teeth inside, just lumpy, grey gums.

'Shiiii...take mushrooms!' Bear shouted, staggering back, and fumbling for something tucked down the back of his pants. Zoey realised it was a "gum". Her cousin Russell had shown her his father's gum once, which he kept in a drawer beside the bed, under some socks. Russell pointed it at some birds out the window for a while, holding it up and closing one eye and shouting got you, got you, got you. When he got bored of that, he pointed it at her. He made her look right into the hole at the front, and she remembered how cold and heavy it felt when he pressed it against her forehead.

They could hear the muffled sounds of the man in the car now, his laugh coming out like a whisper through a cardboard tube. He'd been an old man. He had a bald, spotted head and lots of deep lines all over his face. His eyebrow hairs were very long and drooped over his eyes. She saw the bones in his chest under his dirty overalls. His hands, which were mostly black and purple, scratched at the windows, leaving greasy red streaks.

Bear pressed the gum against the glass. It made a loud tap. He was breathing hard. 'Toothless old goat,' he said to the old man. 'You know what this does?'

The old man didn't seem to know what the gum did any more

than Zoey. He just gasped louder, and pressed against the glass, trying to force his way through. Bear clicked something on the top with his thumb, and Zoey didn't know why, but she was scared of it.

Uncle Bear looked at her, and his breathing relaxed a little. The creases in his forehead slowly disappeared. He lowered the gum. 'Gentle touch first, right?'

Zoey nodded, relieved.

Bear let out a long, long breath, and tucked the gum away again. Then he went over to the bench and found a big container and a piece of hose. The old man tried to follow him, scrambling over the seats, clawing at the windows.

Bear opened the little door at the back where the petrol goes in and put the hose in and blew into it. After a while, petrol started to come out, first into his mouth and then into the container. He spat onto the floor and wiped his beard. When the petrol stopped dripping, he closed the door and walked back to her.

'Let's get out of here,' he said.

Zoey looked back from the doorway at the old man. He was trying to bite through the glass now, and she could see the dark hole of his mouth, and his wriggling black tongue, and although he still frightened her, she was so very sad for him.

April 6

Even with the windows down, the rancid smell of the corpse in the back of Mr Blake's station wagon filled the car. Merry pinched her nose, but it crept down her throat until she gagged, and she leaned a little further out the window. The odour was of decomposing meat, sprayed with some foul fruity perfume. And of course the coppery tang of blood.

She fought the urge to look over her shoulder. With every bump and shudder of the car, the body shifted. A dead hand knocked against the wheel arch. Fingernails seemed to scrape at the tarp that covered her. Don't look, Merry instructed herself. She's not coming back. She's dead. She's dead dead. And she's had her face shot in. And what if the tarp has slipped off? If you look back, you'll be sick. Look ahead. Don't look back.

'You're lucky I saw you when I did,' Mr Blake said, watching them in the rearview mirror. 'Very lucky indeed.'

Neither of them replied—they were holding their breath—but Merry managed a weak nod.

The drive couldn't have taken longer than ten minutes, but it felt an eternity. She breathed a sigh of relief as they pulled up across the street from the Foodmart. Before the wheels even stopped moving, Merry undid her seatbelt and tugged at the door handle. It didn't open. She looked at Claire, who gave her an uneasy frown. She slid her hand across the back seat and found her sister's fingers, giving them a gentle squeeze. Claire's other hand tightened on the grip of her hockey stick.

Mr Blake took his time getting out, slowly unbuckling his seatbelt, smoothing his hair back to the side where the wind had blown it out of place. When he stepped out, he stood for a moment looking up and down the road, then took a small brown bottle from his pocket and tipped it to his lips. Only after carefully screwing the cap back on and replacing it in his pocket did he open the door for them.

They tumbled out, eyes watering, eager to escape the stench, and gulped down lungfuls of clean air. Mr Blake sniffed pointedly and reached to retrieve their backpacks from the rear seat, then slammed the doors and locked them.

'This way.' He dropped the bags at their feet and moved quickly towards the median strip in the middle of the road.

Merry started to follow, but Claire called out to him. 'What are you going to do with her?'

He paused and turned. Even though he was only a few metres away, his voice was so soft it barely carried to them. 'You don't need to worry. I'll take care of her. Come on now, girls. It's not safe outside.' He didn't wait for any further questions, but ducked under the low-hanging leaves of a eucalypt.

He didn't lead them to the front of the supermarket, as she'd expected, but down the alley alongside the adjacent hair salon. He stopped at a solid looking door with peeling grey paint and took out a keyring of coloured keys from his pocket. The door opened into a dark, cramped room that smelled strongly of ammonia. As she stepped inside the salon, Merry noticed bottles of hair dye and bleach and other chemicals she didn't recognise. Blake brushed aside a curtain on the far side and disappeared.

Claire squeezed her hand. Behind them, the door squeaked slightly as it swung closed. The strip of daylight cut rapidly down to a bright splinter on the wall which lingered for a moment, beckoning to her.

She felt a strong impulse to catch the door before it could close. To urge her sister back outside and down the street and as far away from this place as she could go. But she didn't. The click of the latch echoed through the empty space.

'Reckon he's stopping in for a quick cut and colour?' Claire whispered.

'This way, girls.'

Beyond the curtain, a dim light filtered through the security screen on the shop's front windows, broken into a patchwork of dusty gold on the black-and-white tiles.

They followed him through another door and up a tight staircase which opened into a small musty-smelling apartment. The only furniture was a couch that looked like a relic from the seventies, a television almost as old, and a stained coffee table sitting crooked between them. In one corner was hunched a small kitchenette, crowded with cupboards above and below, dishes and tins of food stacked neatly. Pale rectangles, spaced intermittently around the walls, hinted at photo frames recently removed.

Merry walked slowly to the windows that overlooked the street. A dove that had been roosting on the outside ledge took flight, startling her. On each window were decorative twisted wrought iron bars.

Mr Blake stood in the middle of the room, his thumbs hooked through his belt loops, watching them. 'You may stay here as long as you like,' he said. His voice always sounded nervous and effeminate, but when he addressed them directly in such small enclosed quarters, he seemed even more anxious and spoke as though each line had been rehearsed over and over in his mind and which had to be expelled as quickly as possible. 'Outside is not safe. I can protect you here.' His upper lip and nose twitched as if to shoo a fly, and with his right hand he fondled the brown bottle through his pocket, but while the rest of his body seemed anxious, his eyes, shrewd and intelligent, never left them. Away from the stench of death and chemicals, she could detect a hint of liquorice coming from him.

Claire stepped up beside Merry and wrestled the window sash up to let in some air. She gripped one of the bars and shook it.

'I've already checked them,' Blake said. 'They're secure. Nothing can get in.'

'Or out...' Claire mumbled beneath her breath, though a twitch of Blake's brow told Merry he'd overheard.

'Come. I'll show you to your bedroom.'

There was little more to see of the apartment. A sparse master bedroom containing what looked like a hospital bed from the second world war and the world's cheapest wardrobe. The only interesting feature of the room was a fireplace which hadn't been in use since it was last painted, perhaps twenty or thirty years ago.

'I hope the two of you don't mind sharing a bed for the time being.'

He pushed open a sliding door to reveal a tiny ensuite bathroom. A plastic bucket had been placed under the dripping shower-head.

'The water is still running for now, but it won't last long. With the way the pressure has been dropping, I'd say less than a week. Then we'll have to make do with bedpans and jugs of water from the tank until I can find a suitable pump.'

'Sounds lovely.' Claire squeezed past him and stepped back into the hall. 'Hey, what's that?'

She was standing in front of a large rectangle of blue plastic sheeting pinned to the wall at the end of the corridor. Approximately the shape of a door. They both looked at Blake, who was silent for some time. It seemed to Merry that he was debating whether to answer and then choosing his words very carefully.

'When resources are limited, animals will resort to anything to survive. Desperation will turn the kindest men cruel. Strangers would kill us without hesitation for the merest morsel if they were starving. It's natural. The food over there is exceptionally valuable. I'd be a fool to leave it unguarded, but to sleep with gold under your pillow is just as foolish. The hair salon, in my opinion, provides a much less attractive target, and it allows me to secure the supermarket while still being able to access it by less obvious means. This building directly adjoins the supermarket. However, as there was no convenient means of traversing the two, I am rectifying that.'

'Riiight.' Claire peeled some of the masking tape off the sheet and tried to peer into the hole. 'You could just say you're making a secret passage so you can keep an eye on your shit. Are you gonna hide it behind a rotating bookcase on the other side or something?'

'Don't do that,' Blake said, inserting himself between Claire and the wall, forcing her to step back. 'There are loose bricks.'

Claire held up her hands in a mock apology while he carefully smoothed the tape back down.

'I need to leave temporarily. I trust you'll be comfortable here until I return. There are some cans of food by the stove if you're hungry. Don't leave these rooms.'

The girls looked at each other, and Merry nodded. After everything that had happened, she had no intention of leaving and was looking forward to lying down for a moment in a place where nothing more dangerous than her nightmares could reach her.

Mr Blake retrieved a blue duffel bag from the second bedroom, which he locked behind him, and left without another word. They heard his car start and drive slowly away. As soon as he was gone, Claire strode to the door and tested the handle.

'The bastard's deadlocked it. He's fucken locked us in.'

'So?'

'What do you mean, so? You can't tell me you trust this guy, with his creepy moustache and his creepy voice and his "animals will resort to anything to survive". The guy's a nut job. Bars on all the windows? Locking us in? This is a bloody prison. We'd be better off by ourselves.'

'And go where?' Merry shot back with a forcefulness that took them both by surprise. 'We don't know how many of those things are out there. We don't know what to do. And he's right, when people get desperate, who knows what they'll do. At least here we're safe.'

Claire softened. 'I dunno, Merry. I just get a bad feeling about him.'

'I know he's a bit weird, but we need to give him a chance. He's worked in the Foodmart forever, and he's always been kind to us. I think he just wants to protect us.'

'I can protect us.'

Merry looked down. 'If he hadn't found us when he did, we'd

both be dead.'

Claire exhaled softly, but bit her tongue.

Merry said nothing more. Her mind returned to Mum and Kate and Dana, and she felt her chest contract under the weight of a crushing sadness. She turned away so that her sister wouldn't see her cry.

'Okay,' Claire said. 'We'll stay.'

Merry sniffed. 'Okay.'

Claire cracked the knuckles on one hand. 'But if we're gonna live here, I need to know what he's got going on.' She turned sharply and walked back down the corridor to stand in front of the plastic sheet on the wall, and taking hold of the corner, ripped it back in one quick motion. 'Alright you weaselly son of a taint, let's see what you're hiding.'

April 6

Merry hesitated. She could hear loose bricks clattering softly as Claire tiptoed through the hole in the wall.

'Are you coming, or what?'

'I don't think we should. He said...'

Claire's head appeared. 'Merry, the dude locked us in. He's skeevy as hell. You really want to hang around and play Bates Motel with him?' She ducked back behind the wall and her voice echoed in the enclosed space. 'Come on.'

Shivers. Merry took a deep breath and held it and before she could talk herself out of it she ducked under the rumpled plastic sheet and into the passage. The air was heavy with the smell of cement dust and plaster. It wasn't as deep as she'd imagined. A brick wall knocked through on her side, then a dark and narrow crevice bridged by a plank of wood, then a second layer of brick and plaster which was curtained by another plastic sheet. Claire had already passed through, so she hurried to catch up to her. She sidestepped a pile of tools and some sheets of plasterboard that were propped against the wall and found Claire further down the corridor, near the stairs, standing outside a door with a frosted glass window. She was jiggling the handle.

'This looks like an office, I reckon. If he's hiding something, I bet it's in here.' She leaned forward, cupped her hand against the glass and tried to peer in. She thought for a moment, then walked back to the pile of tools and dug around until she found a couple of nails.

'Check that other door, will you?' Claire said as she crouched in front of the office door.

'What are you going to do?'

'Gonna pick this lock...and maybe give myself tetanus.'

'You know how to do that?'

'How hard can it be? Now go on, you're blocking my light.'

Merry swallowed and approached the other door further down the corridor. It was marked with a faded sign: Storage. She watched her hand reach out and twist the handle. It was locked. Thank God.

Claire swore as one of the nails dropped to the floor. 'They make it look so easy in the movies. Time for Plan B then.' She returned to the pile of tools a second time and dragged out a hefty claw hammer.

'Whoa, you can't smash the window. I'm pretty sure he'll notice that.'

'Look, if this guy is making nipple lamp shades in there, I want to know about it. I wouldn't have to go looking in the first place if he weren't such a sketchy bastard. But he is, so here we are. Now, stand back.'

'Claire, wait—'

Before Claire could raise the hammer, she was interrupted by a sound from downstairs. A soft whisper of metal on metal, as though someone had drawn a shower curtain.

'H-he's back,' Merry stammered, pulling towards the hole in the wall.

Claire put a hand on her arm. 'No, we would've heard the car.' She lowered her voice. 'I think there's...th-there must be someone else here.'

She took a step towards the stairs.

'No. Claire...don't...we're not supposed to—'

'Just stay behind me.'

'—we can go back. I don't want to know what's down there. I don't...' She realised she was beginning to cry but didn't care. 'Please. You don't have to prove anything...'

Claire turned to her with a look of resolution and something that was almost contempt before beginning to descend the stairs, hammer raised. Merry hesitated, her hand pressed against the chalky green plaster wall, her vision swimming. Claire had disappeared from sight. She counted her heartbeats. As terrified as she was at what moved downstairs, being alone with her fears was far worse. Her hand trembled as she reached for the banister.

It was nearly pitch black downstairs. With no windows in the room, the only light came, cold and scant, from the corridor above, and barely extended beyond the bottom step. Merry stood, flinching in the darkness.

'Claire...'

'Shhh.'

A moment more of terror then Claire's face appeared like a spectre in the light of a torch. The feeble yellow beam wavered, then swung towards Merry. She held up a hand against the dazzling light, gripping the banister as a wave of vertigo washed over her from the sudden illumination.

'Where did you get that?'

Claire lowered the beam to the floor and joined her by the stairs. 'It was hanging on a hook just here,' she whispered.

They stood shoulder to shoulder as Claire trawled the room with the light. They were in the supermarket break room. A whiteboard showed photographs of all the employees, most of whom she knew by name, with figures and dates written beside them. Positioned above them all, Mr Blake's portrait looked down on them with disdain, like a convict's mugshot.

A table and chairs had been pushed to one side. A refrigerator loomed beside an emptied water cooler. Two doors on their side of the room, one to the bathrooms, and the other which presumably led into the main section of the supermarket.

Another soft hiss of metal drew the flashlight to the door on the opposite side of the room, a wide double-door with circular windows. The kind you'd see in a restaurant. The sign above it read: Meat Prep. Claire aimed the beam at the windows, but they were so grimy that all the light reflected back at them. Merry bit her thumbnail as they crept across the sticky linoleum to the doors. Claire wiped one of the windows with her sleeve and they peered through. She could see the suggestion of stainless steel surfaces, trolleys and the ill-defined shapes of giant mechanical saws and grinders, all obscured by the darkness. Another door at the far end was secured with a chain and padlock.

Claire nudged the door open and Merry, holding tight to her shirt, was dragged in after her. It smelled of blood and bleach, of surfaces stained and sterilised for years in an endless back and forth. Her skin crawled with terror. Her throat and eyes were dry.

'What the hell is that?' The torch beam fell on a wide plastic tub sitting on a counter beside the walk-in freezer. The light turned crimson near the base of the tub where blood had pooled. 'Is that...' They stepped closer. The plastic container was semi-transparent, enough to see the fuzzy silhouette of the objects inside, and the five swollen lumps that pressed against the edge. 'Fuck me dead...'

Even when she stood staring down into the container, Merry still didn't believe what she was seeing. Two human arms, pale with a marbled purplish tinge, severed cleanly just below the shoulder, and resting side-by-side, slightly bowed, as neatly as a new pair of shoes. The left arm still wore its wristwatch.

Merry spun and emptied the contents of her stomach onto the floor. Claire had dropped the hammer and was gripping the edge of the counter with her head bowed, taking short quick breaths. 'What kind of bloody sicko—'

Shhhh.

The metallic hiss came again, and this time it left no doubt in their minds. It was coming from inside the meat freezer. Claire reached feebly for the handle, her fingers stretching, trembling, but halted in the air inches from the door. Merry moved to her side and placed a hand delicately over her sister's. Claire recoiled, eyes fierce for a moment, then all at once the mask dissolved and she was a child again. A frightened girl, just sixteen years old, who had no idea what she was doing. Who wanted nothing more than to curl up on the couch with her mum and sisters and watch a movie. Whose world had been flooded, and who was struggling against the tide of grief that washed her ever further from the shore.

'Claire, we don't have to.'

After a moment, Claire nodded. The relief flowed through her like a drug.

Then a voice from behind them. 'You've come this far. It would be a shame to stop now.'

Merry jumped, digging her nails into Claire's hand as Mr Blake stepped into the room.

'I should have known you'd wander. Girls your age never do as they're told. But since we're all here...' Blake reached out and pulled the handle, releasing the heavy freezer door. Inside was dark, but something at the back of the space was moving towards them, and with it came that familiar hiss of metal on metal, much more forceful now than they'd heard before.

Blake flipped a switch by the door. 'Say good afternoon to Kevin.'

April 6

His name was Kevin Bertram and he'd worked in the deli.

As the light flickered on they saw him, rushing towards them, still wearing his bright orange work vest, lips peeled off in a permanent grin, stomach distended, heavy chains dancing behind him.

Merry leaped back, straight into Claire, and the two of them fell to the floor. She heard Kevin grunt and emit a strange stuttering chuckle and looked up to see his legs kicking out from under him as the chains caught him and pulled taut.

'Kevin was a model employee,' Blake said, making no move to help them. 'Punctual. Reliable. Not overly ambitious. Of course, he spent most of his pay on marijuana, but he had the decency never to smoke it at work.'

Kevin struggled to stand, twisting against the chains, trying to face them. The bloodied stumps where his arms had been waggled at them. Merry sat, pressed both hands into the cool brick tiled floor for a moment, then she and Claire helped each other up.

'He could barely stand from the fever, you know, on the day the virus took hold. He and Patrick McKenzie were the only two that came in. Kevin died right over there, while packaging the gourmet sausages.'

Two meat hooks held Kevin up by the shoulders. They tore bloody holes through his shirt, hooked under his collarbones and protruded another six inches out of his back. Thick chains secured them to rails along the ceiling. On another hook further back against the wall hung the eviscerated but otherwise untouched carcass of a pig.

'Why...' Merry stammered. 'Why is he here?' She remembered Kevin from school. A quiet year twelve boy, he spent most of his time sitting in the library, playing Magic cards with his friends.

Mr Blake stepped forward into the freezer, less than a metre from the grinner's gnashing teeth. 'It's a good question. Why is he here? Why is all of this happening? A good question. The only question left worth asking.'

He turned to face them. 'Did you know Mrs Bertram? Kevin's lovely mother? She drove to church in Bordertown with him every Sunday. Two hours there and back. Praying for her husband. He'd a nasty habit of drinking too much and beating her and young Kevin. She couldn't have minded because she stayed with him, but when he found himself a mistress and tried it on with her, she objected and the magistrate gave him ten years. But still she went to church every Sunday and prayed for his soul. Prayed for his early release. Prayed that he'd forgive her for her role in his incarceration.' At this point he paused and took a sip from the bottle in his pocket. It must have been almost empty, because he held it up for a while to allow the last drops to trickle out, while behind him Kevin lurched against the chains.

'She came into the store a week ago, grief stricken, you understand, and told me that her husband had contracted the virus and died in prison. When I offered my condolences, and some rot about him being with God now, she sneered. She'd stopped believing, she said. Lost her faith. What kind of God would take such a "beautiful soul" before his time? What kind of God would do this to the world He'd created? After all her years of devotion and prayers? I said that perhaps He had answered her prayers. Her husband had been released early, after all. She didn't see it that way.'

Merry frowned. She wasn't sure what he was trying to tell them, or why. It seemed surreal that he could speak so calmly while this creature that shouldn't exist strained against its chains, intent on tearing their faces off.

He walked towards them, rolling up his sleeves, and they fell back until they were pressed against the bench in the middle of the room. He turned to the large container on the counter and picked up one of Kevin's arms. It twisted and bent slightly at the elbow, but the fingers were frozen in the claw-like grip of rigor mortis. Blood had congealed along the forearm and little finger and it wept thick, dark strings. He carried it to the meat saw against the wall.

'Never had much love of the Bible myself. It's nothing but ancient propaganda, controlling and exploiting the ignorant, unquestioning sheep through fear and false promises.'

Blake pressed a button on the saw and the lights dimmed momentarily as the machine hummed. The blade flashed up and down so quickly that its teeth were a blur.

'Isn't it funny to lose faith now? If anything were to convince me of the existence of some awesome and omnipotent being, this would be it. The world has been washed clean of the great disappointment that is our race and only a chosen few have been spared, whose job it will be to remedy past mistakes. The prophesied apocalypse finally comes to pass. Like Noah and the great flood. Biblical, wouldn't you agree?'

He flopped Kevin's arm onto the sliding table of the meat saw and pushed it against the blade and it cut through flesh and bone with a short high-pitched scream. When he'd finished, four thick round slices of Kevin sat on the stainless steel table, like eye fillet ready to be wrapped in butcher's paper. Next he took out a pair of tongs and a small butane blowtorch and held one of the slices under the flame until it charred. Merry covered her nose as the room filled with the strangely sweet smell of barbecue.

She felt as though she was outside her own body. Her empty stomach churned. She looked down and realised her hands were shaking. Claire was gripping her arm, although she couldn't feel a thing.

Blake set the torch down and walked back to the meat freezer where Kevin was still bucking against the chains. Using the tongs, he held the cut of meat up to Kevin's mouth. Kevin snarled at it but was clearly more interested in the living flesh on the other end of the tongs. He tried to lean around, waggling his arm stumps.

'You must be wondering why I've kept Kevin here, restrained like this. We've been given a chance to inherit the world. To start again and make it the place it should have been, free from hate and discrimination and corruption and poverty. We can begin that world. But first we need to reclaim it, and to do that, we need to understand. We need to prepare.'

He returned to the meat saw and took two more slices of Kevin's arm, this time dropping them into a plastic container and covering them with bleach from a big industrial looking bottle. He prodded them with the tongs and flipped them several times.

'There are so many unanswered questions. Why are only some of the dead reanimated? And how? You saw Kevin wouldn't eat infected meat, even after it's been cooked. The pig, too, he won't touch. No good after it's been frozen. But clearly my skin and your skin is far more appetising. You must admit it's fascinating. What is the difference, and how does he know? Is it our warmth? Our smell? Do they hear the blood flowing in our veins? Or something else? It makes sense from an evolutionary point of view. They never attack or eat one another. However...'

He took a dripping slab of meat from the container and carried it back to the freezer. He was just about to offer it to Kevin when he hesitated and walked instead to Merry and Claire.

'Here. You do it.'

He took Merry's arm and forced the tongs into her hand, pressing her fingers closed around it so that she wouldn't drop the meat. A whiff of bleach opened her nostrils with a trail of chemical fire that swept down the back of her throat and into her lungs. She turned away and exhaled forcefully, holding the tongs at arm's length now. Claire was still gripping her arm, but her face was pale and distant.

'Don't worry,' Mr Blake said, placing a hand on her back and pushing her gently forwards. 'You'll be perfectly safe.'

With watering eyes, she stepped through the doorway and into the small, cold room, holding the tongs ahead of her. Kevin's grunts and broken gasps echoed around her. If he'd still had his arms, he could have reached out and pulled her towards him. The slice of meat, wrinkled and white like her hands after a long bath, jiggled and dripped.

Kevin lurched suddenly forwards, snapping down on the tongs and tearing the meat away from her. He retreated back a few steps, hunching as far as the chains would allow him, and worked his jaws around until the meat was gone. Merry put a hand to her chest, trying to calm her shuddering breaths. Mr Blake stood beside her and guided her out of the freezer.

'Good. Good girl.'

The door closed with a snap.

'Sodium hypochlorite,' Blake explained. 'It kills bacteria, fungi and viruses. It's effective and plentiful.' His nose whistled as he took deep, excited breaths. 'There's still so much to learn, and much to do. But that's enough for now. You must be starving. Let's eat.'

They didn't eat their spaghetti until they were far away from the petrol station. Even though it was cold and the noodles were mushy, it tasted wonderful. As they ate, Bear told her stories about her mother.

'My Mum and Dad never had much money, so Jay and me had to make our own fun. Mostly wrestling, torturing each other, terrifying our parents. Y'know, boy stuff.' He chuckled. 'One time I woke up in the middle of the night and found him pinning me down, trying to give me a tattoo with a broken bic pen and one of Mum's sewing needles. He almost finished it, too, see?'

He held out his right forearm and showed her a faded blue drawing of a teddy bear. 'I had to go to the ER. Bled all over the place and was on antibiotics for a month. Yeah, good times.'

When Zoey didn't laugh, he shrugged. 'I guess you had to be there. But Lisa was the golden child. Dad doted on her—that means he gave her anything she wanted—and one Christmas she got this huge doll's house, shaped like a castle, with a little wooden king and queen, and three princesses, and all the furniture, a couple of little horses for them to ride and even a drawbridge that opened.'

Zoey's mouth hung open and her eyes were wide. 'I wish I could play with it,' she said.

Bear laughed. Then he looked down and his face went sad. 'That sounds like fun, doesn't it? I wish I could get it for you. But it's long gone now.' He threw the empty can of spaghetti aside and stood up. 'Time to hit the road again, Jack. Still a ways to go.'

Zoey realised she didn't know where they were going, so she asked Bear.

'It's a little place north of here. Belongs to...an old friend. I used to go there to hide out sometimes when I was in trouble. It's about the only place trouble never found me. A good three hours from anywhere with a name. Peaceful, you know? We'll be safe there.'

They rode past empty fields and farms. It was a long time before they passed another car, and it was empty; an ugly green wagon parked crooked on the side of the road as if the people had just stopped for a picnic and never come back. They saw nobody at all. Further down the road, Zoey spotted a horse in a field and pointed. It was trotting over to them. Uncle Bear pulled the bike over to the side of the road, and they walked up to the fence to meet it. It was brown with a white patch over one ear and white speckles on its legs. It stretched its neck over the fence and nodded its head, asking her for something to eat. Zoey looked at Bear. 'Can we give him something? They eat hay and apples, but not chocolate. Chocolate makes animals sick.'

'I'm fresh out of hay and apples...and chocolate.'

She walked up to the horse. 'Sorry, Pony' she said to him.

'I think it's a horse, sweetie.'

She looked at Bear. 'I know. His name is Pony.'

'Pony the horse, eh?'

Zoey nodded. 'Daddy was going to take me to the zoo.'

She reached up and stroked Pony's nose for a minute.

'Do you think the animals at the zoo are okay?'

'I'm sure they're fine.'

'What happened to everybody?'

Bear sighed and placed a hand on Pony's head. 'I don't know, sweetheart. I really don't. Everyone just started getting sick. It spread so fast...all my friends...there was nothing...' he sighed again. 'Nobody knew what to do. Most people just went home to be with their families.' Pony lifted his head and tried to nibble at Bear's hand. 'I waited to get sick too, but all I got was a sniffle and a bit of a fever. I don't know why. Thought because I didn't get it, maybe Lisa would be okay too...' He looked at her. 'You're too young to hear all this. Too young to see what you've seen...'

'Didn't you give them medicine?'

'Yeah, I tried. The doctors didn't have enough time to make medicine that would work against it.'

'I saw Mummy in the window. After she woke up.'

Bear knelt down next to her and held her shoulders. His eyes were wide. 'That wasn't your Mummy. That wasn't Lisa. Just like that wasn't my friend back there. Not anymore.'

Zoey thought about that. 'Do they all wake up as different people?'

Uncle Bear was quiet for a while. 'No, most don't wake up at all,' he said at last, then added, 'Only the ones you loved the best.'

When she turned to look at him, he met her eyes for a moment, as if he wanted to say more, then looked away.

'But what do I know? Your mum was the only one in our family with any brains.'

She felt cold talking about the laughers. 'I wish they didn't laugh.'

'Yeah, me too.'

'When Mummy gets better, will you take me back home? I'll show you my toy box, and we can play dress-ups.'

Uncle Bear's eyebrows turned down at the edges. 'Zoey...' he began.

Pony's ears flicked and he turned and trotted away. Something was coming along the road behind them. They saw it first as a cloud of red dust in the distance, but soon they could hear the engine and the sound of the tyres on gravel. The green car.

April 6

Merry lay on the thin mattress with Claire curled up behind her. The spaghetti with minced meat he'd served them for dinner sat like a stone in her stomach, posing nauseating questions conjured by the image of the meat grinder downstairs. She closed her eyes tight and listened to the swell of the wind racing through the streets and pressing itself against the windows in great shuddering waves. It whispered in the leaves, hushed at first, then rose suddenly, forcefully, so that it rattled the drainpipes and the bars shook against the windows which trembled in their frames, and the roof rumbled in faraway places, until it fell away in sullen retreat. With her eyes closed it sounded just like the ocean at night, and her bed was a raft, adrift, rocking and heaving at the whim of this dark and daunting ocean. She didn't know whether it was carrying her to shore, or towards jagged rocks, or if it was indifferent to her, and would leave her to drift aimlessly into nothingness.

She opened her eyes and licked her dry lips, watching the unfamiliar room take shape even as the taste of salt from the ocean spray disappeared. When would the nightmare end? She thought back through the days: Today is Friday. The twins have karate class on Fridays. They were supposed to be going for their orange belts together. Tonight. That should have been tonight. Right now they should be celebrating with fish and chips, so greasy it shone through the newspaper it was wrapped in, staying up late watching Honey I Shrunk the Kids, and throwing popcorn into each other's mouths. This was all wrong.

'Claire,' she whispered, a cold panic rising. 'Where are we? What's happening? Tell me it's all going to be okay.'

Across the hall, she heard Mr Blake rise and walk across the room, and a sob caught in her throat. There was a shuffling of papers, a thump that might have been a heavy book closing. The rustling of sheets and the shifting of weight on a mattress. Then the building settled again into silence. At first she thought her sister must have been asleep because for a time there was only the warm, regular touch of each exhalation against the back of her neck. Then a hand found hers in the dark, and Claire's legs drew up against hers, and she whispered back a song she'd made up for Merry after she came home crying from her first day of school.

'Sometimes you fall and scrape your knee,
Sometimes your ball gets stuck in a tree.
It happened to you, it happened to me.
But smile. Smile. Smile and be Merry.'

Merry sighed and closed her eyes, allowing her body to relax a little.

'I patted a dog. Now I've got fleas.
Oh shit, I've been stung by a bee.
You're not alone and never will be.
So smile...Smile...Smile and be Merry.'

Claire kissed the back of her head. The ancient mattress gave a small groan of complaint as they shifted and drew still closer together. The wind, its rage vented, shook the trees halfheartedly. 'It'll be okay, Merry.'

The day after they arrived, he put them to work. First, he had them clear all the food from the shelves of the supermarket and move the remaining non-perishables to the loading bay out the back. He explained that other survivors were bound to pass through town, so if they could create the impression that the place had already been cleared out, they might be left alone. Merry and Claire took a shopping trolley each, loaded them up with tins of preserved fruits and vegetables, bottles of water, honey, cans of soft drink, and other sundries, and re-stacked them on the shelves in the loading bay. Sometimes as they wheeled the trolleys through the break room, they would hear Kevin rattling his chains or chuckling to himself, and Merry would try to forget the smell of the bleach mixed with his acrid breath that her mind seemed so eager to recall. When they needed a break, they'd take turns pushing each other up and down the aisles, whizzing sideways in the rickety trolleys, or they'd sit on the checkout counters at the front of the store, looking out onto the street, eating Vegemite crackers and dried mango.

Claire was quiet. She took to the work without so much as a roll of her eyes, and several times Merry caught her, her hand frozen while taking an item from the shelf, staring with eyes glazed at a bottle of olive oil or white vinegar. When she asked her about it, she'd look up, frightened for a moment, then grin and crack a joke, and hurry on.

Although the work was tiring, Merry relished the chance to occupy her mind with something other than reliving the events of the past few days. It forced her to think forwards instead of back, to a future that had seemed impossible. She'd even entertained thoughts of staying permanently. Perhaps, with Mr Blake, they could survive this. He seemed so organised, so capable. He had a plan for everything, and even though she had to admit he frightened her, he had taken them in and given them shelter, and enough food to last for years.

Sometimes he would appear and update the inventory in his notebook, or tell them to move this or that, or would simply stand and watch them. Occasionally they'd hear the shuffling footsteps of a grinner drifting along the empty street, and Mr Blake would take up his rifle and withdraw without a word, and all the world would pause to listen for that single shot that would crack like a whip a few minutes later and snap it back into motion.

It took them two days to clear all the shelves. During that time Blake continued to work on the security door connecting the supermarket to the apartment. When he'd finished, it looked like a bank vault on the apartment side, while on the supermarket side it was all but invisible, recessed and covered over with plasterboard and painted to blend into the wall.

On the third day, he called them into his room after breakfast. A large map, covered in different coloured markings, was pinned to one wall, and laid out on the bed were three hunting rifles. Blake picked up the largest of the rifles and cradled it against his hip with the barrel pointing to the ceiling.

'Have you ever fired one of these?'

'Yeah, few times,' Claire said. She wandered over to the map while Merry hung back in the doorway.

'Meredith?'

'Uh, no, never.'

'Well, it's important that you learn. One day your life may depend on it. Claire, will you please take that map down? We'll need it.'

Claire crossed her arms. 'Where are we going?'

Blake twisted his lips in a grimace that he may have intended to be a smile. He took a set of keys from his pocket and waved them at her. 'You're going to learn to drive.'

Merry's hair whipped about her as wind blasted through the two open windows. Perched on the back middle seat, her fingernails dug deep indentations in the discoloured vinyl headrests.

'Put it into fourth,' Mr Blake yelled over the straining engine. 'Remember the clutch this time.'

Merry leaned to the side as the wind swept Claire's hair in front of her eyes. The car veered into the middle of the road, straddling both lanes as Claire looked down at the pedals. She stepped on the clutch before releasing the accelerator, and the engine whined before sinking with a crunch into the next gear.

'Can you slow down a bit?' Merry cried, staring straight ahead, watching the white lines of the highway blur into a single, flickering, swaying stroke.

'What for? The road's empty, and the coppers have all taken the day off,' Claire shouted back. 'Just enjoy the ride.'

Yeah, Merry thought, the cops have taken the day off, but so have the ambulances...

'Just up here,' Blake said, pointing.

Claire turned the wheel and the car bent to the left, tore through the grass, still travelling at 60 km/h, and came to a hard stop by the fence bordering an empty paddock. The plume of dust that had been chasing them since they left overtook the car and blew into the paddock. Claire looked around, grinning. Merry could still feel her bones vibrating.

'Good,' was all Blake said, taking a moment to preen his hair back into place.

He handed them each one of the smaller rifles and they followed him over the fence and through the grass towards the far trees. When they reached the tree line, he stopped.

'Look here.' He pointed to a metal switch on top of the rifle. 'That's the safety. Most important thing to remember. Leave it off, and you're liable to shoot yourselves. Leave it on, and it could well be the last mistake you make. Now watch.'

He showed them where to place their hands to balance the gun's weight; how to rest the stock against their shoulder and bring their eye level with the barrel. He stepped back and took a sip from the small brown bottle, watching them. The gun wobbled in her hands, the barrel dipped and swayed, and her shoulder ached. As she tried aiming, a cold pincer grasped her neck and the rifle almost slipped from her hands.

'Relax your neck,' Blake said, stepping around her to adjust her grip. 'Lower your elbow. Let it support the weight of the rifle rather than trying to lift it up.' He released her and turned to check on Claire, who was glancing from Blake to her with a frown of mistrust. Merry tried to smile and went back to aiming the weapon, wondering how long it would take for her muscles to unclench.

'Good. Good. Now let's try it for real.'

He took a box of ammunition from his pocket and showed them how to load the rounds into the top of the rifle.

'Remember, squeeze the trigger, don't pull it.'

The first shot took her by surprise. Not because it was loud—it was quieter than she expected—but the punch against her shoulder came so suddenly that she staggered back, her hands trembling and sweating. She watched Claire take her shot and saw a chip of bark leap from one of the nearer trees.

Merry wanted to leave, but he made them practice until late morning. The air smelled like sparklers, and her eyes hurt from squinting. With an effort, she ejected her last spent casing and loaded the next round. Took aim at one of Claire's bullet holes. Psyched herself up for the shot—

Claire appeared next to her and placed a hand atop her rifle, lowering it. Her face was pale, frightened. Merry gave her a questioning look, but didn't need to ask what was wrong. She'd heard it too. Rising and dipping in the wind, but drawing unmistakably nearer, came a loud and rumbling engine.

April 9

They ducked behind the trees and Mr Blake raised his rifle and aimed it down the road, peering through the scope. Merry crouched, her mind a mix of conflicting emotions. Fear dominated, strangling her with a cord of her own anxiety. Ever since she was little, she'd trained herself to expect the worst. Every tree or playground was an injury waiting to happen. Every fluffy kitten carried tetanus on its claws. She'd dreamed of owning a horse for as long as she could remember, but her fear of falling kept her from ever taking a riding lesson. She'd watched life going on around her, in Claire's impulsive and ever more rebellious actions; read about it in books, seen it in movies, but barely taken part in her own life. She'd always done as she was told, never questioning, never pushing back, hoping when something bad happened, it would be to someone else. Because she was a good girl who always followed the rules. Because that's what you had to do, right?

But now the unthinkable had happened with no explanation or consent from her. That she'd always done the right thing meant nothing.

She stared at the ground. Tiny silken threads lay between the blades of grass by her sneakers—the abandoned parachutes of newly hatched spiders scattered by the wind. She reached down and touched one, and it held her finger for a moment before collapsing into nothing. Ants marched between them, dancing with the invading spiders, swarming them, carrying them away. Of the hundreds or thousands that flew with the wind, how many found safety? Fate, if that's what you wanted to call it, dealt with humans and spiders just the same. Indiscriminately.

Exhaling, she noticed her fear waning.

Fate's pendulum had hit her, despite her best efforts to avoid it, harder than she'd ever imagined, but here she was, still standing, still living. And now the pendulum had nowhere to go but back again.

She leaned out from behind the tree and fixed her eyes on the approaching cloud of dust, fronted by a bright glimmer of chrome. The engine was deep and stuttering—a Harley, or something like it. Soon the bike came into view, though it was too far for her to make out the rider. Mr Blake exhaled softly, his finger sliding down and curling around the trigger. Her heart pounded and she whipped her gaze back to the road. The bike slowed, crawling past the car that Claire had left parked haphazardly by the fence. She glimpsed a black helmet and dark sunnies. A bushy beard. Some smaller shape sitting in front of him. Too far to see what it was. He didn't stop. The engine revved and soon it was out of sight.

Claire stepped out from behind the tree and walked forward a few paces, her golden hair ablaze in the sunlight. 'We should've said something. The first living person we've seen in two days, and we hide from him.'

'Its best to remain cautious,' Blake said. He stood at the edge of the treeline, shadows shifting over his face. 'When survival is at stake, everyone looks out for himself first. People act nice, they might even like to think they are nice, but rules are quickly forgotten when there's no-one left to enforce them. Remember, we have a lot worth protecting.'

Claire snorted, but didn't look at him.

'I know it's hard. Once we secure our resources and fortify the area, we can think about looking for other survivors. But it's not time yet.'

Claire narrowed her eyes. 'There must be years' worth of food locked away in there. More than enough to share. And having something to share is a good way to make friends. Wouldn't this all be much easier with some help?'

'Food is not the only resource I'm protecting. And trust is not so easily bought.' He said this in a tone that made clear the matter was closed.

Claire looked back down the road. She turned, snapping her heels together and giving him a salute. 'Aye aye, Captain.'

Mr Blake's moustache twitched as he stepped toward her. 'There's no need for that tone. Get in the car.'

Merry had to admit she felt a lot safer with Mr Blake at the wheel. The car hummed along the asphalt, but the sound of the road did little to stifle the uncomfortable silence within. Claire drummed her fingertips on the dash and sighed. She fiddled with the knob on the radio, searching through static and dead air, finding only the occasional low-pitched tone or recorded message about the network experiencing technical difficulties. 'Worth a shot,' she mumbled. 'Hey, you got any tunes in here?' She reached out and popped open the glovebox.

'Leave that—'

Merry noticed the revolver first. It clattered forward, almost landing in Claire's lap. But it wasn't the gun that Blake dove for. He jerked across, grabbing for a small pile of what looked like Polaroid pictures. The car veered off the road, throwing them all to one side, and emptying most of the contents of the glovebox onto the floor. Tyres bit into the dirt and they came to an abrupt stop. Blake reached into the footwell below Claire, who drew her legs up in surprise, and scrambled to retrieve the photos. When he'd tucked them into his jacket pocket, he turned on Claire with a look of raw malice. His knuckles were white on the wheel, a thick vein pulsed in his neck, and even Claire had shrunk into her seat, silenced.

Merry was sure he would hit her.

He turned and stared straight ahead, took a sip from the brown bottle. 'You really must keep a lid on your curiosity, my girl. It's going to get you into trouble one day.'

He reached across and snapped the glovebox closed, pressed his hair back into place, checked the rearview mirror, put the car back in gear, and returned to the road. The silence was heavier than before.

Merry looked at Claire, trying to read her sister's thoughts through the back of her head, but Claire just stared out the window, watching the blur of the road.

They passed the biker on the road a short time later. He'd parked under the shade of a small gum tree and was standing by the fence, his hand outstretched towards a chestnut and white horse.

When it heard their car, it turned with a swish of its tail and trotted away. The man watched them. He stood very close to his bike and glanced down several times at something by his leg, but because of the position of the bike Merry couldn't see what was there. Blake slowed as they passed him, and Merry wanted to plead with him to stop. After all, nobody that loved horses could have an evil heart. But the man's hand snuck around his back, like the people do in the movies right before they pull a gun from their waistband, and fear took hold of her again. She craned her neck back, watching him watching her. And then he was out of sight. Another of life's paths unfollowed, another chance gone to dust, and she could only sit and wonder at who he might have been, and whether he might have hurt her and stolen their food as Mr Blake had said, or if perhaps he was just as lost and afraid as she was.

They drove on in silence.

'We're here.'

When Merry looked up, she released a short gasp of surprise. He'd parked outside their house. The door was still wide open, the way she'd left it, and she half expected her mum to step out of the sunburnt shadows onto the porch and wave to her.

'What are we doing here?'

Claire was still sitting with her knees drawn up, her face close to the glass.

'It's time for you to eat the frog,' Blake said.

Merry frowned. Had she heard that right?

'There are a lot of bodies left in the houses around town. Before long they will begin decomposing, and if we let that happen we'll be at risk of all manner of other diseases. They need to be retrieved and burnt as soon as possible.

'Mark Twain once said that if you eat a live frog every morning, you can be confident that nothing worse will happen to you the rest of the day. We're starting here because this is your frog. There are many bodies to be moved, but for you, this will be the worst. If you can do this, you'll have no problem with the others.'

Merry looked back at the house. The edges of her vision blurred and the gaping doorway seemed to race towards her. 'Please...no...I can't.'

'You must.'

'You don't understand...I can't go back in...they were eating her...they were...and their eyes...there was nothing left in them. I can't...I can't.'

He wasn't listening. He'd already got out of the car and opened the back. From his duffel bag he took two plastic white biohazard suits, goggles and face masks. 'Try not to come in contact with any blood, or other fluids. I suggest wrapping them in sheets. If you work together, you will manage.'

Her mind slowed to a crawl and stepping out of the car without falling took all her concentration. Nobody spoke as he helped them into the suits, except the occasional word of direction from Blake. Turn around. Tuck your hair in. Pull the gloves over your sleeves. Breathe through your mouth. But Merry's eyes never left that doorway. Before she knew it, her feet were taking her across the lawn towards the house.

April 9

The plastic biohazard suit crinkled with every step. Her breath was caught by the mask that covered her nose and mouth; held there until it died. Every thought scrambled by heat and fear.

She looked back over her shoulder. Mr Blake was leaning against the car, watching them, his rifle slung over one shoulder. There were tears in her eyes, but she tried to match Claire's pace, who strode boldly ahead. Not for the first time, she wished for just a taste of her sister's bravery. Nearing the porch, her nausea grew, and she had to catch herself on one of the wooden columns.

The empty shell of a cicada clung to the dry wood above her hand. Its eyes translucent and sightless, its wingless form hunched, preserved in a state of frozen fragility. Could it have known about the transformation it was undergoing, or would it have felt like death? Trapped inside its own skin, constricting and petrifying in the sun, with no hope of escape, until the very force that seemed about to destroy it instead set it free. The neat split down the back of the husk an epitaph not of a life ended, but of rebirth.

'Hey, you okay?' Claire stood in the doorway. Her voice was muffled and unfamiliar through the mask. 'Here, come on inside and sit down. I know this sucks, just...let's not give him another reason to be pissed off right now, okay? Just get out of sight. I'll take care of this.'

Merry forced herself through the door and part of the way down the hallway. She listened for any sound of the twins, that telltale clicking of teeth, but the only sound was the kitchen clock, still ticking, echoing through the house, dutifully keeping track of the time though neither the dead nor the living had any use for it. They must have moved on. She slumped against the wall.

'How can you do it, Claire?' She tried to breathe through her dread. 'How come you're not afraid? How come everything is so...darn easy for you?'

Claire laughed. 'You're kidding, right? Not afraid? I'm shitting myself right now. I have been since old man Harrison dropped dead in the kitchen. But I don't have a choice, do I?'

'I can't believe he's making us do this.'

Claire looked down the hall toward Mum's room, pulled the mask down to her chin. Tiny beads of sweat shone on her upper lip. 'It's karma. I was a crappy daughter. I didn't mean to be...most of the time. But staying out late and not telling her where I was going...coming home drunk...not giving a shit about school.'

Her gloved hand clenched, relaxed, clenched, relaxed. 'Do you think if I do this...if we bury her...the nightmares will stop?'

Merry thought. 'No.'

Claire smiled at her. It was a strained smile, the kind for holding back tears. 'You're probably right. Anyway, better get on with it. You can wait here—'

Merry stood up. 'I'll help you.'

'You don't have to—'

'Yes, I do. I think...I'm glad we're doing this. He's right. We need to do this.'

Claire nodded, and they both pulled their masks back into place.

Thankfully the room was too dark to see anything clearly, but Merry was sure that what she did see would haunt her forever. She tried to keep her gaze averted, concentrate on the cues Claire was giving her, but as she pulled the corners of the fitted sheet off the mattress to cover the body she was caught and held by her mother's dead, sunken, milky eyes.

She stopped breathing. A second became an eternity. Her mother's pale freckled skin had become yellowed tissue paper, pulled taut over jutting cheekbones. Blisters had erupted along her neck and shoulders—above the crusty hollow and protruding ribs—swollen pale islands on a marbled purple and green sea. They'd eaten a little more of her, emptied her of her organs, stripped some more skin from—

She tore her eyes away and pulled the sheet into place.

'You take her legs,' Claire whispered.

Together they hoisted the dead weight off the bed and into the hall, taking short, shuffling steps. Claire paused on their way back to the front door, then veered into the living room.

'He's not having her.' She shifted the weight against her stomach. 'Let him burn the rest—ugh—I don't care, but we're not gonna just...toss her into a bonfire—shit...my hand's slipping, hold up—We're gonna bury her here. At home—'

A corner of the sheet caught under Merry's foot and the body slipped from Claire's hands, falling headfirst onto the tiles with a heavy crack. Merry was pulled forward, her foot slipped on something wet, and the next moment she was on the floor, one hand buried in the clotted viscera beneath the sheet.

She scrambled back for the safety of the counter, trying to wipe off the thick, tar-like fluid that covered her gloved hand. Her jaw trembled. She ripped the gloves off, threw them down, closed her eyes, but the image persisted.

Claire hurriedly covered the body, as though the sun's touch might awaken it.

'Are you alright?'

Merry shook her head.

'Yeah, stupid question. Sorry.'

'I just...need a minute.'

'I know. Just...don't think on it too long. The more you think, the worse it gets.'

Merry lowered her head to her knees, took some deep breaths, and, realising it did nothing to soothe her nerves, reluctantly stood. Some of the blisters must have torn open in the fall because the sheet was blotted with newly wet patches, and the air had taken on a new foulness.

They wrestled the body into the open air and laid it on the lawn. While Claire went to find the shovels, Merry stood vigil, standing with her back to it, looking at the house.

Blake was standing in the doorway, watching her. His gaze flat, questioning. The drumbeat of her heart quickened. She swallowed, trying to hold her ground, but found herself stumbling over her words.

'We're...burying her. It's not right...I mean, I know we can't just leave the...bodies...lying around, but she's still our Mum...and she would want to be buried here.'

She couldn't tell if he was frowning, or just squinting in the sun. His face revealed nothing.

Claire's footsteps came back, and there was the gritty chomp of a spade being thrust into the dirt. His eyes shifted to a space above Merry's shoulder, but Claire didn't speak and Merry didn't dare turn around. His face twisted with agitation, as if he'd been trying to bend a spoon with his mind and had just now realised it was beyond his powers.

'Don't take too long,' he said, before sliding the door closed and disappearing.

'Shivers.'

It took most of the afternoon to dig the grave, and it was barely two feet deep. Merry sweltered and itched like mad inside the plastic suit, but she wouldn't allow herself to complain. She felt that if she began she'd break down and wouldn't be able to stop, so she put all her anger and helplessness into digging, driving the blunt metal blade into the earth, pressing it into the clay with all her weight, rocking it back and forth until it came loose, throwing it on the pile. Soon her hands were raw with blisters, her back ached and she had splints down her shins.

As they were clearing out the last of the clay the glass door trembled open and Mr Blake emerged carrying two bottles of bright orange sports drink. He set them down on the bench by the lemon tree, pausing to watch them dig for a moment before going back inside. As soon as the door slid closed they set their spades down and drank thirstily. It was warm, tasting vaguely of oranges, and bitter, but Merry didn't care, guzzling half the bottle before coming up for air.

When the job was done they stood side by side on the lawn, looking down at the shrouded figure in the earth. It was difficult to believe it was their mother. The wind bent the grass and scattered some loose dirt back into the hole. Her head was throbbing. The cicadas seemed to trill an endless, unbroken tune from inside her skull. She thought maybe she tried to say some kind of eulogy as Claire shovelled the dirt, but she couldn't remember—

—she was back in the car, watching the house recede into the distance, a large black 'X' spray-painted on its closed door.

The world outside seemed to flash by in repeating coloured shapes she couldn't quite distinguish   her eyes refused to focus   once or twice she heard Claire's voice, but there was something funny with her ears too and the words sounded like they were being spoken in a different language   her forehead pressed against the glass thumping against it   exploding with every bump in the road.

The moon was still out on the morning he'd left, Merry remembered. Daddy. The sky was blue, but the moon was still up and she'd asked him if it was daytime or nighttime.

(What's happening to me?)

Telephone poles flashed past the window flash   flashflash

Did the moon forget to go to bed this morning, Daddy?

Maybe it stayed up so it could say goodbye to Daddy as well, Mummy had said.

(Something isn't right)

                A car door slammed and she staggered into the street   the air was warm and she was floating on it   her head tilted upward by the pull of the pink and orange expanse of sky   her eyes not nearly wide enough to take it all in   and he was dragging them along by the elbows.

'What did you…do to us?' Claire's voice.

'It's heat exhaustion. You were in the sun too long.'

'Bullshit—'

'I'm going to be sick…' Was that what her voice sounded like? Now she was staring down   down at the artificially orange vomit decorating the cement around her shoes   like a child's painting of the sky

I'll only be gone a few days. And I'll call you from the hotel.

Say goodbye to Daddy, girls

Goodbye, Daddy!

Goodbye Clairebear. Goodbye Merry. Bye, hun.

Don't forget the moon, Daddy. He stayed up to see you.

Goodbye Moon

Footsteps coming   running   the grip released from her arm and she was floating free on her own legs

'Shit, how did she get out?!'

Something hit her and she was spinning   falling   the sky was so big   so big   but there was something blocking it   it was jerking twitching snarling like an animal   pain in her chest in her legs in her hand   he was behind it   holding it back (Daddy?)   he dragged it away   the sky was back   but where was the moon?

He was grunting   fighting hard   the other one was strong stronger than it looked   Merry remembered how strong it was she tried to tell him that but all she could do was smack her lips

The other one was panting too but not because it was tired because thats just what they did   she could hear its jaws opening and closing as it gasped

'Yah, yah, yah, yah.'   Was it laughing at him?

We talked about this. You know I wouldn't go if I didn't have to. But its a big conference, some big names will be there. Its all about connections. I'll call you in a few hours

'yah, yah, yah—ugh—'

it fell   bumping against her shin   then its fingernails were digging into her calves   digging into the muscle as it pulled itself up her leg and back onto her chest. This time she saw enough of its face before it was ripped away again. Dana.

and there was the moon   a pale sliver   a thin crack in the darkening sky

a thud as a small body hit the hard wall   again   a sharp crack another crack less sharp   meatier   the gasping had stopped. Teeth sprinkled on the ground.

Maybe the moon stayed up so it could say goodbye to Daddy as well

Goodbye, Moon

Merry licked her lips. As the sky darkened, the moon grew brighter. His ragged, furious breaths were all she heard now.

'The moon got up early to say goodbye,' she mumbled. 'Say goodbye, Dana. Say goodbye to the moon. Don't forget to—'

She was on her feet, moving, shoved along, dragged. Each time she blinked the scene had changed. The street. The door with its peeling grey paint. The hair salon. The stairs. The room that was now her room and the bed that was now her bed.

'Sit,' he ordered. 'Drink some more.'

He held the bottle of orange liquid to her lips, pressed on the back of her head when she tried to pull away.

'Drink. Good. Now sleep.'

Her eyelids grew heavy, but she willed them to stay open, waiting for the comfort of Claire's body to settle into the space behind her. Two sets of footsteps left the room

the latch clicked
　　　and she fell asleep　　still waiting

April 9

Zoey watched fairy-floss clouds swimming through the darkening sky. It was much bigger out here than it was at her house—the sky—and the clouds had more room to chase each other around without the telephone poles and buildings to get in their way. She rolled her head back, trying to take in the whole gigantic thing, wishing that when they went home, she could take this sky with her.

They stopped only once since seeing the green car. Uncle Bear followed a path that led off the main road into a flat, dusty area with no trees, and only shreds of grass and wood chips in the wide tyre-tracks. Some cars and a big truck with two long trailers on the back of it were parked around the edge, almost making a circle, and in the middle were sticks linked with coloured string, like tiny fences. Someone was building something here. The cars were more like baby trucks, white and covered in red dust, with big tools and shovels in the back. The daddy truck had some big yellow diggers on its trailers, a bit like Scoop from Bob the Builder.

Uncle Bear was very excited at first and went to each one with his hose and container, trying to suck out the petrol. Zoey pulled a stick out of the ground and started winding the string around it.

'Come on,' Bear shouted when he'd reached the last car. Red faced, he threw the container to the dust, where it bounced and skidded past Zoey's feet. 'How can they all be empty? How, goddamit?' His shoulders slumped, and he ran both hands through his beard and up the sides of his head, before rubbing his eyes. 'What am I supposed to do now?'

Zoey fetched the container and brought it back to him, but when he didn't move to take it from her, she just stood by his side, swinging the container in one arm and watching him. She thought maybe he was waiting for an answer so she whispered, 'We could play I Spy. I'll spy something and tell you its colour, and you have to keep guessing until you spy it too.'

She felt Bear's hand fall on her head, gently ruffling her hair.

'That sounds like fun...but not just now, okay?'

Zoey stopped swinging the container, pouted her lips, and followed him back to the bike.

As the sun disappeared behind the hills, the bike's engine gave a hiccup and a rattle. Uncle Bear muttered something to himself. She tilted her head right back to look at his face. He glanced down and must have seen the question in her eyes because he gave her a little smile and a quick squeeze with one arm.

'Gonna be dark soon, sweetheart.'

Zoey nodded. 'Are we nearly there yet?' she asked.

'Not quite,' was all he said, giving the little clock another tap. The red needle was pointing to the letter 'E', which Zoey guessed must mean it was time for bed, because bed had an E in it. At bedtime Daddy would call out to her, 'Stop playing now, it's time for B-E-D, bed,' and she would run away giggling.

Night came quickly, and soon all she could see was the ground racing beneath them under the bike's headlight, and flashes of grey trees among the shadows. Bear was muttering to himself more and more, but Zoey's eyelids had forced themselves closed and all the sounds were mixing into a soft buzz. When they flickered open again for a moment, the sound of the bike's engine was gone and there was only the sound of footsteps crunching along beside her. The stars and the moon looked down on her from the sky.

When Zoey opened her eyes, she saw a ceiling with peeling white paint and a dusty lampshade hanging from a fan. Her body ached. It must have been morning because there were birds singing outside the window. She reached a hand out for Hopkins, who always slept tucked in beside her, and instead found nothing but more of the cold, lumpy mattress. Like a jack-in-the-box, she sprang up and sat on her legs, bouncing on her heels as she looked around the room in a panic. Her pink unicorn curtains had turned grey; her drawings of the Little Mermaid and Rapunzel had been taken down and replaced with an ugly picture of some mountains. And her door—

She stopped.

In a small plastic chair with his back against the door sat Uncle Bear, watching her through half-closed eyes. Now she remembered. This wasn't her room. As Bear heaved a great sigh and looked up at her, she breathed again but the tight feeling in her tummy stayed.

'Mornin' Sunshine,' he said. His voice sounded like he'd been eating rocks, and his eyes were dull, drooping, pink around the outside and gray underneath.

'Where are we?'

With an effort, Bear pushed himself out of the chair and stood, tucked his gum down the back of his pants, and rolled his shoulders, causing his big tummy to stick out. He cleared his throat, but the crunchy sound was still there.

'We must've had a guardian angel watching over us last night. Couldn't see a thing after the old girl ran out of diesel and the lights went out, 'cept the odd dirt track that led off to God knows where. Figured we'd have to camp out under a tree or somethin', which I didn't fancy much, when I saw this sign. Look out the window.'

Zoey scooted to the edge of the bed and tottered over to the window. The curtains were thick and heavy, but she got her head around them, and the window was set low enough for her to peer over the sill. The bright light dazzled her for a moment, but as she blinked away the spots she saw a dirt carpark edged by wooden posts, some picnic tables beside a large brick barbecue, and one, two, three, four, five big white vans. One of them was leaning up against a tree, balancing on two wheels and almost tipped over.

There was a swishing sound as Uncle Bear came up beside her and pulled the curtains all the way open. 'This place has seen better days, for sure, but it beats sleeping in the dirt. Tucker Hills Caravan Retreat.'

'What happened to that carry-van?' she asked, pressing a finger against the glass. It came away covered in brown dust and cobwebs, which she inspected, then wiped on Uncle Bear's pants.

'They're called car-a-vans, sweetie.'

'Car-a-van,' she repeated. 'What happened to that caravan?'

'I'd guess someone drove off in a hurry and forgot they were still hooked up. See, the front there's all mangled.'

Zoey looked around the rest of the park. A big black crow was pecking through a rust hole in the bottom of a metal rubbish bin, pulling out something that might once have been a sandwich, while pink galahs waddled around on the grass behind it. Across the far side, behind a line of trees, were dotted a few little cabins with dark green roofs.

'I'm gonna look around, see if any of these vans are carrying some extra diesel, or even some food. You better stay here—'

'No,' Zoey shouted. 'Not by myself. You said, bemember? You pinky-sweared.' She felt a lump growing in her throat and tears stinging her eyes.

'Okay,' Bear said, lowering a hand onto her trembling shoulder. 'I remember. I just don't want...if anything happened...'

Zoey stared hard at him, tight-lipped, and pulled her eyebrows down as low as they'd go.

Uncle Bear gave a little laugh and looked away, shaking his head. 'Fine, fine. You can come with me. Gee whiz, you don't half look like your mum. She used to give me that same death stare...'

Together they went from one caravan to the next, Zoey clinging to a corner of Bear's t-shirt, while he dragged along the red container and hose. It smelled of morning, with a quiet dampness hanging in the air, but now and then as the wind changed her breath would turn sour in her throat, as if someone had waved rotten fruit in her face.

Most of the caravans were empty, their doors flapping open, rubbish and odd socks lying on the hard carpet inside. They found a few tins of food, crackers, water, and some glass bottles that Uncle Bear called 'brews'. In one, they even found some colouring books with only a few of the pictures already coloured, crayons, a book of fairytales, and a little blue nightlight shaped like a bunny rabbit. Zoey sat cross-legged on the floor, flipping through the colourful pages with pictures of smiling princesses, witches and funny looking knights. There were so many pages. It would take longer than forever to look through them all.

Bear found some brown and white shirts in a cupboard and gave one a sniff. 'Smells like my granddad.' When he tried one on over his t-shirt, he couldn't get the buttons to meet in the middle. He made a popping sound with his mouth and groaned. 'Ooh, almost fits. And it's only an XL. A few more weeks living like this and maybe I'll finally get rid of this spare tyre.' He slapped his belly with both hands so that it shook.

Zoey's eyes widened as she stared at Bear's middle. 'I thought that was just your tummy sticking out.' Then she added in her most thoughtful voice, 'But you should probably keep the tyre in case of we'll need it one day.'

Bear looked at her for a moment, a wide grin creeping up out of his beard, then he roared with laughter. He put an arm around her and squeezed her against his side. 'Okay,' he said, still chuckling. 'That's fair. In that case, we'd better finish up and have something to eat. There's a tin of pineapples with your name on it.'

She followed him down the steps of the caravan and back into the sunlight. 'Last one,' Bear said, as they crossed the lawn to a white caravan with blue stripes parked by a gum tree. A large branch had fallen on top of it, covering most of the windscreen.

'I'm betting we'll find some juicy steaks and sausages, still on ice, maybe a shepherd's pie, a cake or two, whadda' you reckon?'

Zoey nodded. 'And ice-cream!'

'Well of course ice-cream,' he said, reaching for the handle. 'Strawberry for you, maybe some pistachio—'

When he yanked the door open, the smell hit them like a wet towel in the face. Bear staggered back, trying to pull the collar of his t-shirt up over his nose, coughing and making a sound like he was about to be sick. Zoey stared into the dark caravan, her eyes stinging. There was nothing but grey shapes at first, with a burning bright patch from the window on the opposite side, but as she looked the darkness seemed to creep out, or the sunlight crept in, she wasn't sure which.

The air inside was thick with flies.

On the bed she saw two people. She knew they'd been old because of their white hair. The man lay behind the woman with his arms around her waist, and his head resting on her ear, like he was whispering secrets to her. Their eyes were closed, and their skin white and papery, with dark black bruises all over. The woman's mouth was open and moving slightly, and it looked like she was trying to talk, but there was something in her mouth, something wriggling, swollen, moving, like grains of rice.

Bear was coughing into the grass, but he drew himself up and slammed the door again. Without another word he took Zoey's hand, and their bag of supplies, and led her back to their room.

April 10

The first thing she noticed when she woke was the smell of her hair—vomit and oranges. When she moved, a gritty layer of dried sweat cracked on her skin. The room was empty. She eyed the window—a cold, grey dawn. A few birds were whistling tentative morning tunes at half voice.

Merry sat up and immediately regretted it. The movement shook her head like a snow globe, and everything came loose in a swirling storm of pain and confusion.

'Ow.' She wrapped her hands over her temples to stop the nauseating motion. As the storm cleared, she opened her eyes. 'Claire?'

The apartment was silent. Turning, she slid her legs out from under the covers and onto the floor. The bathroom door was open. Empty, too.

Eating breakfast already?

Another burst of dizziness hit her as she stood up. A darkness closed in like she'd just entered a tunnel. The room hummed. She waited, wobbling, trying not to panic, until it cleared. She shuffled across the room and into the hall. In the dining room, the small table sat silent and untouched from the previous morning. Breakfast dishes were stacked by the sink. Hadn't they eaten dinner here last night? She paused and tried to think back to the previous day. What had happened after they left the house? Her memory of the car ride home had been spliced together with this morning; and everything in between was blank.

Blackbirds chittered outside, drawing her towards the barred windows. Claire couldn't have gone outside, could she? No. Not by herself. Not at this time of the morning. She tiptoed around the couch and nearly fell over Claire, who was sitting on the floor beside it, a blanket drawn around her shoulders, staring up at the window.

'Claire?' Even whispered, her voice seemed much too loud for the fragile silence. 'What are you doing?'

She didn't answer, didn't turn her head.

'Claire?' Merry knelt beside her and touched her shoulder. She flinched and turned slowly from the window.

'Sorry,' Merry said. 'What are you doing down here?'

Claire looked back out the window. 'Couldn't sleep.'

'I was out like a light,' Merry said. 'Guess I fell asleep as soon as we got back yesterday and slept right through. I...don't remember much. I just know I'm starving. You want some breakfast?'

'Hmm? Sure.'

Merry took two bowls from the cupboard, poured them each some Froot Loops and opened a carton of long life juice. Tropical Blast. As she was setting their places at the table, Mr Blake's door opened and he appeared in the doorway, dressed in his usual neat white shirt and pressed trousers, but with the new addition of an oversized belt buckle emblazoned with a crocodile. Claire didn't move from her place by the window.

'We have a lot to do today,' he said. 'More houses to clear. Things to prepare. I...where is your sister?'

Claire raised her arm and extended her middle finger. Merry flinched. Blake stared at Claire's raised hand with the expression of someone who'd just stepped on a bug and lifted their boot to find it still twitching.

'Come downstairs when you've eaten.' He returned to his room, then left carrying two large bags of supplies.

Once she heard the door click closed, she slammed a spoon down on the table. 'Shivers Claire, why do you do stuff like that? You know what he's like. Why do you have to make things more difficult? He's helping us. He's on our side.'

But something was wrong about him. You know something's off. No, she couldn't think like that. They had to trust him. He might be weird, but he was only trying to protect them. He'd proven that much already.

Claire snorted and turned back to the window.

'Fine, don't eat then.'

There was blood in the alley outside the salon. A red star on the bricks and a short coagulated trail on the ground, already partially covered by dust and dirt.

Teeth sprinkling the ground. Gasping breaths cut short. Crack. Say goodbye to the moon, Dana. Say goodb—No! Bury it. Bury it. Whatever can't be cleaned can always be buried.

Claire trudged past, her arms crossed, holding her elbows. When they reached the car Blake handed them a map of the town. He had circled a row of houses in red marker.

'Do you know these houses?'

Merry looked at the street names. 'Yes.'

'Good. Yesterday was a demanding day, but I'm proud of you for facing it. You both did well. It will get easier now.'

Merry swallowed and asked the question she already knew the answer to. 'So...all these houses...you want us to...'

'Move the bodies out. Yes. Here, this will help'

He lifted the hatch at the back of the car and showed them some sort of trolley.

'It's a hydraulic table cart. We use them in the store. You pump this pedal here, see, to raise it up, and this lever lowers it. You should be able to slide them right off into the back of the car. If you hear movement in any of the houses, mark it on the map and move on to the next.'

'We should? You're sitting this one out again, are you? And what will you be doing while Merry and I are having a meet and greet with the neighbours?'

'It needs to be done,' he said. 'And unless you know how to install a generator or a water pump, I suggest you bite your tongue and start doing as you're told.'

Claire looked ready to explode, but Merry elbowed her. 'Don't. Please?'

Claire didn't look at her. 'You gonna give me the keys then, or what?'

'There's enough petrol to get you there and back. No detours unless you want to walk home.' He held out the keys and Claire snatched them from his hand. Merry let out a breath and slid into the passenger seat, tugging on her seat belt as Claire spun the wheels and tore, zigzagging, up the road.

* * *

They knew as soon as they entered which houses had bodies inside—with shades and curtains drawn, locked from the inside, most of the houses had become tombs, trapping the smell of death until they broke a window and released it. It only took a few before she became accustomed to the smell and sight of dead bodies. Mr Blake had been right—it did get easier.

Most of them were in their beds, blistered and yellowing as Mum had been, and they could wrap them in a sheet, slide them onto the cart, and wheel them to the car. They could fit three side by side in the back of the station wagon—sometimes four if there were children—then they'd drive back to the Foodmart, dump them on a wooden pallet, refill the petrol from a small jug he'd left for them, and go find three more.

Claire parked outside the fourth house on their list. Merry's body refused to move. She stared, eyes unfocused, at the peeling paint on the white weatherboard house. Coloured plastic windmills lined the path through an overgrown lawn, spinning idly. 'This is Mrs Fitzgerald's house.' Her grade four teacher. She was one of those teachers most kids loved, but for most of that year Merry's fingernails were chewed almost to the bone. Mrs Fitzgerald would wear the loudest, flowiest clothes, never showed a hint of having a lesson plan, and would often interrupt herself to lead the class off on a tangent. They'd be in the middle of a spelling test and she'd slap her palms down on her desk and announce, 'Nothing exists but this moment! Come on, 4F, we're going outside to make a Nature collage.'

Claire sat with her for a moment, then saying nothing popped the car door open and went up to the house. Merry watched her go, sank forward until her head rested on her knees. Her fingers scraped the carpet beneath her chair. Maybe Mrs Fitzgerald was right. Nothing existed outside this moment. The tingling feeling of coarse fibres on her fingertips. The press of the seatbelt into her belly. Prickles of sweat on her temples. That's all there was. Everything else was as tangible as a memory. The grinners. Mr Blake. Even Claire. None of them real. In this moment.

Her finger found the corner of something under the seat. She caught it between two fingers and slid it out. A faded, dog-eared Polaroid photo. The blurred top of a fence and some bushes obscured most of the foreground, but just off-centre, sitting in the sun in an open backyard was a girl. About Merry's age. She wore a pale sundress and had her long hair pulled to one side in a ponytail. She appeared to have been reading a book, but at the moment the photo was taken she'd lowered her arm and was scratching her leg, or perhaps swatting a mosquito. Unaware she was being photographed—that someone had been behind the fence watching her during this unguarded moment. Written along the thick border at the bottom: Annabel, Summer 1981.

A screen door slammed and Claire emerged from the house, straining to push the trolley along the weed-choked path. Merry took one last look at the photo and stuffed it into her pocket.

When they had emptied a house, they spray-painted a large X on the door or front fence and moved onto the next. She found a strange satisfaction in crossing off the last house on a street and from the knowledge that she was helping do something important.

A few of the houses were given circles instead of crosses. Those were the ones they could hear movement inside—bumps, scrapes, snarls, gasps. Mr Blake returned to those houses with a jerry-can full of petrol and matches. Merry and Claire would sit in the car parked a little way down the street and watch as the flames reached up the walls, climbed over the eaves and engulfed the house, leaping and crackling like firecrackers while Blake stood outside with his rifle raised, ready to take down the flaming, screeching figures that would emerge once the front door collapsed or the windows blew out, and Merry would press her face against the window, feeling the cold glass heat up, finding a kind of peace as she sat and watched her nightmares burn.

The days ran together. Mornings were the hardest. She'd often wake up groggy and disoriented, and smelling slightly of over-sweet artificial orange. The old Merry might have convinced her it was a brain tumour, begged Mum to bring her in for a CT scan, and then even more exotic tests when they failed to detect anything wrong, but that idea was laughable now. Instead, she buried her concern by focusing only on their task. She and Claire barely spoke, except to direct each other when lifting the bodies. There was no more reminiscing about the time before, of Mum or the twins or school or anything. In the evenings, she'd read an old copy of Nietzsche's Thus Spake Zarathustra that she found in one of the houses, which, although difficult to understand, she found strangely uplifting.

It was as though her entire life had been a dream. It had been a pleasant dream. She'd been happy. But she was awake now, and all dreams, the good and the bad, no matter how vivid and convincing they might have been, eventually erode under the current of time, stripped of their colour and their edges and their importance until there's nothing left.

April 15

Claire pressed the point of her knife into the table and spun it with one finger. Her potatoes and tuna sat untouched on her plate, cooling until they were as cold as the atmosphere between them. At last Mr Blake set down his cutlery and wiped his mouth and moustache with his napkin.

'You're intoxicated,' he said.

Claire let the knife fall to the table. She stared for a moment, one eyelid lower than the other, stifled a burp, then shrugged. 'And you're ugly, but we can't change that either.'

'Consider this a warning. I understand you've been through a lot, and dealing with it isn't easy, but this doesn't happen again. I won't have alcohol in my house.'

Claire rolled her eyes. 'Oh, right, you understand. Please. You're such a hicco...hycoprite. Don't think we haven't seen you swigging that cough syrup every chance you get. You're lit ninety p'cent of the time. I bet you're loving all this. This little power trip you're on. You're living your fuckin' wet dream right now, aren't you?'

'That's enough—'

'No, I'm just getting started. You're pathetic, you know that? You think you're some hero, chosen to cleanse the world and rebuild it "in your image". You keep Kevin down there chained and drugged so you can feel like God. Well, I got news for you, you're nothing. You're just a skinny, cowardly, greasy, big-headed, perverted psychopath who can only get his jollies from—'

'I said enough!' He slammed a fist down, rattling the plates, and even Claire sat bolt upright. 'I took you in when you had nothing. You'd be dead if it wasn't for me. This is MY house, and this is MY food, and you cannot speak to your father like—' He cut himself off abruptly, his face already burning red. But the words were out. 'I mean...you cannot speak to me like that...'

Merry could feel her mouth hanging open and snapped it shut.

Claire rocked forward in her chair. 'Geez, you're even more fucked up than I thought. I mean, our Dad was a piece of shit, but if I knew any part of me had come from you, I'd kill myself right now.'

'Claire, please stop...'

'And you...' Claire turned on her, her eyes bloodshot and cheeks flushed, jabbing a finger in accusation. 'Isn't your arse getting sore from sitting on the fence all the time? Stop trying to please everyone and make up your damn mind, because I'm tired of doing everything just so you can sit back and act like you're so perfect. Open your fucking eyes, Merry. You can't even see how much shit we're in right now. Everything I've been through for you. Or don't you even care? Is that it? You don't care what happens to anyone else so long as you can stay in your little Merry bubble. Everyone else gets covered in shit so that you can stay clean.'

Merry's stomach clenched in anger. She pursed her lips and looked away. 'Why are you saying this?'

'Why? Because it's time the blindfold came off. Rip it off quick like a Band-Aid, yeah? Here's a good one. You always thought Dad was so great. Well, when he died in that car crash he wasn't on his way to a conference. He was going to a hotel with some bimbo. They blamed the rain for the crash, but when they pulled him out of the wreck, he had his pants around his knees, so you tell me. Can you imagine how that was on Mum? "Sorry Ma'am your husband's dead, and by the way he was having an affair. Now I'll just be off with th' future you thought you'd have, and leave you to plan the funeral for your cheating husband instead." Don't look at me like that. Yeah, the truth hurts. I had to overhear it from Mum crying to Auntie Gwen. At least you got to live in a Disney movie for a few more years.'

Merry could feel the hot tears breaking over her cheeks. It couldn't be true.

'After I told Mum I knew, she could never look at me the same. I had to promise I'd say nothing so you and the twins could go on remembering him as a good dad who loved his family, while I was stuck with a deadbeat who was willing to throw us all away for some slutty intern. That's some shit, huh?'

She looked like she was about to burst into tears or burst a blood vessel. Her knuckles were white on the edge of the table. She opened her mouth to speak again. Her eyebrows softened, but a sideways glance at Mr Blake seemed to rob her of her nerve.

'Perhaps you should excuse yourself before you say something you'll regret,' he suggested. 'You've done such a good job keeping Merry out of harm's way. Let's not do anything to jeopardise that, shall we?'

Claire pursed her lips and stared at her hands, then leapt up, sending her chair toppling over. She dashed from the room, swaying and catching herself on the doorframe before disappearing.

Mr Blake watched her go, then resumed slicing his boiled potato into neat quarters. Merry picked up her fork, put it down again. Her stomach was a knot and her back ached.

'I should...I'd better...'

She couldn't look at him, but when he didn't seem to object, she slid awkwardly out of her chair and scurried after Claire.

Claire was curled up on the bed with her back to the door. Merry stood in the doorway, not sure what to say. She was ticked off, of course, but more than anything she was frightened. She'd seen Claire drunk plenty of times, seen her swear and curse about Mum or her friends or the world, but she'd never turned on her like that. Part of her wanted to shove Claire off the bed and demand some answers. Even if it was true what she'd said about Dad, and she couldn't be sure it was—Claire had been known to over dramatise—she shouldn't have told her like that.

A tiny sniff came from the bed. 'I'm sorry,' Claire whispered.

Merry exhaled and sat down. 'Where did you get the alcohol?' After everything Claire had just spouted, that's the question she went with? What did it matter where she got it from? She really was a wuss.

Claire reached a hand under the bed and rolled out an empty bottle of tequila. 'Mrs Fitzgerald had more booze stashed away than a bottle-o. Who knew? No wonder she was always so happy to come to class.'

Merry smiled. She reached a hand towards Claire's shoulder,

but stopped as another cramp seized her. 'Ah...' She doubled over. It was lower than her stomach. What was it? Her bowel? Spleen?

'What's wrong?'

'Nothing. I think just...too many carbs...' She stood, placing a hand below her belly. Something didn't feel right.

'Oh shit...'

'No, I'm okay...it's nothing.'

Claire's face was as white as death. She wasn't looking at Merry, but at the half dozen spots of red that stained the sheet where she'd been sitting. Merry's own confusion at what she saw made the effect of Claire's panic all the more terrifying.

'What's wrong? What is that?'

Claire was shaking her head, glancing about as though looking for an escape. Her eyes settled on Merry. 'Oh, shit!' she said again.

April 15

'We have to leave. Tonight,' Claire said, scrambling off the bed and going to the door. She pressed her ear to it for a moment, then stalked back to the bed, whispering to herself like a madwoman. 'Okay...okay...it'll be alright...we'll, we'll wait until he's asleep...sneak out...but the outside door will be locked...so we get his keys...take some food...we can do it...no choice now...'

'What are you talking about? We can't leave—'

'Shh! Don't—' Claire gripped her by the shoulders and stared hard into her eyes. Merry could still smell the alcohol on her breath. 'This isn't a discussion. You don't need to like it. You don't even need to understand why, but I'm making the call this time. We're leaving. Got it?'

'No, Claire, I don—'

'Shhhhut up. Merry, you know I love you, but you need to shut up now. Just please trust me when I tell you we're not safe here.' She rubbed her temples. 'Here, follow me.'

Claire picked up some clean pants and underwear and led her into the bathroom and handed her a little coloured box from the cupboard under the sink. '...There're instructions inside...with pictures and stuff.'

Merry flipped open the carton and stared, open-mouthed. She looked up at Claire, who shrugged, and slid the bathroom door closed. 'You're smart. You'll figure it out.'

She stared at the back of the door for a moment, then frowned as she fumbled to unwrap one of the cotton bullets, breathing out slowly.

Claire's words about her needing to grow up, to take off the blindfold and see the world as it really was, came rushing back. She thought of the way Mr Blake's eyes always wandered up and down her body, the way his hand would linger just a little too long when he'd touch her shoulder and tell her she was a good girl. But it wasn't like that. It meant nothing. He was just a lonely man who wanted a family of his own, wanted children of his own. And if she was being honest, she liked the praise. The way he trusted her, treated her almost like an equal, gave her a brief nod of approval when she did as she was told without complaint. She liked the fact that she had a job to do, that she understood it, that it was important. If they left, what would she have then? It wasn't fair that Claire was going to make them leave just because she didn't like him—because she's jealous that he likes me more.

She caught her own reflection in the mirror, brow knotted in an ugly grimace, and it took her by surprise. Was she really taking his side over Claire's? She turned her back on the mirror.

As she took off her blood-spotted pants, she felt the Polaroid in the pocket. She took it out and studied it. Annabel, Summer 1981. Her legs were folded up beneath her, causing the hem of the sundress to creep above her knees. A hint of her smooth, white thighs. Merry watched her from behind a tree branch. The girl turned a page, leaned forward to scratch her leg. With the flash of the bulb and a burst of chemicals, the private moment that would otherwise have slipped by unobserved, was captured forever. A plastic window into the past that was even now sending its ripples out into the future.

You're letting your imagination get out of control, she scolded herself. There are a thousand innocent explanations for the photo. Like...maybe she's his sister, and he was just taking snaps of his whole family that day. Maybe the next photo in the pile is his mum knitting, or his dad cleaning the gutters. Maybe it wasn't even his. It could have been someone else's car, someone else's photos...

Or maybe it's time to take the blindfold off.

Alright. She pulled on the clean clothes and washed her hands. Alright.

When she came out Claire was busy sorting through their clothes and stuffing them into backpacks. She stopped and looked up as Merry closed the door behind her.

'Okay, Claire,' Merry said. 'Tell me what you need me to do.'

Claire smiled, her relief plain. 'The tricky part is going to be getting out without him waking up. We'll need to get his keys for the outside door, and the car. The windows are no good, those bars won't budge, and now the generator's up and running the exits will be alarmed...'

Merry looked at her backpack open on the bed and thought back once again to the day she'd seen Blake in the pharmacy. 'I...I might have an idea.'

They sat together in the dark, waiting. Mr Blake was a man of strict habits, and they'd come to know his routine well over the past weeks. He always spent an hour or two after dinner going over his maps and writing meticulous notes and plans in a binder he kept on his desk. When he was done, they'd hear him grunting and panting behind his closed door as he did his push-ups, squats, stretches, and whatever else, before going across the hall to shower. That was their window. The plan was simple but terrifying. Merry closed her eyes and strained her ears. Were they really going to do this?

They heard his door open and bare feet pad across the carpet to the bathroom. Moments later, the sputtering spray of the shower head came on. Claire stood, wobbled, and headed for the door, but Merry grabbed her wrist.

'You're still drunk,' she hissed. 'I'll do it.'

Claire looked ready to argue, and if they'd had more time, Merry might have let herself be talked out of it, but Blake's rule was that none of them take more than three minutes to shower. There was no time to waste.

Holding her breath, she tiptoed down the hall to the main bathroom. Before she had time to process what she was about to do, she'd turned the handle and nudged the door open just enough to slip inside. Her heart was thumping so hard it shook her entire body. This was insane. She was going to get caught. He could be out at any moment. She focused her gaze straight ahead, ignoring the shower curtain to her right and the shadow that moved across it, to where his clothes hung on the towel rack. Carefully, she slid a hand into his pants pocket. A moment of panic at first when she thought it wasn't there, then her hand went deeper and closed around the bottle of cough syrup.

She took the small paper envelope from her pocket and unfolded the flap. Inside was a pale blue powder. They'd crushed six tablets the best they could, but there were still some larger chunks in the mix.

Would six be enough? He might only drink a little...say...a tenth...but it was already more than half empty. Would it be too much?...

With shaking hands, and one eye on the shower curtain, she tipped half of the blue powder into the neck of the bottle, hesitated, then tipped in the rest. She covered the bottle's opening with her thumb and swirled it around vigorously. The room seemed to spin. Out of time. She shook the bottle some more, praying the powder had dissolved.

Come on, Merry. Time to go. If he catches you in here...

She didn't dare finish the thought. She spun the lid back on the cough syrup bottle and slipped it back into the pocket...just as the water shut off. Merry bit her lip to keep from crying out as Mr Blake's hand reached out from behind the curtain and started groping for his towel.

Covering her mouth and nose with one hand, tasting blood, she backed up until she felt the doorhandle with her other hand, expecting the curtain to fly open at any moment. Shaking now, she stepped back into the hall and eased the door closed behind her. It took all her self control not to break into a run. She threw open her bedroom door, straight into Claire, who was waiting on the other side.

'Well?' Claire asked, rubbing her forehead.

Merry wobbled over to the bed and collapsed. 'I think I'm having a heart attack...' She pressed a hand to her chest and tried to calm her breath. 'Sh-shivers.'

'But you did it?'

'I...I think so...but I don't know if it will work...oh God, what if he tastes it and knows something's wrong? What if I didn't put enough in?'

Claire sat behind her and started plaiting her hair. 'Well, then we go to Plan B.'

Merry looked back at her. Claire nodded to her hockey stick propped against the bed, just within reach.

'Oh no, oh no...why did you let me do that?'

The bathroom door opened and footsteps came down the hall, stopped outside their door. Merry thought she might throw up, but Claire just held a finger to her lips. He stood outside for several agonising minutes, while they watched the two dark blots of his feet in the light that shone beneath the door. A small cough. The rattle of the plastic lid spinning off the bottle. Claire's grip tightened on her shoulder. The soft plip, plip, plip, as he took a long draught. Merry found Claire's eyes in the dark and they stared at each other without breathing.

Another plip, plip, plip before the lid was screwed on again and his footsteps shuffled away.

Merry realised she had her hand around her own throat, lowered it.

They heard papers shuffling. A cough. A soft moan. Then the thud of his body hitting the floor.

Claire looked at her.

'Shit, Merry. You've killed him.'

April 15

They stood outside his closed door. There wasn't a sound from inside the room. Not a snore, not a groan, not a breath. It was Merry who broke the spell and reached for the door handle.

'Mr Blake?' she called meekly. 'Are you alright? We're coming in...'

He was lying face-down on the carpet, arms by his sides, legs askew. She bit her lip as she tiptoed around him and knelt by his head. He didn't seem to breathe. When she touched his neck, the skin was cool, his hair still damp from the shower.

'I...can't feel a pulse,' she said, her voice trembling. 'Where is it supposed to...Claire, help me. This wasn't supposed to happen.'

Claire, rummaging through the desk drawers, didn't even turn around. 'Leave him. Us being here in the first place wasn't supposed to happen...Aha!' The large keyring jingled as she raised it over her head in triumph. 'Let's go.'

Merry turned back to the body on the floor. She put two fingers on the inside of his wrist and tried to hold still. There, was that something? Or just her own heartbeat? Oh my God, what have I done?

His chest gave a sudden heave and Merry fell back on her hands, 'I...I...I...I...' but he didn't wake. She could see the back of his shirt rumpling now with each shallow breath. Thank goodness she wasn't a murderer. But she couldn't just leave him like this.

Hooking her hands over one shoulder, she yanked him over onto his back, then rolled him onto his side, propping his knee up in the recovery position. Claire's feet appeared by his head. Looking up, Merry saw Blake's revolver in her sister's hand. She stood, not taking her eyes from the gun. 'Claire?'

'He'll come after us. You know he will,' she said to the gun. 'He'll never stop.'

'Claire, don't.' She stepped over his splayed legs and stood next to Claire. 'He'll never find us. We...we can go anywhere. You don't need to.'

Claire closed her eyes and let Merry's hands close around hers, relaxed her hand, lowered the gun. 'You don't know what he did to me. What he'll try to do to you now. He deserves it. He...'

She turned her back and looked at Merry. Eyes red. Lips tight but trembling.

'I know he deserves it, but you don't deserve what will happen to you if you pull the trigger. Please, let's just go now.'

Claire looked at nothing for a while as the silent tears trickled down her cheeks. At last, she nodded and went out into the hall.

They left the apartment in darkness. Outside it was cold, a cloudy night thick with shadows. Far away, a dog barked twice and stopped. Their fingertips brushed the coarse brickwork as they navigated by touch down the alley and around back to where the car was parked. They set their bags on the backseat and Claire started the engine. She leaned over the wheel, crawling around the corner and out into the road. 'Dammit, I can't see a thing.'

'The headlights.'

'Oh, right,' She fumbled with the switches on the dash. 'I've never driven at night before. Where the hell is it?'

The hazard lights came on, lighting up the street with an eerie blinking orange, while the car rolled forward inch by inch.

'Try that one—'

'I tried that one already.'

'Can you twist it? We're just sitting here...'

'I know, I know...'

Merry's head spun to look out each window in turn. Under the flashing lights it seemed as though the entire street was moving, circling in on them. Claire pressed the hazard switch again and the blinking light stopped...except there was another light on now. Outside, above them. Merry leaned forward. It was a light from the apartment. She slapped Claire hard on the leg. 'Just go,' she shouted. 'Just go! He's awake!'

Claire turned, saw the light, gaped for a second, then stamped on the pedal. The car's engine whined and strained as they fishtailed down the road in first gear.

'Shit shit shit.'

There was only darkness ahead. Through the windscreen a mash of grey and black shapes rushed at her. There was a thump, and they were jolted from side to side as the car hit the curb, leapt up, then bumped away. Merry moaned and held the seatbelt while Claire leaned forward, pulling the car blindly to the right, driving by mere memory of the road. At times, they came close enough to the side of the road that she'd see power poles and street signs flying past her window. She was too terrified to blink.

Claire fumbled with the indicator lever again and the headlights came to life, and the road was back, and there, standing in the middle of it, pale and stooped, was a person. The face rose to look at her, a face stripped of its skin and muscles and human features so all that remained was a shining red skull and two oversized milky eyes above two rows of gleaming white teeth. In that instant of light she saw Death himself standing before her, and she was rushing to meet him.

Claire spun the wheel and the skeletal face passed by her window. Tyres screeched. Her nostrils filled with the smell of burning rubber and her ears with the sound of screams. A pole leapt towards the car, then the world shattered.

Silence.

Her head felt swollen. Waterlogged.

Her chest was cement.

Death stood by her window. A bloodied hand picked a hole through the shattered glass, peeling off its own skin like the flesh of a rotten fruit.

Claire...

Merry turned.

Blood on her face...blood on the wheel...darkness.

Her neck was too stiff to move, locked in a downward stare. At one edge of her vision, the limp hand of the grinner protruded through the window. No longer moving, dripping thick stings of blood down its slender fingers onto her jeans. Pat...pat...pat...

Dead. How?

To her right, the empty driver's seat and the door standing open.

Claire...

'Put the gun down...' Blake's voice sounded distorted through the static in her head.

Claire was hysterical, screaming something unintelligible at him.

'I said put it down...'

A gunshot rang out. Feet scuffed on the glass strewn road. Gasps. Grunts. They sounded too close to be real. He's hurting her. He's hurting her. Claire was crying out her name in a strangled voice.

Claire...

Merry tried to work her hands, but they were so heavy. So heavy. The seatbelt refused to release her.

'Don't touch her,' she tried to scream, though it came out as a whimper. 'I'll kill you if you do anything to her.'

I have to get out. I have to get out. Have to help her...

Darkness swam into her vision like ink in a pool of water.

Claire...

April 23

Rapunzel was her favourite story, and she made Uncle Bear read it to her every day. The bad witch still scared her each time, especially the drawing of her coming out of the shadows at the start of the book when she caught Rapunzel's father stealing her vegetables, but Zoey loved the ending, where Rapunzel and the prince escaped the tower and the bad witch, and lived happily ever after.

After the first night in the caravan park, they'd found a bigger room with two beds, so Bear didn't have to sleep in the chair by the door anymore. Together they filled all the pages in the colouring book, taking one page each and sharing the colours, and when there were no pages left Bear drew cartoons of himself and Zoey for her to colour, and made animals out of folded paper. Soon the boring grey walls of the room were covered in colourful pictures, and all the surfaces with paper rabbits, birds and turtles.

Their days were filled with games and adventures—from chasey to pirates and princesses to bowley-ball—everything but hide and seek. She hated hide and seek. They found an old cricket bat and ball, and Bear taught her how to swing it to 'hit a six'.

On the far side of the caravan park was another building that had some offices and a kitchen in it, and in the kitchen they found more potatoes than they could eat in twenty-nine years, and enough tomato sauce to even make them taste good. They ate chips, and hashybrowns, which Bear cooked on the barbie-cue with a pan and some golden-coloured oil from a huge plastic jug, and baked potatoes, and mashed potatoes, and sometimes for a treat, he would open a tin of fruit for dessert.

Before bed each night he would read to her, and she would pull the blankets up to her chin and look at the pictures in the book and around the room, lit up by the pale blue light from her rabbit nightlight, until the sun went down and the world went to sleep. She loved it there.

Except at night.

Night was the only time she hated. Because every night she had the same bad dream. She'd wake and sit up in bed, and there'd be just enough light to see that Uncle Bear wasn't in the bed next to hers. The curtains, which they always closed at night, were gone, and the glass shook and wobbled against an angry storm outside. Then the door would creak open, and even though she flew out of bed and pushed it with all her muscles, and shouted for Uncle Bear, she could never stop it.

Sometimes it was the old lady from the caravan, her eyes empty holes, and her mouth full of rice. She'd shuffle into the room, reaching for Zoey, and trying to speak, and little bits of wriggling rice would spill out onto the carpet. Sometimes it was Mummy or Daddy, or some stranger, but worst of all was when it was Uncle Bear, his hair and beard in tatty clumps, his arms, the safest place she'd ever known, reaching, grabbing, hurting.

* * *

141

Zoey woke screaming, trying to escape the sheets that wrapped around her. In a second, Bear was beside her, holding her shoulders, trying to calm her down.

'Hey, hey, easy. Zoey. I'm here.'

She just screamed harder and pushed his hands away. His eyebrows creased with hurt, and he half lowered his hand. When she realised he was the real Uncle Bear, not the eyeless, lipless monster from her dream, she crawled to him and pressed her head to his chest, allowing his big arms to wrap around her.

'You were gone, and she didn't knock, but the old lady came with rice in her mouth, and I didn't want her to but she was there…and then she was you…she was…' With her face against his shirt, she couldn't even understand her own words.

'Shhh, it was just a dream. You're safe.'

His breath felt cool on her head, where her hair was wet with sweat. She peered around Bear to check the door. It was closed. A crack of grey light between the curtains told her it must be morning. As she shifted on the bed, the sheets clung to her skin, and she realised she'd had an accident.

She gasped and tried to sit back on the wet spot, to hide her mess, but he had already seen.

He wiped the tears from the corners of her eyes with his thumb. 'It's not your fault, my little one. Don't you fret about it. There's plenty of spare sheets and mattresses around. Easy fixed. Okay?'

She nodded, but couldn't look him in the eye.

'Hey, you hear that?'

Zoey sat back on her heels and listened. She shook her head.

Uncle Bear turned to the side and cupped his hands to his mouth. 'Cock-a-doodle-doooooo.' He spun to face her, his eyes wide. 'You must have heard it that time. Sounds like a rooster right outside. He's saying it's time for breakfast.'

Zoey giggled. 'That's not a rooster. That was you!'

'Really? Are you sure?'

She nodded, bouncing up and down.

Bear slapped a hand to his forehead. 'I bet I know what happened. I ate an egg last week. It must have hatched in my stomach.' He pounded his chest twice, swallowed, then let out another loud cock-a-doodle-doo.

Zoey stopped bouncing and stared. She scooted over and pressed her ear to his tummy. It was big enough to fit a rooster inside, but the sound was too gurgly and ribbitty, like it was full of frogs. She frowned and looked up at him. 'Did you eat some tagpoles too?'

He laughed and ruffled her hair. 'You know, I think maybe I did. Now come on, let's get you cleaned up.'

Uncle Bear stood at the barbie-cue, and smiled at her through the wiggly, smoky air that came off the top of it. He waved with the tongs, then nudged one of the potatoes wrapped in metal paper. Zoey wished they had some Froot Loops, but then again, she supposed she was happy it had been potatoes they'd found, and not six giant bags of broccolis. She waved back, then returned to the lawn, crouching down and creeping up on the lazy galahs that were waddling around hoping to get some of their breakfast.

The birds didn't seem frightened of her. They pecked through the grass, puffing out their pink chests, occasionally spreading their wings and skipping away if she came too close.

'You'll have to be quicker than that if you wanna catch one, little miss. Mind you, there's not much meat on 'em. We'll need two or three for a decent meal.'

Zoey giggled. 'People can't eat birds, silly,' she said, ducking down as another galah squawked at her and flapped over to the other side of the lawn. It would be like trying to eat a feather duster. 'You're silly, Uncle Bear.'

He shrugged. 'We bears can eat anything if we're hungry enough.'

The image from her dream came back all at once—Bear reaching for her, clicking his teeth hungrily, laughing. She stood up. Smoke blew from the barbie-cue into her eyes, and she closed them. She wished she could stop thinking about things like that. Deep down she knew he would never ever hurt her.

As she thought this, the galahs took off all at once, and for a moment everything was feathery flashes of grey and pink. Bear was by her side, his head turning this way and that as he searched the trees and the dirt road leading out of the caravan park.

'We need to go,' he said, and dashed back to the barbie-cue. He twisted off the knob on the gas bottle and clanged the cover back on top. Smoke was still spinning out of one corner, but Bear left the potatoes there and grabbed her hand. He was breathing a lot faster than usual and still looking all around as he walked.

'Why do we have to go? I'm hungry.'

'Shh. We just do. It's probably nothing, but—'

She heard the crunch of wheels coming down the dirt road and knew then that it wasn't nothing. Someone else was here.

April 16

Outside it was raining. Merry watched, watched a drop trickle down the glass, sliding snakily between the other drops, slowly falling, pausing, coming together, snaking down, slowly, quickly, down down, out of sight. Another. Another. Each took a different path but came to the same end. Always different. Always the same.

She rolled her neck to look at the ceiling. Where was she? Her collarbone and chest felt out of shape. Collapsed. Expanded.

'Claire?' Her voice was a scratch of a whisper. Mouth so dry. She found a glass of water on the table by the bed, but when she tried to raise her arm found it was too painful. She sat up, swung her legs around so she could reach with the other arm. Half the water ran down her mouth, down her neck, into her shirt. She left the empty glass on the bed and went to the door.

The handle refused to turn. Puzzled, she blinked the fuzziness away and looked closer. Locked. But their door didn't have a lock. Someone had put a new handle on, one with a keyhole on the inside. She closed her eyes and ran her fingers through her hair, scratching her scalp. It felt good.

Where was Claire? She was so tired.

It was still raining. Dark outside now. The click of the latch had woken her. The man with the moustache came in, carrying a tray. Warm buttered toast with marmalade. When he set it down on the table, she could see scratches covering the backs of his hands. More on his neck. A Band-Aid on one cheek. He looked over and saw her watching him, froze. Expecting some reaction from her?

'You're hurt...' she said.

'I'm alright.'

'Who are you?'

He stood upright. The question had caught him off guard. She knew his face. He cleared his throat.

'I'm...your father,' he said, placing a hand lightly on hers.

Yes, of course.

'Rest now.' He turned and left her to eat alone.

When she next woke, there was a girl sitting at the end of her bed. It was dark, but she could see her clearly. She knew this girl at once. Her long blonde hair falling nearly to her elbows. Her intelligent eyes and rebellious smile.

Claire.

'Where have you been?' Merry asked.

Claire pointed out the window.

'Oh. I'm glad you're back. I missed you. It's lonely here by myself.' She rolled onto her side and closed her eyes. The rain, stroking the window pane became a whispered voice.

'Ssss   sss   sss

Ssss   s   st

It   me
Sssssssmile   ssssmile   be Merry
Merry smiled, allowing the pain in her shoulder to sink down into the mattress.
'Not alone   never will be
You're not alone, and never will be'
Not alone.
Smile   smile
Merry

It might have been the next day. Merry wasn't sure. She stood, squinting in the alley, her baggy Loony Tunes T-shirt flapping about her.

'Father?'

'Yes, Meredith?'

'Where are we going?'

'There's something I need you to see.'

'Okay.'

As she followed him down the alley, she felt an intense sense of loss that she couldn't explain. As though the world had been irreparably damaged. Everything she saw, she was seeing again for the first time. Every sound, though familiar, was new. She stopped. The green car that was normally parked behind the salon was gone, replaced by a little white hatchback. But now that she thought about it, maybe it had always been there. Maybe there had never been a green car.

'Merry.'

Her head snapped to the side. Father was calling her. She felt as though she'd just woken from a daydream in which she'd been falling. Looked around. Confused.

'Come on now.' He held the passenger door open for her.

'Yes, Father.'

She sat down and stared straight ahead, tuning in and out, switching between the present and her muddle of memories, unsurprised by the constantly changing view outside her window.

'Where do you think he's taking us?' Claire whispered by her ear.

'I don't know.'

'What did you say?' Father asked.

'I said I don't know where you're taking us.'

He turned and looked at her. 'You'll see soon.'

'We'll see soon,' Merry repeated to Claire. Her ears were ringing.

'He's scared, you know. All the time. That's why he drinks the cough syrup. He's hooked on the codeine. He was scared of me too…before. You'd better be careful.'

'Yes. Better be careful.'

'What?…Who are…?' His eyes darted between her and the road. She looked at him with her head tilted. Then returned her attention to the window.

The car slowed and stopped near a pile of dead bodies in the middle of the road. Flies erupted off them as they came close, swarming, filling the sky like a black mist, circling, settling, refusing to leave, pelting into Father and her as though defending their claim.

Father carried a large plastic container that sloshed when he walked, originally made to spray weed killer, but which he had now filled with petrol, and sent a jet of liquid into the midst of them.

'This may be difficult to understand, but it's a necessary measure.'

Merry peered into the dead, bulging eyes. Limbs protruded at odd angles, reaching, pleading for help. Too late.

'The virus that killed them could still be in the bodies. Although we're immune to this strain, viruses can mutate. We can't take any chances now. Burning them is the only way to make sure it's destroyed. And...this will also warn others away.

'You're extremely...important to me Merry. Others might come here and try to hurt you, but I'll never let that happen. I promise you that. Do you understand?'

'Yes. He'll never let others hurt you. Nobody else will hurt you.' Claire circled the pile of bodies, brushed the matted hair out of an old woman's eyes. Only him.

'Of course, Father.'

He lit a match, cupped it, shielded it from the wind, threw it into the pile. There was a whoosh and the blue flame front spread over them. The clothes blackened first, some shrivelling, some flaking off, some melting into the skin.

Merry felt the heat on her face as the flames took hold. Some of the limbs twitched as pockets of gas trapped in their joints burst—the flourishes one final, feeble, futile attempt to claw their way from the pile, out of the clutches of Death. Or perhaps they were waving goodbye.

Or beckoning for her to join them.

She inhaled acrid, sweet, charcoaly air.

Kevin in the meat freezer. Grinning. Bleeding. Gnashing. Gasping. Kevin. Orange vest. Chains. Burning. Eating.

She frowned.

A blackened face tipped back, mouth wide, orange flames licking the inside of its throat.

Claire. Death in the road. Glass. Blood. Screams. Claire...

Claire was standing behind him again, silent, her arms folded.

'Meredith? What's wrong?'

'Where...what happened to Claire?'

His face showed signs of doubt for a second, but then again it might have been the shadows dancing over his features in the shifting light.

'You don't remember what happened?'

Claire stood by the fire, silent, her arms folded.

'I...' Merry squeezed her eyelids shut. The buzzing of flies seemed so loud.

'She took the car. She crashed it—that's how you got hurt. When I caught up to you, she was hysterical. She threatened to shoot me. You tried to calm her down, but she was so angry. She wanted to leave. I told her she wasn't a prisoner and that I wouldn't stop her. The two of you argued about it for a long time, but her mind was made up. Before she left, I insisted she take the car, some provisions, one of the rifles. It was all I could do. She...I know this must be difficult to hear...but she said she was better off alone.'

Merry looked down. It couldn't be true. Claire would never leave without her.

'I'm sure she'll be back in a day or two. She's strong. She'll be alright. I know the first instinct is to rush off and look for her, but you need to stay strong, too. She knows where to find us, when she's ready.'

When she looked up, Claire was standing beside him.

He's lying, she mouthed.

Smoke blew into her eyes and burned. 'Take me home please,' she said. 'Father.'

It was hard keeping up with Bear as he ran. His hand swallowed hers and wouldn't let go, pulling her so fast her feet kept losing the ground. After this happened a few times, he picked her up and ran with her against his chest. She could see movement on the road, flashes of sunlight on glass and a cloud of dust filling the spaces between the trees.

All the birds had fallen silent, as if they were waiting to see what was coming too, or maybe they were pretending they weren't home.

They reached their room and Bear dropped her on the bed and kicked the door closed behind him. He drew the curtains, then pressed his face against the little peeping hole in the door. Behind the sound of his whistling nose and gasping breaths, she could hear the vehicle moving around the park. First it was faint as it passed the kitchens and office buildings, then a little louder as it travelled down the row of caravans towards them, then grinding loudly as it turned down the gravel track that ran outside the cabins.

Zoey slipped off the bed and went to the window, nudging the corner of the curtain aside and standing on tip-toes. A dirty yellow truck with red and brown stripes and big letters on the side was rolling past their room. The driver was hunched over the steering wheel, turning his head from side to side, but the glare on the front windows turned him into a dark shape with no face. She tried to read the letters before they got too far away: F-O-O-D-M—

Bear mumbled to himself. 'What are you doing out here, you nosey bugger?'

The truck finished its loop and crawled back around the corner out of sight. She wondered if the man was going to stay at the caravan park too. Maybe he had some kids. It would be nice to have some other kids to play with—

'Zoey! Get away from the window!' Bear cried at her, stepping up next to her and pulling at her arm.

Her head snapped to the side and she stumbled. She saw horror fill his eyes, and he immediately got down on one knee and placed his hands gently on either side of her head.

'I'm sorry…God, I didn't mean…Did I hurt you?'

Zoey could feel the tears coming; couldn't stop them. 'I just wanted to see…' she whimpered as sobs shook her voice.

'I know, darlin'. I was the one that did wrong, okay? I shouldn't have grabbed you. We just gotta be careful. Some people out there, we can't trust…'specially with everything that's happened…people get desperate. Dangerous. I've seen it. I don't know what I'd do if…' He took a deep breath. 'Please just promise me you'll stay away from the window. Just for now. Until I can be sure it's safe.'

Zoey said nothing, just stared down at her shoes, feeling the tickly tears slide down her cheeks and into the corners of her mouth. When he lifted her face with a gentle hand under her chin, she saw that he was crying too.

'Please?'

'Okay,' she mumbled.

They stayed in the room for the rest of the day. Bear spent most of it by the door, peering out the peeping hole, or pacing back and forth, biting his nails.

'Nothing for you here,' Bear whispered to the door. 'Get on. Get on out of here and leave us be.'

A few times his hand reached for the gum tucked down the back of his pants. They heard a door slam in the distance, faint footsteps, the door to the kitchens creaking open and closed.

Zoey lay on the bed, coloured a picture Bear had drawn of her as a fairy, ate some stale crackers, then when there was nothing else left to do, she fell asleep.

A truck door woke her some time later. At first she thought it must be night, because the room was so dark, but then the curtain moved a little and she saw Bear's tired, lined face lit up by a triangle of orange sky. The truck's engine coughed and puttered for a while, then it gave a mighty roar, a wall was sprayed with gravel as the wheels spun, and the truck raced away.

Zoey wanted so much to break the terrible silence that followed. But she'd learned a long time ago when it was best to keep quiet. Bear had that same look on his face that Daddy used to have after he and Mummy had a fight, when she would yell and slam the door to the bedroom and leave Daddy and Zoey to eat dinner alone. His eyebrows crouched low over eyes that didn't quite see, and if she dared to try to cheer him up with a funny face or a silly noise, those eyes would turn to her and flash danger.

She was used to those looks from Mummy and Daddy, but didn't think she could stand it from Uncle Bear, so she just sat on the edge of the bed, waiting, swinging her legs and rubbing her fingers over the stiff, white sheets.

At last Bear moved away from the window and sat beside her with a sigh. 'It's gone,' he said. 'Probably just passing through, skimming the place for food and fuel. Doubt he found where I stashed most of the food, though. If we're lucky, he just took the couple of cans I left out on show. Won't know until the morning. Not enough light to go looking now.' He gave her a tired smile. 'You doing okay, little miss?'

She nodded, but her tummy growled at her for lying.

'I hear you,' said Bear, heaving himself up and walking stiffly over to the bag on the table where they kept a few extra cans. 'What would you say to some cold baked beans?'

Zoey giggled. 'Nothing. Beans don't even have any ears.'

He smiled at her. 'You're right. How 'bout we just eat some then?' Though his eyes were red and puffy, there was no sign of the anger she'd feared. Only kindness and warmth.

Was she dreaming, or was she awake? It was so dark that the room seemed to flicker like the fuzzy static on an old TV. The wind shook the leaves. Bear snored softly on the bed beside hers. And outside, slow footsteps scraped through the gravel.

Zoey sat up and stared at the door. Scrape. Scrape. There was nothing it could be but feet dragging along the rough ground. More than one set of feet. At any moment, the door would creak open, and the old woman would step into the room. Any moment.

And that was when the screaming started.

April 16

The sound of buzzing flies followed her everywhere. Worst was when she tried to sleep. The room was full of them. Her head was full of them. And the sound was full of secret, whispered voices. Always whispering, whispering, whispering to her. Sometimes she could tune them out for a while, the way one can tune out a ticking clock in an otherwise silent house, but they always came back, and just as the clock, always louder than before. Often just when she thought she had gained control, she would hear someone shriek by her ear, like a waking nightmare; like a drill boring through her skull; like a dying scream, half-remembered.

She balled her hair up and pressed it against her ears, but it offered no relief from the buzzing, whispering silence. Claire was there sometimes, standing by her bed in the darkness, facing the window. She didn't respond when Merry called to her, and she vanished in a blink.

Sssshhhhheee's dead...

He's   lying

Make   him   confesssssssss

Make   him   pay

'Claire?'

Claire? Claire?   Claire's not here   teehee   she's
gooooooonne.   And we know whyyy   why   why you need
to blame   him   hehe   hee   he is a tiger   and tigersssss
do what tigerssss doooo   but it was youuuuuu   youuuuu
who led her to himm   youuuuu who wouldn't let her   go
and when he   pounced   you loooked awayyyy   you ran away
and when he   pounced   you ran   awayyy

'Stop it!'

Stop it?   Stop it?   Only youuuu   can stop   it

Merry threw back the covers and started pacing the room. The
whispers drowned her footsteps out, drowned each other out.
Drowning. She was drowning…

A sound downstairs. The whispers stopped. Had she imagined
it? No, he was down there. What time is it? Middle of the night.
Follow him? Yes.

The dread hour   all the innocent abed   all the innocent are
ddeadd the dread hour is made for those who have something
to   hhhide   like youuu   like hhhhhim   mischief   and
sin   mischief   and sin

She opened the door a crack and waited for the static-filled
darkness to withdraw. The door to the supermarket was ajar. She
waited a moment more, then crossed the hall in her bare feet,
nudging the door open. A faint light shone up the stairs, guiding
her down the dark corridor. With somewhere to focus her
attention, the whispers faded to the back of her mind. When she
reached the stairs, she saw Claire standing by the door to the
meat prep room, her face level with the greasy window through
which shone the light from a battery-powered lantern. She

moved aside as Merry approached the door.

She heard Kevin rattling his chains, moaning and gasping, but his cries sounded sluggish, passionless. Blake stood with his back to her, sleeves rolled up, black rubber gloves up to his elbows which moved in small gyrating motions over the bench. After a time, he set aside a mortar and pestle and walked to the freezer carrying a tray piled high with pinkish grey meat.

Merry turned away from the window and leaned back against the wall. As she listened to the soft squelches of fist-sized gobs of raw meat being chomped and chewed she would have welcomed nausea, but all she was left with was a terrible emptiness. All her internal organs had dropped out of her and she was collapsing in on herself. The sound was soon consumed by the familiar escalating, droning buzz—a can of soda poured into her skull. She retreated to the darkest corner of the room and sank down, pressing her forehead to her knees, crunching fistfuls of hair over her ears.

That meat…could that be…NO…fffffzzzzzzzzz

Need   to…see…could   he   have?   NO
NO…ffffffzzzzzzzzzzffffffzzzzz

Need to see. Need to know. Need to see. But…if it's her…if he's done that to her…ffffzzzzzzz…he couldn't have…nobody could…not…even…him…fffffzzzzzzzffffffzzzzzzzzzzzzzfffzzzzz…

She felt rather than heard the door swing   ffffffzzzzzz Can't see. can't know. can't see. His footsteps slowly climbing the stai— can't can't can't

Merry!

Her body jolted. All sound gone. She felt Claire standing over her. Now, Merry, now. You need to see for yourself.

Can't can't can't. If you're in there, if you're really gone, it'll break me and I won't ever be able to go on. Please don't make me...

Nobody makes it through unbroken. Go now. He will be back soon.

A floorboard creaked overhead. Merry opened her eyes to a dark and empty room. She forced herself to her feet and through the door. The room was quiet now; not so much as a clink or rattle from Kevin. With no lantern or torch of her own, she had no choice but to turn on the light. The fluorescent bulb glowed for a moment, then began flickering, throwing the room in and out of darkness.

She passed by the freezer without looking in, focused entirely on the meat grinder on the bench opposite, and the few glistening worms hanging out the end. The air smelled of blood. She looked in the pan at the top—saw only a red, watery stain— then began searching amongst the items on the bench, looking for anything that might confirm her worst fear. One of the cheap rings Claire always wore, perhaps. Some of her hair, or clothes...

She turned from the bench, all at once short of breath. The buzzing whispers came back in force and she struggled to keep herself upright.

Find herrrr   find herrr   find   herrrrr   what will you do when you find   hhherrrr?

Her gaze fell to the rubbish bin and she staggered over to it. A frightened face, dark-eyed, pale-skinned, stared up at her. Her own reflection deformed by the curved stainless steel lid. She lifted it, reached in, pulled out a large polystyrene tray. The plastic wrapping, still attached, bore the label "Kangaroo Steaks".

She let out a breath that became a sob. So that's what the meat was. Nothing but some rancid, unrefrigerated kangaroo. Out of the corner of her eye she saw feet step out from the other side of the bench and tread silently towards the freezer. Claire paused in the doorway, waited for her to lift her head, then went inside. Merry wanted to lay her head down on the cold tiles and never get up, but she knew the whispers wouldn't let her rest so, reluctantly, she stood, wiped her eyes on her sleeve, and followed Claire.

Kevin was hanging from his chains with his head drooping. A red thread of drool connected his bare teeth to a pool of blood and meat on the floor. The tray, with its half-eaten contents, was discarded to one side. Merry took another cautious step forward. He wasn't moving. Was he asleep? Did they sleep? It didn't make sense—

Something stung the side of her neck. Merry gasped and tensed as a hand clamped over her mouth.

'Shhhhhh,' Mr Blake whispered. 'Fascinating, isn't it? They came from us, and yet they are so much more. They feel no pain, or if they do, they don't show it. They don't tire, don't sleep, don't complain. They do nothing except what their nature directs them to. Their singular, predictable nature.'

Still holding her by the head, he walked forward until they were less than a metre from Kevin. She felt the needle quiver in her skin and flinched as he withdrew it. A cold, painful throb spread through her neck.

'But the virus still relies on the body's infrastructure. They don't draw breath, but the heart still beats. Did you know that? Oh so slowly, but enough. The tissue may decay post-mortem, but the muscles still function, which means the nerves must also function. And anything with nerves can be paralysed.'

Merry felt herself sinking. He held her up.

'Ah, not yet. Not yet.' He took her hand and, with it, lifted Kevin's chin so that his dead eyes looked into hers. The skin of his jaw was like thick, half-dry paint, rubbery on top, but fluid beneath.

'You gave me the idea,' Blake said. 'Given orally, a high enough dose of triazolam, combined with alcohol to enhance its effect, can reach the brain, cutting it off from the body. He looks dead, doesn't he? Will the effect wear off, or is it permanent? I suppose we'll find out.'

Her eyelids fluttered, fought to stay open. Even the whispers were muted. She could hear the excitement in his voice.

'You see, Meredith, the thing Claire didn't understand is that we have a responsibility. We are on the precipice of extinction, and our survival depends on our ability to learn, to adapt, to sacrifice. I think you understand. Our genes make us immune to the sickness, and we have a responsibility to   continue the species fffffzzzzzzzzfffffzzzzzzzzzzzz   that's the most important thing. None of the old rules apply. No matter how unpleasant we might…ffffffzzzzzzzzfffzzzzz.

Her head drooped.

When she looked up she saw his face looking over her. She could smell the liquorice cough syrup on his breath. The room swayed behind him as he carried her up the stairs   down the corridor into the locked room.

April 23

Uncle Bear leapt from the bed like it was a trampoline, fumbling in the dark for his gum on the table beside the bed. The screaming filled the room—sharp, terrible shrieks, so full of pain, sending shivers through her body even worse than the squeal of chalk on glass. Whatever it was, had to be right outside the door.

She tried to cover her ears with handfuls of hair, but couldn't block out the sound. It was already inside her head, scraping on her eyeballs from the inside.

Then it ended. There was a deep crunch, and the window shuddered as something wet sprayed against it.

'Dear God,' Bear was saying, over and over. 'Dear God...'

By the dim blue light of the rabbit nightlight she saw the gum was shaking in his hand.

'It...sounded like...some sort of animal,' he whispered. 'A cat...or a possum, maybe...'

The room was silent, except for their own breathing, and the echo of the scream in her head. Zoey closed her eyes and rubbed her hair over her ears, filling her head with the sound of it prickling and rustling. Her chest heaved and twitched with every breath, and even though she tried to take big breaths, to calm herself down, she couldn't get enough air. The bed shifted as Uncle Bear sat beside her and wrapped her in a hug. Through her hair, she could hear his rumbling whisper.

'—have to stop crying…Please, baby girl…stop crying…have to stop—'

The door shook as something slammed against it. Zoey lowered her hands and stared. Slam. The little chain bounced and rattled. Slam.

Each time the door shook, she jumped. She knew who it was. It had to be the old lady, finally come for her. Her dream had come true.

Bear raised the gum, pushed a button on its side, and popped out the round bit in the middle. Zoey saw six little holes. Three of them had gold circles in them. He snapped the gum back together and turned to her.

'I know you're scared—'

Slam.

His eyes squeezed shut for a second, then he continued. 'I'm scared, too. But we just—'

Slam.

'We just need to stay put. We're safe here. Not even I could break down that door. Whatever's out there—'

Slam.

'Can't get through. We just have to wait until they go away.'

The slamming stopped, and they heard the voice of a laugher. The sound was so close, as though it had its mouth pressed right against the edge of the door.

'Aah, yaah, yaah, yaah…' Its rattling, squeaky voice seemed to come closer and closer. 'Aah, aah, AAH.' Behind it, another one was walking around. The old man too?

She shook her head as hard as she could. 'Go away,' she whispered. Then screamed, 'Go AWAY.'

'AAH, AAH, AAH—' Slam. Slam. Slam.

She curled up against Bear's chest and sobbed.

The laugher stopped hitting the door after a while, but it didn't go away. They could hear it walking around outside, crunching the gravel, clicking its teeth and laughing. Uncle Bear pulled on his boots and jacket and made her do the same. 'Just in case,' he said.

'I want them to go away,' Zoey said as Bear took off her shoes and put them back on the right feet. 'You said they would go away.'

'They will,' he said. 'They can't get to us in—'

There was another slam, this time on the window. Uncle Bear turned white and stood up.

Slam.

Crack.

'No...'

Slam. There was a pop and little pieces of glass pattered against the curtains. Slam. Crunch. Crunch. A hand reached through the gap in the curtains. It was covered in blood, with skin peeling back like a rolled-up sleeve, and stringy bits dangling from the wrist.

'Get up! Move!' Bear shouted, taking her by the shoulder and pulling her towards the bathroom door.

The window fell in all at once, and a small body, trailing a tangle of long, yellow hair, tumbled in with it. It wasn't the old woman after all, but a girl, wearing a pair of dirty pyjamas. Zoey skidded into the bathroom, and the door swung closed between them and the laugher.

Hurried footsteps pattered on the carpet, and Bear clicked the lock just as the laugher crashed against the other side of the door.

In the small, echoey space of the bathroom, the crashing sound was even worse than before. The door shook and creaked with each hit.

Uncle Bear was standing with his boot and shoulder pressed against it. He was looking around the room. It was very dark, but outside in the sky the moon was shining brightly, and some of its shine came in through a small frosty window above the toilet.

'Mother fff...father brother sister...' He closed his eyes for a moment, then stepped away from the door and snatched a towel from the rail.

'Stand back,' he warned as he wrapped the towel around his fist and climbed onto the toilet. With one punch, he shattered the glass, and wiped around the frame, knocking out all the sharp bits. Some fell inwards, tinkling on the tiles by her feet.

Bear threw the towel, which was now ripped and covered in red splotches, into the bath.

'Grab me another. One of the big ones.'

She stood for a moment, unable to think or move, until a crash against the door startled her.

'Quickly now, darlin'.' His voice was calm and patient, and his dark eyes, bright now with moonlight, held hers with a kind look that somehow told her without words that everything would be okay. He glanced to the side, and she followed his gaze to a large towel hanging crooked on the rail by the door.

She nodded and ran to it, jumping again as the door pounded against its lock. Bear spoke in that same calm voice as he took the towel from her and folded it over the bottom of the window, covering the bits of glass, and dangling it outside.

'Now, when you get out, I want you to run as quick as you can over to the kitchens. You know the way. Get inside and go to the back office. You remember where we hid the rest of the food? Lock the door and stay there. Real quiet.'

Zoey frowned as he helped her up onto the toilet seat. 'But you can't fit out the window, Uncle Bear. How will you get out?'

'No, sweetie. I can't. It's time to be a brave girl. I know you can do it. I'll…meet you there.'

He picked her up by the waist, and before she knew what was happening, her legs were out the window into the cold night air.

'No!' she cried, grabbing hold of one of Bear's hairy arms. 'No, not by myself!'

'I'm so sorry,' He whispered, pushing her further through the window while she kicked and squirmed.

'No, you promised,' she cried. 'You promised!'

'It's the only way—'

There was a loud crash, and a few long brown splinters flew from the door frame. He grunted and pushed his arm so that she was all the way outside.

'Hold on to the towel. I'll lower you down. Be careful…ugh…there's glass on the ground.'

Tears blurred her vision, but all she could do was grab the towel and hang on. It lowered quickly, ripping as it slid over the sharp glass in the window frame. Before her feet touched the ground, she heard the door crash open and slam against the wall. Her stomach jumped as she fell the rest of the way, landing on her ankle and toppling over.

'Come on then, you little bi—'

A loud bang swallowed the rest of Bear's words. Zoey scrambled to her feet, felt something hard and sharp sticking to her hand as she pushed herself up, and ran. The moon was bright, painting the tops of the trees and patches of grass silver. In one patch, a tall boy with a bright orange vest and no arms was down on his knees, his face lowered to the ground, biting into a dead possum. He didn't seem to notice her as she ran past on the soft grass, and she made it as far as the barbie-cue before stopping to look back. The curtains of their room were partly open from where the laugher had crawled in, and the room glowed a pale blue from the nightlight. Shadows danced inside. Grunts and growls and thumps upset the otherwise quiet night. Zoey held on to the side of the barbie-cue and watched. She couldn't go on without him. There was no going on without him.

Her heart beat like a drum played too fast. There was a roar of pain from Bear, and Zoey stepped forward.

'Uncle Bear,' she cried.

The boy with no arms looked up, and a face appeared in the window. All hair and blood and teeth. The laugher reached its arms through the broken window, scrambled at the bricks below, and tipped itself over. It was on its feet again so quickly, kicking gravel in all directions as it found her in the dark and charged, its legs moving in a way that didn't look right. The boy had struggled to his feet too, and both of them were lurching towards her.

'Uncle Bear!' Her legs wouldn't work, so she just held onto the barbie-cue.

Another huge bang came from the room, and the girl's shoulder exploded into a purplish mist. She fell and skidded across the ground, tripping the boy, both of them laughing all the way. As the monsters lay there, clicking, kicking at the ground, trying to right themselves, Zoey heard a much heavier set of

166

footsteps and looked up to see Uncle Bear running to her. His shirt was ripped at the sleeve, and scratch marks covered his arms and face.

He didn't stop when he reached her, just scooped her up and continued running. He stumbled a few times in the dark, almost ran straight into a tree, but soon they saw the large grey shape of the kitchen building ahead. They heard other cries through the darkness, some coming from behind, some in front. More laughers. She couldn't tell how many.

Bear ran up the concrete ramp and pulled the door closed behind them. With no nightlight and the only windows boarded up so the moon had no way in, it was darker than the inside of a monster's mouth.

Bear stood in the doorway for a while, panting and sniffling. Listening. There was nothing from outside, but the slow tick tock of the kitchen clock seemed to come out of the darkness, and grew louder and louder. She heard Bear check the lock again, then he lowered her to the floor.

'We should keep going,' he whispered. The words struggled to get out of his throat.

With his hand on hers, he led her through the dark kitchen. By feeling their way along the walls they found the corridor that led to the back offices, and then the room where they had hidden the rest of the potatoes, and tins of food, and the big jug of oil, and tomato sauce. Bear closed the door and locked it and they huddled together in the space between the wall and a filing cabinet.

Zoey's body was still shaking, but she couldn't remember why. Couldn't remember why she was out of breath. Why her hand hurt. Why she wasn't in her own bed listening to Mummy and

Daddy argue downstairs. She tried to remember, but none of the answers seemed important, and so she let herself slip into a deep sleep.

April 16

Thick blinds covered the windows   black blinds   black sky   the sky   the stars   all blind to her pain   she prayed she would black out

He gently laid her on the bed, flipped on a small bedside lamp. She closed her eyes.   Stay blind.   Her body was numb, but she felt a distant tugging as he removed her clothes.   Let me fall asleep and never wake. Let the darkness enclose me. Save me or erase me, I don't care as long as it ends. Let it end in agony or let it be painless, I don't care. Just let it end. Please let it end.

Merry

She let her head fall to the side, but couldn't open her eyes. When Claire touched her cheek, her hand was warm and real and comforting.

Help me, Claire.

Her head filled with the roar of static, a disorienting cacophony.

Come with me, Claire said.

The static subsided, settled to a steady crunching hum. Tyres on a dirt road. Birdsong crept out of the darkness, hollow at first, then full, vibrant. Her body bumped and jostled.

Where am I…?

'Open your eyes, Merry.'

Claire was beside her. Much younger. Hair just past her shoulders. Head propped up on a rolled-up sleeping bag. Overhead, the clear blue sky with branches rushing past.

'Do you remember this?'

Merry craned her head back. She saw the dust-covered rear window of Grandpa Pat's truck. He looked back at her and his face wrinkled in a quick grin, before returning his attention to the road.

'This was…we went camping with Grandpa Pat…he took us to his cabin in the hills. You talked him into letting us ride in the tray at the back…but…Claire…Mr Blake is…'

'Shhh.' Claire touched her shoulder. 'Look.' She pointed to the sky, her arm wavering as the truck bounced beneath them. A pair of rainbow lorikeets chased each other through the canopy. 'This is all there is in the world right now.'

'But it's not real…it can't be. This is all in my head. I'm losing my mind…'

'Why isn't this real? Reality is relative. You can hear the birds, can't you? And the stream down below? You can feel the wind on your face. Smell the mud and rust and exhaust of the truck.'

As Claire spoke, the sounds and smells came to her one after the other, washing over her, through her, but never quite washing away reality.

Claire, seeming to hear her thoughts, sat up and punched her in the arm.

'Ow.' The flare of pain shocked her and she rubbed her arm.

Claire was looking at her smugly, as though she'd just proved her point. 'If a tree falls in the woods, and Merry isn't around, does it make a sound? Something only becomes real once it's in here.' She reached forward and flicked Merry between the eyes. 'Stop looking for excuses to suffer more.'

She lay back down, folding her hands behind her head. Merry did the same.

'How long can I stay here?'

She felt Claire shrug. 'Probably not as long as you'd like. Nothing lasts forever. Even here.'

Grandpa's truck slowed to take a bend in the road, and when it straightened the sun was above her, intermittently blinding her as it dodged through the branches. She looked back at Grandpa Pat again, and again he turned and gave her an identical grin.

'I remember this trip.'

'Of course. That's why we're here.'

'Do you remember what we talked about on the way? You were trying to scare me telling me—'

A burst of static cut off her voice, crackling through her head, and she was back in the room watching the ceiling through teary eyes, watching his disproportionately large shadow lurch back and forth, surrounded by his laboured breaths.

No. Claire. Take me back. I can't. This isn't happening. This isn't real!

Have you finished all your homework? Claire, what about your maths sheets?

We're the disease. We're the disease and it's the fucken cure.

The itsy bitsy spider climbed up the water spout

He's living at the Foodmart now? That's pretty weird, right?

She went to church every Sunday and prayed for his soul...prayed that he'd forgive her...

Drive carefully, okay, Dad? There's a lot of twists and turns on those roads. And don't let them ride in the back again. It's too dangerous.

The itsy bitsy spider...

Please, Grandpa?

Okay, but don't tell your mother, she'll skin me alive

It escaped from the zoo and now it lives in these hills

Smile.   smile.   and be Merry

Down came the rain

Down came the rain

'You're just trying to scare me.'

'No, it's for real. It escaped from the zoo and now it lives in these hills. I even saw it once.'

'Nuh-uh.'

'Ya-hah. You were only three last time we came, so you wouldn't remember, but I was playing on the tyre swing and Grandpa Pat was making sandwiches and I saw it in the trees, a real tiger, and it even looked right at me, but then Grandpa came out and I looked away and when I looked back I just saw its tail disappearing into a bush...'

Merry craned her eyes up and eyed the trees nervously, looking for any hint of orange and black.

'Hey, imagine if when Grandpa stopped the truck it smelled us, or it smelled the peanut butter sandwiches in your bag, and it even jumped right in here with us. Tigers like peanut butter, you know.'

While she was talking, the brakes squeaked and the truck rolled to a gentle stop. They looked at each other, wide-eyed.

'You girls okay back there?' Grandpa Pat called through the dusty window.

'Yep,' Claire said. Then she whispered to Merry, 'Don't worry, I know how to stop a tiger. We just have to kick it in the nuts. Rachel said that God made boys stronger than girls, but he also gave them nuts for us to kick if they're being too mean, so it evens out. One day at lunch Ryan pulled down Lucy's pants in front of all the boys, so I kicked his nuts and he had to go to sick bay and missed all of fifth period. I got detention.' She said this with a gleam of pride.

Merry nodded, letting this sink in. 'But...what if it's a girl tiger?'

Claire crinkled her brow in deep thought while Merry watched on hopefully.

'Well, I guess we'd better ditch the sandwiches, just in case.'

Merry dove for her bag and pulled out the peanut butter sandwiches. As hungry as she was, even one of Mum's peanut butter sandwiches wasn't worth a tiger attack, so with one quick shake of the bag she jettisoned them. Her stomach grumbled as she watched the little white triangles spin and fly apart in the road.

'That should do it,' Claire said. '...unless...the tiger finds the sandwiches and wants more, and follows the road right to us...'

'What?'

'Well, you never know...'

'I hope the tiger doesn't find us.'

Claire flicked a spider from her shirt. 'Don't hope for anything. Hope is pointless. It's just another way to say "doing nothing". You can't hope a tiger away. You just need a plan, like kicking it in the nuts.'

'Stop saying nuts. It's rude.'

'Okay...plums, then.'

Merry snorted with laughter, then tried to pretend she hadn't.

When she looked over, Claire was older.

The car had stopped moving.

We never did see the tiger.

'I kind of wish we had. I remember being scared for that whole camping trip, but maybe if I hadn't been scared I wouldn't have remembered it.'

She looked up. The lorikeets were suspended against the blue sky, frozen, living brushstrokes on an insubstantial canvas. The air was still. Somewhere in the back of her mind came the dusty echo of a man breathing heavily through his nose, sighing sharply.

'Did you make the whole thing up, about the tiger? You never saw it, did you?'

Claire shrugged. She looked over her shoulder as though someone was calling her away. 'I have to go now,' she said.

'No, not yet. Please. Just a little longer.'

The surrounding trees began to swirl and fade, like a chalk drawing in the rain.

'I don't want to go back. It's too soon...'

Claire gave her a sad smile and sat up. 'Everything good is gone too soon.'

Merry clutched at her sister's sleeve as Claire too slipped away. 'No, you can't go. You can't leave me...'

The world fell out from under her. The bright day faded to night. And every good thing was gone.

It had rained hard in the night, but now the only sound was the splash of water overflowing from the gutters. He'd changed her clothes, placed her back in her own bed and tucked the blankets around her after—nothing happened nothing happened nothing happened nothing—a glass of water and some glossy teen magazines had been left on the bedside table. She frowned at the flawless, smiling faces on the cover. They promised her advice on how to "nail her first kiss," how to "get that perfect pout," how to "dress to catch his eye"—nothing nothing nothing happened—the absurdity of it made her sick. All those celebrities and people in the media shouting over each other for attention when none of them had anything to say. All dead now. Dead people giving advice to dead girls. She reached over and tipped the magazines onto the floor.

She didn't need to check the door handle to know it was locked. Trapped.   Trapped   trapped. It's all gone   No way out   but nothing happened   nothing happened   what happened?   all gone

Trapped?   Hope   for a way out?   for safety?   Hope? Hope is stupid   Hope is death   Hope is nothing   Hope is suffering   falling   falling   so far   so deep   always further to fall   always deeper   finally   finally   finally   Is this the bottom?   Or is there further yet to fall?

A plan   a plan   No way out?   No such thing as trapped there's always a way out   look   inside   turn over your wrist   there   you see it   there is the road to freedom

Merry sat up slowly and picked up the glass of water. It left a ring of condensation on the already-stained wood. She carried it into the bathroom. Looked at herself in the mirror for a long time.

The shower-head was dripping. Plip   plip   plip   do it do it   do it

She held out the glass and dropped it into the sink where it shattered. Picked up a long, curved shard and went into the shower, sitting with her back against the corner

Nothing happened nothing happened nothing happened do it do it do it

She looked about for Claire, but found herself alone. Spoke anyway. 'Will we be together now?'

The whispers whispered but did not answer. She closed her eyes and wished. Wished one last time for blue skies and lorikeets, and the cabin in the hills, and sandwiches and stories of tigers. Everything good is gone too soon.

Holding the glass delicately between her thumb and forefinger, she pressed it to the outside of her wrist and slid it quickly across.

'Claire. Can you forgive me now?'

April 24

When she woke, it was light outside, but only a little of it squeezed through the gaps in the boards that covered the window. Her body rose and fell slightly with Bear's breaths, and she drew her legs in tighter, snuggling against his warmth.

'Morning,' he whispered.

'You make a good pillow, Uncle Bear,' she said.

He chuckled, making her head bounce up and down. 'You were out like a light. Sleep well?'

She yawned, nodding. 'What are we doing in here?' she asked. Her memories were fuzzy, and she had the feeling she'd been in a terrible dream last night, but couldn't remember any of it.

'You don't remember?' He sighed, then said to himself, 'Well, that's one blessing.' He turned her so she was facing him, a serious look in his eyes. 'Listen, Zoey, it's time for us to move on from here.'

Zoey pouted. 'You mean leave? I don't want to leave. I like it here.'

'Me too, kiddo,' he said, sadly. 'But our food's gone. Our friend in the truck cleaned the place out, apart from the vegetable oil, and a half-empty bottle of ketchup. I thought maybe we'd found a little haven for ourselves. Wanted to believe we'd be safe here for a long time. But I was stupid. We're exposed here, is what we are. Now the…uh…chocolate pudding has hit the fan, and we're stuck out here with no wheels.' He heaved a great sigh and shook his head. 'I should've stuck to the original plan. I really stuffed everything up.'

'Your bike has wheels.' She was only half concentrating because now all she could think about was chocolate pudding.

'Yeah, but there's nothing in the tank. Without a good drink, this is the end of the road for the old girl.'

'What do bikes drink?'

'Mine likes diesel. But there's not a drop around. Trust me, I've looked. It's like someone's been through the whole area and siphoned everything with an engine.'

Zoey didn't quite understand, but nodded as though she did. 'Sometimes, when we run out of milk, Mummy puts water on my cereal.'

Bear smiled at her. 'It's not quite the same, is it?' Then suddenly he frowned and looked up at the shelf across the room. 'But…it might just get the job done…'

'It's yucky,' Zoey went on. 'It tastes better without anything.'

Bear wasn't listening. He was staring at the big plastic container of vegetable oil on the shelf. 'It might just…' Without a word he stood up and went to the shelf, picked up the container, and started swirling the thick, golden liquid around inside. 'She won't like it. Not one bit. But just maybe…'

A shuffling shadow moved past the window, and all at once Zoey remembered everything. The screaming possum. The laughing girl crawling through the window. Running in the dark. She sank to the floor and hugged her knees.

'It wasn't a dream...'

'No,' Bear said softly, crouching next to her. 'No, I wish it was. I wish I could take those awful memories away for you, little miss. I wish I could make this whole nightmare go away. But it's no good wishing for the impossible. All I can do is get you out of here. How's that sound? You and me get out of here and go some place safe.'

Zoey nodded.

'I'm gonna need your help, though, angel. Do you think you can be brave for a little longer?'

She tried to swallow the sick feeling. She wasn't sure she could be brave. Not when it came to those monsters. But she nodded. Uncle Bear needed her help.

'That's my girl. Come on.'

With the jug of oil in one hand, he led her down the corridor to the kitchen and into the big pantry where they'd hidden his bike. He ran a hand over the silvery handlebars, pausing to scratch off some speckles of dried mud with his thumbnail.

'We'll need a funnel. I think I remember seeing one in the cupboard by the oven. Can you run and grab it for me?'

Zoey nodded and trotted into the kitchen, happy to have a job to do that could keep her mind off the things walking around outside. She pulled open the cupboard—it creaked noisily—and pulled everything out. Funnel. Funnel. Now that she thought about it, she didn't know what a funnel was. She put back the bowls, because they weren't funnels, and the cheese grater, and some different sized saucepans, which only left a plastic thing that looked a bit like a volcano. When she got back to Bear with the plastic volcano, he was unscrewing a lid on the front of the bike.

'Well done. Now, the next thing we need is a couple of pots and pans. Think you can find some?'

'I know where they are,' she said, and scurried off.

She returned to the kitchen and headed for the cupboard, but a flicker of movement caught her eye. Zoey stopped and held her breath. Lines of dusty sunlight came from the boarded-up windows, but the gaps were too small and too bright for her to see anything outside. Galahs in the trees called to her, wondering where she'd gone. From the pantry, she could hear the thick gloop, gloop, gloop sound as Bear poured out the oil.

They would leave soon. She could be brave, she told herself. She would be brave.

As she took the pans from the cupboard one slipped from her hand, but as she tried to stop it falling, she lost her grip on the other two, and all three of them clattered to the floor. It was the loudest sound she'd ever heard, and she covered her ears to try and block it out. Bear appeared in the doorway, looking white in the face, with splashes of oil down his shirt.

'Are you alright?'

'Yes…I'm sorry.'

'It's okay,' he whispered. 'It's almost time. There's just one—'

Some slithers of light disappeared and reappeared. Bear held a finger to his lips as the dreadful clicking of teeth passed the window.

'When I start the bike, it's gonna make one heck of a racket, and it might take me a few tries to get her going…So…here's where I need you to be really brave, little one.' He looked deep into her eyes, and she knew what he was about to ask was hurting him a lot.

'I can do it, Uncle Bear,' she whispered back.

'I know you can. Take these.' He picked two of the saucepans up off the floor and handed them to her. 'If we're gonna get the bike out of here, we'll need some time. And we can't do it if...those things...are waiting right outside the front door. It's the only way out. I need you to take these to the back office and make as much noise as you can. Get their attention. Get them over the other side of the building. I'll get the engine going and manoeuvre the bike outside. Then I'll call you when it's time to go.

'Those boards on the windows are strong. They'll hold. But if you think for a second one of them's getting in, you drop everything and run back to me. Understand?'

'Yes.'

'Okay. Now come here.' He pulled her close and hugged her tight. His hair still smelled of smoke from the barbie-cue they'd never eaten, and metal-y from the dried blood on his neck. And now there was the oil smell too. He kissed her hair twice, then sighed.

She didn't say anything else, but tightened her grip on the pans, and headed into the dark corridor.

Zoey stood in the small office and waited. Birds were chirping as though nothing was wrong in the whole wide world. She heard Bear rolling the bike out of the pantry and over to the front door. Then she raised the pans and swung them together as hard as she could. Her eyeballs shook with the sound, and the birds outside scattered. She crashed the pans together again twice more, then stopped to listen. There they were. Footsteps and gasping breaths coming towards her. Fingernails explored the outside of the window. Crash. She whacked one of the boards with the bigger of the two pans, and the creature outside cried with excitement.

'Haaaaaah.'

Miles away, the bike's engine was rumbling and choking out, but she hardly heard it over the crash of the pans.

Crash crash, clang clang. She walloped big chips out of the wooden desk, smashed dents into the filing cabinets, flung all the folders from the shelves.

'Hey, hey, hey!' She yelled. 'Heeeey!'

Her hands were numb and shaking, but she didn't stop. Glass from the window shattered and rained down. Squirming fingers slipped between the boards. Zoey stared into a yellow eye, circled with blood. The nails holding one of the boards groaned and squeaked, then peeled away on one side, letting a slippery, shredded arm in. She could see the light moving, hear the bangs as more of them pounded at the windows.

Zoey dropped one of the pans and turned to run, but stopped. She turned slowly, stepped closer to the arm and swung the pan like a cricket bat, just the way Bear had shown her, and 'hit a six' right into those reaching fingers. Hammering down on those red and purple nails. They popped, like the sound a big sheet of bubble wrap made when you jumped on it, and the hand bent backwards. She ran from the room.

Uncle Bear met her on the way back. Over the grunting growls of the laugher, she could hear the low rumble of the bike's engine, not as smooth as it used to be, but still the best sound she could imagine. Bear picked her up and ran outside to where the bike was waiting. He threw his leg over the side, squeezed Zoey tight with one arm, revved the engine twice, then set it free. They swerved around the caravans, skidded onto the dirt road, and soon it was all behind them—the old lady in the caravan, her drawings of princesses and fairies, the laughers—all swallowed up by a growing cloud of red dust.

* * *

The view never changed. Red dirt and white grass either side of the narrow road, sometimes trees, a fence, a field, and hills in the distance. Whichever way Zoey looked, it was the same. The shaking from the bike made her whole body numb, except for her bottom which hurt all the time. She tried looking back a few times, sure that the laughers were right behind them, but each time there was nothing.

When Bear started slowing down, she looked up. Though the world was shaking, she could see a big blue sign by the side of the road. She didn't know all of her letters, but the first word started with a W. Most of it was scribbled out, though, and someone had written something else over the top in red paint. That started with an F.

'Hold up,' Bear said to himself. 'Looks like someone really doesn't want visitors.'

They rode on slowly. Some other streets crossed over the main road now, but all had been blocked with cars and big, white caravans. Zoey could smell smoke.

'What the...' Bear slowed down further, leaning forward.

There was something big in the road ahead, right in the middle where two main streets crossed. It was mostly black on the bottom, but she could see lots of other colours on top, like a big pile of dirty laundry, and there were things sticking out of it in all directions.

'Dear God,' he whispered, trying to cover Zoey's eyes with his hand, but it was too late. She'd already seen. It wasn't laundry. It was a pile of people.

April 22

The woman was lying on her back beneath a wide coolabah tree. Middle-aged with long dark hair and plump cheeks, wearing a purple dressing gown, she might have looked normal, peaceful, if not for the lipless grin and blood on her chin. Above her head, suspended on a thread of fishing line tied to the tree branch, a half-eaten slab of kangaroo meat twirled slowly. It had worked exactly as Mr Blake planned. They crushed up a few dozen triazolam tablets, dissolved them in a tub full of chloroform, and soaked the meat. The bait was then hung at strategic points around town overnight, and in the morning they drove around in Blake's truck collecting the unconscious grinners.

There were no signs of life from the woman on the ground, but that was how it worked on them. The heart and breathing seemed to stop completely for several hours, then as the drug wore off it was as though they were coming back to life all over again.

Once the woman was tied, muzzled and locked safely in the back of the truck, Merry took a fresh piece of meat from an esky in the truck's cab. As she threaded the fishhooks through it, its juices ran down her hands and into the bandages that bound her wrists. Pink stains bloomed where they met. Merry stepped back, absently scratching at her scabbed wrists through the bandages. She looked down at her hands. The creases on her palms, the pores of her skin, around and under her fingernails were all stained a deep red. She tried to rub it away.

You stupid girl. What have you done?

It burned when he pressed the gauze to the gashes in her wrists.

Don't you understand anything? The more you fight, the more it hurts. How dare you try to leave me after everything I've done for you.

Do you hear me, Annabelle? I am your entire world now. I am everything. Your father, your saviour, your lover, your only friend. Me! Your life belongs to me, and I decide when you die.

He pulled the cap off a syringe with his teeth and jabbed the needle into her arm. His eyes were distant, full of rage and fear.

Stupid girl. You're not going anywhere. I'm all you have. All you'll ever have.

Behind her, the truck started and she heard him pop open the passenger door for her. The sun was sinking, and he'd be impatient to get home before dark—this was one of his rules. Her body started to turn, but her eyes stayed fixed on the horizon, searching, searching for...what? There was nothing out there. No escape. Nothing to hope for. Hope is pointless.

'Meredith, come. You know the rules.'

She sighed, pulled the sleeves of her heavy woolen jumper until it covered her bandages. It was warm out, but she always wore the jumper because it hid the shape of her body. With her eyes downcast, she returned to the truck.

* * *

It had been a long day. They'd spent the morning siphoning petrol out of all the abandoned cars around town, transporting it in small jerry-cans to huge, thousand-litre IBCs, which Blake kept in a warehouse near the Foodmart.

She felt his eyes on her always, but she could no longer meet them. When he spoke, she studied the ground. When he touched her arm, she flinched and looked away. When he took her to the black room, she left her body behind and went to another time, another place. It was the only way she could find to go on—to deny what he'd done, what he was, what he'd turned her into. So she did as she was told, she ate with him; she slept beside him; she numbed herself to his touch and the voices in her head that tried to whisper their dark truths, that mocked and ridiculed and blamed her and pushed at her to try again, to cut deeper...

Her .270 calibre rifle rested by her knee, always within her reach. He'd shown her how to clean it and oil it and make sure it was loaded—another of his rules—and he'd placed it in her hands and turned his back, knowing she was too broken to ever pull the trigger on him. Because living with a monster was better than being alone.

April 24

The bike's engine puttered and stuttered as they sat in the middle of the road, with the smell of burnt people in their noses. Zoey's eyes were closed and covered, but she could still see them, piled on each other as high as a car, some of them arched like gymnasts, legs sticking out like they were made of wood. Some had the lipless grin of the laughers, but most were just normal people, only the skin on their faces was too tight and yellow.

She felt Bear turn the bike around and drive back the way they'd come. When the smell had faded, he stopped and got off.

'Cover your ears, darlin',' he said to Zoey.

When she did, he walked a little way down the road, took off his helmet, then slammed it against a tree, over and over, shouting words she didn't understand. Chunks of bark sprayed onto the road and Zoey started crying.

When he came back to her, his face was still red, but his voice was calm. 'I'm sorry about that, sweetheart. I...lost my temper. Didn't mean to scare you.' He took out the map and unfolded it on the seat, sucking in a few deep breaths. 'We're okay, though.

It'll all be okay. We just need to go back the way we came for a bit, double around, and take this other road up through Jamestown. It will just take us a little longer, is all. We might not make it by nightfall, but we'll be fine. Nothin' bad's going to happen to you, okay? Not a thing. That's a promise.'

Zoey understood enough to know they wouldn't be going back to the pile of people, so she forced herself to stop crying, but her tummy still hurt. 'I don't feel berry well,' she said.

'I know,' was all he said back. 'Me neither.'

The shadows of the trees grew longer and colder, reaching across the road to join hands, and Zoey shivered whenever they passed through one. As they rode, she dozed, leaning back against Bear's warm belly, and she felt safe with his great paw across her like a seatbelt. She dreamed, even though she never quite fell asleep, always aware of the hum of the tyres on the gravelly road, and the flash, flash, flash on her eyelids as they rode in and out of shadows...

But she was also back home in her garden, playing with Hopkins. She pushed him down the short, plastic slide, then slid down after him, landing on his head and laughing. She dragged him through the uncut grass, climbed onto the lawn chair, and threw him into the air. She held out her arms to catch him, but he landed in the fairy bush.

Mummy was there, dressed as Cinderella in her poofy blue dress, and she picked up Hopkins and dusted him off. Come along Zoey, she said, we mustn't be late for the Ball. Zoey had completely forgotten. Mummy helped her into her own pink dress. It had white ruffles along the bottom that swooshed on the grass as she walked. They arrived at the palace, and were greeted by the prince—Hopkins in a dark blue suit, with those yellow tassels on the shoulders that she always thought looked so nice. He bowed to her, and they danced together under the moonlight while Mummy looked on, smiling. Prince Hopkins leaned close to her and whispered something...

'Holy...hell.'

Zoey opened her eyes. It was almost dark, but she could see houses on either side of them...and roads blocked with cars and caravans. Ahead of them, lighting up the road and trees around them, was a big fire, and inside the fire she could see arms, legs...faces.

They'd gone back? Her eyes filled with tears from the burning smoke in the air.

Bear tightened his hand on the handle and the bike lurched forwards. 'The Devil take you all,' he roared.

Zoey screamed. She felt the heat of the fire on her face as they sped past and into the town. The bike's headlight flashed off street poles and shopfront windows, dazzling her. Bear was breathing heavily, his head twisting from side to side. It was a small town, and it wasn't long before the buildings were behind them, and they were back on the familiar road lined with gum trees, only now the branches looked like twisted limbs, and the clumps of leaves like huge hairy animals dangling from them.

As darkness closed in, Bear slowed the bike and pulled over to the side. He was still breathing quickly.

He swallowed. 'I didn't see anyone there. Someone just wanted to scare us, that's all.'

'Why did you take us back?' Zoey demanded, tears in her eyes.

He looked at her. His eyes were wide and glistening. 'I didn't go back,' he said. 'This is Jamestown. Someone put 'em here, too.'

Zoey shuddered and closed her eyes. She didn't want to open them ever again. She was so tired. The wind through the leaves sounded like the ocean. But it felt like there was a storm coming.

She kept her eyes closed until Bear shook her. He must have thought she was asleep. They were coming up to another town, he said, but she didn't open her eyes. She couldn't. She couldn't see it again. The bike slowed down to a crawl, then stopped.

Zoey opened one eye and saw they were outside a small supermarket. She opened the other and looked around. There was no pile of people this time. But still, she didn't want to get off the bike.

'I know you're scared, sweetheart,' Bear said as he unclipped the belt. 'But we don't have any food left. We've still got a ways to go and I don't know what we'll find when we get there.'

The shop's windows were dark, and it was impossible to see anything but their own reflections. The Uncle Bear she saw in them looked tired, too. He was blinking fast, rubbing his eyes. She took his hand and looked up at him. 'Are you okay, Uncle Bear?' she asked.

'Aren't you somethin'. Everything you've gone through and you're worrying about me. I'm fine, angel. We bears are hibernators. I won't rest 'til winter.' He smiled and gave her a wink.

They walked up to the front door, which was covered by a big shutter with a brick pattern on it. Bear tried to pull it up from the bottom, but it was locked.

'Don't think I'll be able to kick this one down, somehow. But locked is good. Means we might still find something inside, if we can get in. Come on, let's try around back.'

The alley behind the supermarket smelled like the cupboard under the sink at home, and most of the walls had been painted with big colourful letters and drawings. There were stacks of cardboard boxes by a big garage door. Uncle Bear tried to lift it, but it was locked, too. He looked around some more and found a smaller door behind a dumpster.

'Fire Door,' he read. 'Do not obstruct. This door is alarmed.' He looked at Zoey with a grin. 'It's not the only one, right?'

Zoey blinked at him.

'It's alarmed? See, it's a pun because…ah, nevermind.' He put his shoulder against the dumpster and gave it a shove. The metal wheels crunched and squealed loudly on the concrete, and it fought him hard, but eventually he moved it out of the way. It didn't matter, though, because even when he rattled the handle and kicked at the door, it wouldn't budge. At last, he sighed and stepped back.

'Well, it was worth a shot.'

Zoey shivered as a gust of wind swept newspapers through the alley, and a tin can clanged against something out of sight. Above her, telephone wires swayed and twanged, and something made a tinkling sound. She didn't see it at first, then there was a glint of light off something shiny. It was a little silver cat hanging from a string by a window. Below it, different sized metal sticks swung, dinging softly as they bumped one another. A wind chime. Zoey pointed.

'What is it, darlin'—?' Bear followed her finger. 'The window? Good thinking.'

Zoey clasped her hands together as Bear climbed up on the dumpster and reached for the window. She didn't like him being up there without her. It felt like something was pressing on her chest whenever he was out of her reach, and the shadows around her seemed to creep a little closer. He gave the wooden window frame a shove and it moved up a little.

'We're in business,' he whispered.

With another shove, he pushed it all the way up. Chips of white paint flaked off the wood and sprinkled down like snow.

Bear hoisted her up onto the dumpster beside him, then scrambled through the window. He was only gone for a second, but Zoey's breath stopped until he reappeared and reached down to pull her up.

It was too dark to see anything inside. Bear took out a small flashlight and shone it around the room. The first thing she saw was the ugly green paint on the walls. Then the desk in front of them. Everything on it was lined up with everything else. The yellow notepad, the old-fashioned black telephone, the little lamp, the pens all in a row. Pinned to the board beside the desk was a photo of four smiling girls with yellow hair. The two younger ones looked the same, but their shirts were different colours. Zoey thought she knew one of the girls from somewhere.

Hand in hand, they crept over to the door. When they heard nothing, they stepped out. There were two other doors on the same floor, both locked, and a set of stairs leading down. Downstairs, they passed through a room with a couple of round tables, chairs, and a fridge in it.

On the wall was a big board with photos of smiling people. Most of them were dressed in white, with dark green aprons on, and next to each photo were numbers and words that she couldn't read. The face at the top looked familiar. He was a thin man with a neat little moustache and small eyes, and hair that started too close to the top of his head. He wasn't smiling like the others.

Through another door they found the main part of the supermarket where all the shelves were. Bear's shoulders slumped when his torch found rows and rows of empty shelves. They walked up and down the aisles, checking under the shelves as they had at the petrol station, but there was nothing left.

As they passed back through the room with the tables, they saw another door, flat with the wall, and painted the same ugly green colour so it almost disappeared. When they pushed it open, Bear gasped. There were more shelves in here, but they were stocked full of cans and boxes and bottles. Zoey spotted a big packet of Cheetos, with the grinning cheetah.

'Hold up,' Bear said. 'Something ain't right here...'

But she didn't hear him and rushed over to grab the bag off the shelf. Her tummy, remembering how hungry it was, growled loudly. Bear came up behind her and took the bag from her. He was looking around the room, shining his torch over the shelves.

'Someone's put all this here. Recently. We better take what we can carry and get—'

There was movement in the next room, and a light overhead flickered on. Bear grabbed her arm and dragged her behind the shelf. Zoey heard the door open and a soft step on the concrete floor.

April 24

Night. It was unusual for him to be out after dark. But he'd been out a lot the last few days. Going off by himself in the truck. Merry sat on her bed and peered through the bars on her window, down into the alley that became a sunken chasm in the darkness. A moment ago, when the wind shifted, she thought she'd heard an unfamiliar engine, a deep-throated rattle, though it was impossible to tell its direction. Now, though, the world outside was silent again, and she convinced herself it was just another trick of her malignant mind.

But there it was again, definitely an engine, very close now. She closed her eyes and tried to visualise where it was and where it was going. It had to be inside the town, coming from the west. She could hear it slowing down to navigate through the blockade of cars and caravans they'd set up. It must be a motorcycle, nothing larger could make it through. The engine rolled evenly along and stopped, as she'd known it would, out the front of the Foodmart.

She went to the door and tried the handle—not locked,

strange—and tiptoed into the living room. The windows overlooking the street glowed yellow from the bike's headlight. As she reached the window, the engine and the light faded away. She tried to listen, but the noise in her head made it impossible to hear anything else.

What should she do? She could hear Mr Blake's voice clearly: Never attempt to contact outsiders. Rule number one. She should go back to bed, where she'd be safe. They had to be looking for food, but even if they broke in, it wasn't likely they'd find anything. The shelves were all empty, all the fresh food was long gone, and everything that could be saved was safely hidden away in the loading bay. She should keep quiet, stay in bed, let them go on their way. Silently, she slipped back under the covers and pulled the pillow over her head.

Yess hide hide little girl. Who knows what new dangers this midnight rider bringsssss. Hmm? I heard that. You wonder how anything could be worse than what you've already been through. How could anything be worse than thissss? Surely you see by now...It can always always always get worse. Head down, little girl and preserve your personal Hell.

Movement in the alley. A rattle at the door. It was only when she heard the scritch scritch scritch of a window sash being forced up that she opened her eyes.

Could it be him? Could this be a test? Another of his games to see how she'd react? Whether she was willing to defend their territory. Her door left unlocked; Him staying out later than usual. What would he want her to do?

She bit the edge of her thumb in the dark. Childish laughter filled her head. Go? Stay? Run? Hide? Afraid to move. Afraid not to move. She felt her chest would burst and the voices in her mind laughed at her pain and she lay staring up at the ceiling, thinking nothing, thinking nothing.

At last she lowered her feet to the floor, reached under her bed, and pulled out her rifle.

'You're trespassing,' a voice said.

It was a girl's voice. She sounded like a kid, maybe a little older than her cousin Russell. 'I know you're in there. Just make this easy on yourself and come out.'

Her voice was trembling, and they could hear her quick breaths. Bear brought his face very close to Zoey's and held his finger up to his lips. Then he put both hands on her shoulders firmly. She understood he wanted her to stay still. He stood up and stepped out from behind the shelf, still holding the bag of Cheetos.

'Don't move,' the girl squeaked.

'Easy,' Bear said. 'No need for that. Crikey, how old are you, girl? Do you even know how to use that thing?'

'I grew up on a farm. I can bulls-eye a rabbit from fifty metres...I'm not going to miss you, don't you...don't you worry about that.'

'Alright, I believe you.'

Zoey stared up at the long lights on the ceiling above them, transfixed. They hummed like far away insects. She could hear something else, a muffled engine rumbling somewhere below them.

'You're not supposed to be in here,' the girl said. 'He...said nobody would come. Didn't you see the warnings we left? You weren't supposed to...this, this is our place. There's not enough to go around anymore, he said. We need to make it last.' Her feet scuffed across the concrete floor. 'He'll be back soon, so you need to put those down and leave!'

'Warnings?...You mean that was you? Those piles of bodies? Why?'

The girl cleared her throat. Her voice was a little quieter now, but it still trembled. 'They were...already dead, or worse than dead. Father told us we needed to move them away. Away from our home, or they'd make us sick, too. And we needed to keep the others away. He said they'd bring the sickness and take everything from us. We had to close off the town fast, he said.'

Zoey didn't understand the girl, so she started looking around the room. There were cans of baby corn on the shelf next to her. Baby corn was one vegetable she liked.

'Look, we didn't know anyone was in here. We weren't going to take everything. We just need a little to get us through the next couple of days. You have plenty of food here, and power. Is that a generator I can hear? You're set for a long time. You can spare just a little, can't you? Then we'll be gone, I promise.' Bear took half a step forward, then stopped as something clicked.

'We?' Her voice squeaked again 'What do you mean...who else is in here? Show yourself, of I'll shoot him, I mean it!'

Zoey understood enough to know they were in trouble. She stood, but Bear turned to her and shook his head.

'No, sweetie...' Then he turned back to the girl. 'It's not like that. It's just me and—'

Outside, a car door slammed. The girl screamed and the bag of Cheetos burst with a loud pop, sprinkling orange fingers on Uncle Bear's shoes and across the floor. He groaned and tipped over sideways.

April 24

The girl was screaming, but Zoey's ears were ringing so loudly that it sounded like her head was underwater. When Zoey stepped out from behind the shelf, the girl stopped screaming, but her mouth stayed open. Zoey stared. It was one of the girls from the photo upstairs. Her long yellow hair hung over her shoulders almost to her tummy, partly covering the horse pattern on her knitted jumper. She dropped the thing she was holding—some sort of bat with a long black tube on one end— and ran from the room.

Uncle Bear was trying to stand up. There was some ketchup on the floor around his feet, which she hadn't noticed before, and that must have been what he'd slipped on. She took one of his hands and tried to pull him up, but he was too heavy. Eventually, he sat up against a shelf, and dragged himself to his feet, with Zoey tugging on his collar to help. The shelves shook so much that most of the neatly stacked cans toppled over. His eyes were scrunched closed and he seemed to be saying something, but Zoey still couldn't hear through the ringing.

He stumbled over to the wall and grabbed some green shopping bags, then returned to the shelves, running his arm along them, blindly tipping in boxes and cans and bottles until they overflowed. Zoey watched as bottles of olive oil silently shattered on the concrete and thick golden pools spread across the floor, making islands of the Cheetos.

Bear headed for the door they'd come in, but he only made it a few steps before he stopped and bent over. She thought he was going to fall down again, but he just picked up another bag of Cheetos, and put it in one of the green bags. He staggered, hugging the walls as they went back past the stairs and into the main part of the supermarket, Zoey trotting anxiously a few steps behind. He must have hurt his tummy when he fell because he was holding it a lot.

All the lights were on now. The empty brightness of the supermarket and the sound in her head made her feel like she was floating—like she wasn't really there at all.

That feeling ended as Uncle Bear crashed through the door with a picture of a fire on it, and they were back in the alley, and her ears filled with a new noise. An alarm. Bear didn't stop, though. He lurched down the alley so fast she had to run to keep up. She could hear him grunting now, and the noises he was making scared her.

He stopped at the corner and stared. Zoey stared too. There was a green car parked half up on the curb. The same green car they'd passed on the road that day, except the front of it was all dented in. Bear lurched forward again, heading for his bike, but he seemed to change his mind and instead opened the door of the green car. He threw the shopping bags over the passenger seat into the back.

'Get in,' he said through his teeth.

As he turned to face her, Zoey noticed the hole in his shirt, and the big red stain around it. She pointed to it. 'You need a Band-Aid.'

He stepped towards her and grabbed her arm hard. 'Get in,' he said again.

'I'm not asposed to sit in the front...' she said, barely louder than a mumble, as he dragged her to the car. She climbed up and he slammed the door. She wasn't sure why he was being so mean to her, and she pinched her tongue, trying not to cry.

As he walked around to the other side, the supermarket door flew open and a man ran out. It was the man with the little moustache. With his clean white shirt and neatly combed hair, he was the exact opposite of Uncle Bear. If he was an animal, he would be a cat. One that sits up on a high shelf, cleaning itself all day, and only looking at you if you got in its way. He stared at them for a second, then calmly pulled a gum out of a pouch on his belt and pointed it at them.

Bear cried out in pain as he slid into the driver's seat and slammed the door, ignoring the man. As the engine started, there was a loud crack, and suddenly a hole appeared in the windscreen right in front of her.

Zoey slid across the seat as the car bumped down off the curb and into the street. With another crack, the little mirror on Bear's side flew off. Two more rang out, but the sounds were fading behind them as Bear sped away.

Mummy leaned forward, stamping out her cigarette in the ashtray and blowing smoke at the TV. The windows were all closed, so the smoke had nowhere to go, except into Zoey's eyes.

'Geez,' Mummy said to the man on TV. 'Geez Louise. It's in

Adelaide now. Zoey, go get Mummy the phone.' She opened and closed the empty box of cigarettes. 'And some more of my smokey treats.'

Zoey slid off the couch. 'Is it lunchtime yet?'

'There's cereal in the pantry. Your idiot father left the milk out again last night, so you'll have to have it with water.'

Zoey went to the kitchen and got Mummy's phone and cigarettes from her purse and brought them back to her. Then she went to the pantry and found a box of Froot Loops. She didn't like them with water, so she just took the whole box back to the living room and started munching on them dry. Mummy had the phone between her ear and shoulder, and was lighting another cigarette.

'Hey, Candice, yeah, it's me. You watching this?...I know, right?'

The TV was showing pictures of the hospital. Lots of people lying in beds, sleeping in the chairs, even lying on the floor. Then it showed a doctor giving an old lady a shot in the arm.

'You believe this? Yeah, the vaccine...ha, please, girl, it's for show...Nah, they don't know what the hell it is, or where it came from. No way they got a vaccine out this quick...More than you. I took Biomed for two years, remember...Yeah, so what? I don't see a degree hanging on your wall either, but at least I went to the classes...'

The picture changed back to the man reading the news. Beside him there was a yellow circle with black rings in it. "...hospitals and doctor's surgeries in Melbourne have begun turning people away in the hundreds stating that they are already over capacity. A statement from the Royal Melbourne Hospital advised anyone experiencing sudden, severe flu-like symptoms to remain in their home, and minimise contact..."

Zoey had an idea, and put down her cereal to find Hopkins. She found him in the playroom with his head stuffed in her plastic oven. 'Those brownies will have to wait, Hopkins,' she told him, firmly. She also grabbed her doctor bag and Daddy's old brown hat, and took them all back to the living room. 'Mummy, do you want to play doctor with me? Hopkins is sick—'

'Shhh,' Mummy said. 'Yeah, she's home. Pre-school's shut down, too. So whaddaya think, you getting out of town?...Yeah, good...He's at work!...I know...Well, they're paying triple rates, he says. Ha. Fat lot of good that does if you end up dead...'

Zoey put on her hat and took Hopkins' temperature, then checked his ears and throat. 'Hmm,' she said. 'You're berry, berry sick. You must take your medicine and go straight to bed.' Then she hit him in the knee with a hammer because that's what doctors do. 'Mummy, can you get some medicine for—'

'Come on Zoey, shut it for a second, Mummy's talking...Yeah, I'll tell him tonight...Well if he doesn't then I'll just take Zoey and go by myself...I don't know, to my brother's maybe...' She coughed, shooting smoke from her nose in little puffs. 'Nah, not Barry. He's probably so stoned he doesn't even know it's happening...Yeah, Jay...Nah, trust me, it's coming here too, but when it does, I'll be long gone.'

The car swerved from side to side, trees and fences appearing in the car's headlights for a second, then vanishing as Bear pulled them back onto the road. His skin was turning white and he looked like he was about to fall asleep. Zoey knew he was very sick. If only she had a Band-Aid, she could make him better. She didn't know how long they drove for. She tried talking to him, but he didn't seem to hear her.

The car started slowing down, and when she looked over, Bear had his eyes closed, and his head on the steering wheel. They rolled off the road and slowed down even more as they went onto the grass, then came to a stop against the fence.

The engine chugged and ticked along, but inside the car it was quiet. Bear's mouth was open a little bit, and his chest was hardly moving.

'Uncle Bear?'

His eyelids flickered, but didn't open.

Zoey sniffed and touched his arm. It was colder than usual. She climbed into the back seat and started searching through the food that had spilled onto the floor and under the seats. She found the Cheetos and squeezed the bag until it popped open, but when she took out a puff and tried to put it in Bear's mouth, he wouldn't take it. Maybe he didn't like them. So she went back for something else. He wouldn't eat the chocolate biscuits, either, or the peanuts. Suddenly, she didn't feel like eating, so she crawled into his lap and rested her head on him. His mouth twitched as she moved against his tummy, but still he didn't wake up.

A little while later, the engine started making a funny sound, then it gave a little hiccup, jumped forward against the fence, and went quiet. Zoey didn't care. She just closed her eyes again and snuggled against Bear's tummy.

But she didn't sleep. Sometimes she heard flapping wings, and little clicks as bats flew through the darkness above them. Another time she heard a scratching sound and opened her eyes to see a possum running along the fence. It stopped in the headlights and looked at her for a while, its eyes flashing yellow and green, then it went on its way.

Zoey looked around the car. She saw the glove box in front of the passenger seat and remembered what Daddy told her one time. 'You can find just about anything in the glove box, except gloves.'

She slid off Bear's lap and across into the passenger seat. The glove box popped open easily and inside she found a heavy torch, a book with maps on every page, a small box of tissues, two pens, a spanner and a screwdriver, and…a doctor bag!

Her hands were trembling as she took out the little white case with the green cross on it. The clip on it was hard, and it took her a long time, but eventually she got it open. Inside, she found what she was looking for. She peeled the stickers off the Band-Aid and slid back over to Bear. Carefully, she lifted his shirt, and, after unsticking it from her finger, pressed the Band-Aid against the hole in his tummy.

Bear gasped and opened his eyes. His hand went to his tummy, and he stared at Zoey.

'I found a Band-Aid,' she said. 'It will make you better.'

Bear was gasping and squirming in his seat. He just blinked at her for a minute, then he smiled a little. 'I feel better already.' His voice was so dry and croaky. 'You're an angel,' he said. His chest gave a big heave, and tears ran down his cheeks into his beard. 'I'm a goddam useless bum, and you're my angel.'

'You're a burden,' Mummy said, leaning close to Zoey, and spilling her grown-up juice down her fingers. 'Tha's what you are.'

She looked at the dark red stain on the carpet, laughed to herself, and reached for the green glass bottle on the coffee table. 'If it wasn't for you, I could have stayed at uni, I would be making th' money I deserve, and we wouldn't even be here. We'd be living in the States, or Germany, I always wanted to go to

Germany. Jus me and Mark. Not you. You'd be nothing more than a glimmer in your daddy's eye. D'you see?'

Zoey shook her head and took a little sip from her apple juice.

'Course you don't. Cos you're jus a stupid little girl. Nobody's getting sick in Germany. Nope. But instead, we're here, and it's too late now. Bloody Mark had to take that job at the factory working for peanuts, and now he's not coming home, okay? Daddy's not coming home, and I'm stuck here with you.' She tipped the glass to her mouth and drank until it was empty.

Zoey couldn't understand most of what she was saying, so she nodded this time and hugged her knees tighter.

'Ha,' Mummy said, and tried to stand up. It took her three tries to get off the couch, then she staggered off to the bathroom, and Zoey heard her throwing up. When she came back, she was holding a plastic bottle, rattling it up and down.

'So, darling daughter, apple of my eye. It's almost time to go. The old pale rider is on his way to collect us, one way or another. Whadda you want to do for our last night on this Earth?' She rattled the plastic bottle in Zoey's face. 'Hey, I've got an idea. Let's play Sleeping Beauty. Pass me your juice.'

She passed it, and Mummy tipped a handful of little white medicines into the cup, then started stirring it with her finger. She held it out to Zoey. 'Drink up, princess.'

Zoey took the cup and looked at the juice. Some of the medicines were floating on the top, bubbling a little as they broke apart. 'I don't want to,' she said, looking back at Mummy.

'I don't care what you want to do. Good girls listen to their mummies, and I said drink it!' Mummy lunged forward and grabbed the cup, pressing it against Zoey's mouth. Zoey scrambled back, and the juice spilled onto the couch as Mummy lost her balance and fell forward on her face.

Zoey ran to the corner and stood there, expecting the cup or Mummy's glass to come flying at her. But Mummy just picked herself up slowly. She found the plastic bottle of medicine and gave it a rattle to make sure it wasn't empty. Then she took her bottle of grown-up juice from the coffee table and stood up. Without looking at Zoey, she started walking down the corridor to her room. 'I'm going to sleep,' she said. 'Don't wake me.'

'I'm going to sleep soon,' Bear whispered. He held Zoey's hand in his and stroked it with his thumb. 'But don't you cry for me.'

But Zoey was crying.

'It'll be okay,' he said. 'We almost made it, little miss. It's not far from here. Pass me...that pen.'

She found the pen from the glove box and handed it to him. Bear took something out of his wallet and started writing on it. As he wrote, he mumbled to her.

'All you need to do is keep following this road...Just wait until morning and keep on walking. Stay close to the fence...an if you hear anyone coming, you get down in the grass an' you hide till they're gone, you hear me? When you come to the white tyre...big ol' tyre off a tractor, half buried in the ground, and painted white...when you see that big ol' white tyre, right next to it is a narrow road...turn down that road...It goes off into the trees...jus keep on that road and you'll see it...the house I told you about...It's the only one there...You got all that, sweetheart'?'

Zoey nodded. Follow the road. White tyre. Find the house. 'But you can show me. We can drive there in our car.'

Bear shook his head and swallowed. 'Not this old bear. Not

this time. Winter's here for me...came on quicker than I thought...but there's no runnin' from it when it's time...time to hibernate...you know what hibernate means?'

Zoey did. She remembered it from an episode of Play School. They read the Three Bears, and made a bear out of paper plates, and talked about hibernate. 'When you sleep a long time.'

Bear smiled and nodded, coughed, and closed his eyes. He struggled to open them again. 'Now, when you get to the house, there'll be a man there...give him this.' He tucked a folded piece of paper into her pocket and gave it a pat. 'He'll look after you now.'

Zoey shook her head and crawled over to Bear. 'I don't want him,' she sobbed. 'I don't want Mummy...or Daddy, or anyone. I just want you, Uncle Bear. You promised...you promised you'd never leave me alone.'

He squeezed her tight, and rocked her gently in his lap, and there she fell asleep.

Zoey woke up two times that night, or she thought she did. Both times she was so sleepy that she couldn't tell if she was awake or dreaming.

The first time she woke to Bear's heavy breathing. Her eyes flickered open and she looked up at him. His mouth was wide open, and he was holding something inside it. The metal on it flashed in the moonlight, and she realised it was his gum. He was crying, and his breaths were whistling into the hole in the end. She closed her eyes again and fell asleep.

The next time she woke, she saw the stars and the moon. They were swaying from side to side behind Bear's face. His eyes were scrunched up from pain, and he was grating his teeth. He's okay, she thought. The Band-Aid worked, and he's got better, and we'll go to the house and be safe together. Everything was going to be okay. She went back to sleep smiling.

It was morning. The birds were singing and chirping to each other already. Those same old birds. Wherever she went. She opened her eyes and stared at something she'd never seen before. Pieces of metal running up and down and curving around, some thick, some thin, some rusty, some covered in grease. She turned her head to the side and saw the ground, and a big black tyre. After puzzling on it for a while, she worked out where she was. Under the car. Beside her were the plastic bags filled with food.

Zoey rolled onto her tummy and crawled out into the sunlight. A startled blackbird flittered away when it saw her. She rubbed her eyes on the back of her hand and tried to remember what had happened. Why was she sleeping under the car?

She reached up and tried to pull the handle. It clunked up and back down. Locked. She walked around to the other side and tried again. Clunk. Locked. She tried them all, a panic growing in her chest. She pulled the handle again and again. Again. Again. Again. Clunk. Clunk. Clunk.

Through the window she could see the top of Uncle Bear's head. It was tilted forward. He wasn't moving. Zoey banged on the door to wake him up. 'Uncle Bear!' She hit the door until her hands hurt, and then she hit it some more. 'Uncle Bear, Uncle Bear, Uncle Bear!' Her throat closed from crying and she couldn't talk anymore. She collapsed to the ground, unable to see through the tears. 'Uncle Bear,' she whispered.

She curled into a ball under Bear's side of the car and cried until she couldn't cry anymore. She was alone again. Really and truly and completely alone.

April 24

The rifle slipped from her hands and clattered to the floor. The little girl blinked at her for a moment, her wide dark eyes transfixing. With wild hair and a dusty, sunburnt face, she looked as though she'd just emerged from the wilderness. Merry's heart turned to lead and fell into her stomach. She couldn't. She couldn't. She couldn't look any longer. Pried her eyes away from the little girl's. What have you done? What have you done? Your only chance of escape—gone. She bit her lip and raked her nails down her arm, drawing beads of blood. The fact that the little girl didn't seem to understand—held no blame or resentment in her eyes—made what she'd done so much worse. Merry turned and ran from the room.

She sat on the stairs while the world fell in around her. At one point, the bearded man stumbled past dragging the little girl behind him and crashed through the emergency exit. The clamour of the alarm. Moments later Father was standing over her, shouting at her, demanding from her, shaking her, then, when she didn't respond, he disappeared towards the front of the store.

A thousand damning voices swirled in her head, crippling her with self-hatred and despair. You're a coward   you're a nothing less than nothing   it should have been Claire that lived   what have you done but cause more pain   you've orphaned a little girl

Two gunshots popped in the night, but even that couldn't rouse her from her spiral of self-destruction. Maybe if she focussed her mind hard enough, she could bring her heart to a stop. That had to be possible, right? She'd heard of people who could slow their heartbeat at will. The instructions for a quick and painless and completely deserved death had to be in there somewhere. She just needed to keep digging into the wound—

'What the hell happened? How did they get in?'

She hadn't heard him come back in. His voice was coming from far away, up from underwater. Or was it she that was underwater? Yes. Drowning.

'Meredith, I'm speaking to you.'

She opened her mouth, but forming any words seemed impossibly difficult. He softened slightly, stopped pacing and knelt before her, reaching one hand into her hair to cup the nape of her neck. His breath reeked of liquorice cough syrup.

'Did he hurt you at all?'

Her skin crawled at his touch, but she managed to shake her head.

'Good. Can you walk? We need to go after them immediately.'

'They...got away?'

'Hmm. He stole my car. They won't get far, though. You saw to that. You did very well.'

Something like pride bubbled up inside her, and she immediately hated herself for it.

'But they stole from me. I won't allow it. They took the A-32

213

heading north. There's no turn-offs until after Franklyn so unless they pull over to hide somewhere, that's where we'll overtake them.'

He snapped his fingers at her. 'Meredith, fetch the map from my room. Quickly.'

She jumped up. Fear, as it always did, overcame her self-hatred, added to it, and so she placed a hand on the bannister and hoisted herself up. Why was she still afraid of him? Afraid of disappointing him? She took the steps quickly, shakily, headed back down the corridor, through the secret passage, and into Father's room. It was neat and orderly to the point of compulsion; the bed made with military precision; the trunk aligned squarely with the dresser to one side and the bed to the other. The map was pinned to the wall above his desk. She unpinned it and folded it neatly and set the pins in the top drawer. Turning, she struck her shin on the corner of the trunk, knocking it off its perfect alignment.

The pain barely registered, but she bent at once to straighten the trunk. Stopped. Instead undid the clasp and lifted the lid. Her mouth felt suddenly dry as she stared into the box. With a trembling hand reached inside and turned over some of the objects. Feelings of loss seemed to seep out of them, staining her hands. Lightheaded, trying to forget what she'd seen, she backed slowly out of the room, leaving the trunk open and askew.

She hadn't been this far from town since it all happened. The night was eerily quiet, and black, everywhere but the under the moth-speckled beams of the headlights. Merry held her own light, a high-powered torch that lit up the farmland and houses they passed. The car rattled along the uneven asphalt, doing no more than twenty. Father peered forward over the wheel, while she sat in the back seat scanning out one window, then quickly sliding across the seat and scanning out the other. The shadows came alive as her light travelled through them, peeling away but revealing nothing.

Darkness unbearable   the light even more so
Peel back the darkness   peel back the light
what's left?

Hours passed. In her mind she returned again and again to the abandoned motorcycle outside the store, the dirty, frayed couch cushion resting on the seat, the brightly coloured child's backpack hanging from the handlebar, and again and again she sent prayers to all the imaginary or indifferent gods of the universe. Please. Please don't let us find them. Please. And she knew that if Claire was there she'd tell her that prayers were even more useless than hope.

Dawn found them still on the road, still scouring the unchanging farmland for any sign of the stolen car. Of course, it wasn't about the car. Father could take his pick of any car in town, and the strangers couldn't have taken more than a bag's worth of food. Practically nothing. But he would hunt down this man and kill him for his hubris. Father was God, and he had been defied.

Shortly after dawn they saw it. Nestled against the roadside fence. She heard his breath quicken, and his fingers tighten on the wheel. A sense of triumph radiated out of him.

'Imbecile didn't even try to hide,' he snickered.

He leaned forward on the gas and the speedometer needle climbed quickly as they closed the distance between them and the stalled green car. The green car...

Merry's breath quickened. She hadn't seen the green car since the night she and Claire had tried to escape. And he'd said...what had he said? When she left, he insisted she'd taken the car? That was it.

When the car skidded to a stop she looked up to see him watching her in the rearview mirror, a cold, smug smile on his lips that said: Yes, I killed her. What are you going to do about it?

She looked away, grabbed her rifle. They got out of the car and went over to where the green station wagon rested, growing hot in the sun. The bearded man was in the driver's seat, his head tilted forward slightly. As they approached, the head turned to face them. She could see from the colour of his skin and the blank look in his eyes that he was dead, but not quite a grinner. Not yet. The change was still happening. His mouth opened and closed, clicking teeth, biting into blue, fleshy lips which bled black tar into his beard. A soft groan from between those lips.

Without pausing, Father stepped up beside her, raised his revolver and fired two bullets in quick succession through the glass and into the man's face. Merry gasped and flinched as glass rained down around her feet and the man slumped forward. The wind blew and the sun beat down.

'There was a girl, too,' Father said, lowering the revolver and turning to her. 'Find her. I want her.'

Merry swallowed, but nodded.

'Search over there. I'll take this side. And Meredith...'

He fixed her with that same smile that chilled her stomach. 'If you try to run again, I will be very...very disappointed.'

Her mouth hung open for a moment. He was inside her head. He knew her thoughts. 'Yes, Father.' Tearing her eyes from him, she passed behind the car and climbed over the splintering wooden fence into the long grass.

April 25

Zoey sat with her back against the car's wheel, watching ants crawl on her leg. They had been following the road, going in and out of the cracks in the dry, red ground, until they found her leg blocking the way. At first they seemed confused. Some went back the way they'd come, some went in circles or looked for a way around, and others just stood there, talking to their friends. She gave them names. Daddy Ant was the first to turn around and go back the other way.

'I'm going to work now,' she said in Daddy's voice. 'Bye everybody. Don't beget my dinner, Mummy Ant.'

Mummy Ant was running in a figure-eight. She was carrying a little white piece of sand for some reason. 'Oh, okay, Daddy Ant. I just need to find somewhere to put this. It's very, very heavy.'

Zoey took a chocolate biscuit out of the packet next to her and took a bite. She dusted the crumbs from her fingers over the ants and watched as they scrambled about.

'Brrrm, brrrrrrrrrrm. I'm Uncle Bear Ant. Do you want a ride on my motorbikyle? My motorbikyle can drive over this mountain...'

She had to stop and take another bite of the biscuit to keep herself from crying. She couldn't think about him right now, still sitting there in the car right behind her. She covered Uncle Bear Ant with a leaf so she wouldn't have to look at him.

Zoey Ant was just standing there, next to Zoey's leg, as everyone else ran around.

'You can't just sit there, Zoey Ant,' she said. 'You'll be left behind.'

Zoey Ant thought about this for a moment. Then there was a little tickle as Zoey Ant started running up her leg. She almost took a wrong turn into Zoey's shoe, but eventually made it to the other side. Soon, all the others were following the trail. She gave them all another sprinkle of crumbs as a prize.

The sun was right over her head now, and the skin on her hands and arms was turning pink and itchy. She stood up, brushing the ants from her leg, taking care not to squish any of them. Then she stepped over them and climbed up on the wooden fence. It looked very old. The wood was almost black and bits crumbled away where she touched it.

On the other side of the fence was a field of tall, dry grass. It was an orangey white colour and grew almost as tall as she was. When she climbed a little higher on the fence, she could see it bending in the wind, as waves moved across it like an ocean of straw.

If she looked back now, would she be able to see Uncle Bear's face? Would he see her? Would his lips be peeling away from his teeth already? Would he laugh at her?

She stared at the grass even harder. She thought she'd used up all her tears already, but she found some more for him. He'd told her to walk down the road. She was supposed to find the house. But she couldn't leave him.

When her tears dried and her eyes cleared, she spotted

something across the field, behind some trees. It was a house. She leaned forward. The fence creaked under her. It had to be the house she was supposed to find. All she had to do was jump down and run to it and she would be safe. Uncle Bear said there would be a man there that would help her, but she was scared—

A car was coming. She could hear the hum of its wheels on the gravel road, and she saw the glint of sunlight off the windscreen. It was coming fast.

She forgot about her bags of food, and jumped over the fence, running into the long grass. She crouched down so that she couldn't see the road.

The speeding car stopped suddenly; three long scrapes on the gravel. Two car doors slammed. Footsteps crunched and stopped. There was a pause, two loud pops and shattering glass, then nothing but the wind.

'There was a girl, too.' The voice sounded like a man's, but it was high and soft, a bit like a woman's. 'Find her. I want her. Search over there. I'll take this side. And Merry...' There was a long silence. 'If you try to run again, I will be very...very disappointed.'

'Yes, father.'

One set of footsteps went away, but the other came towards her. The old wooden fence creaked under someone's weight, then she heard two feet landing together on the grass. Zoey turned and started crawling away.

The ground was hard on her knees, and dirt built up under her fingernails, making them feel heavy. Tiny grasshoppers jumped ahead of her, flittering through the grass, their white wings flashing as they leapt from one stalk to the next. They must have thought she was chasing them. The footsteps were always right behind her, stomping the grass flat, snapping twigs.

The field went on forever. Her arms and legs were moving by themselves now. If she thought about which went where, she would tangle herself and end up with her arms crossed, and then she'd panic and have to scramble to get moving again.

Then the grass seemed to shrink and she could see the trees ahead, and the house beyond it. She stood up, not even daring to look back, and ran as fast as she could.

She hardly registered the broken windows and rotten, peeling weatherboards as she ran up the path. She didn't notice the weeds sprouting between the boards as she dashed across the porch. She reached up for the handle of the fly-screen door, never seeing that the screen had been slashed to shreds.

Zoey ran inside and let the door clatter shut behind her.

April 25

The grass was wild and strawlike, and it bent in the wind like waves on the ocean. As Merry passed through it, taking long careful steps, she held out her hands and let the rough blades brush across her fingertips. Dragonflies zipped across her path, hovering and swooping like daredevil pilots. Ahead, she saw a patch of grass moving against the wind, parting, making way for the tiny runaway.

Merry looked over her shoulder to where Father was prowling the other side of the road, bent over looking for footprints, she guessed. She could pretend to do the same for fifteen minutes, then go back and say she'd seen nothing. But would he believe her? Did he already know which way the girl had gone? Was this another test?

But then...she couldn't just leave a little kid alone out here. Even living with a monster like Blake was better than being alone. She followed the path the girl had left, slowly now because she didn't want to get too close. Ahead, behind a row of paperbarks, sat an old, dilapidated farmhouse. The Compton place, she realised, where Claire and Rachel used to sneak off to sometimes. They used to scare her with stories about it, and although she knew they couldn't be more than half true, she hesitated.

Did you ever hear about Mad Old Compton? Claire asked, spinning slowly back and forth on Merry's desk chair while Rachel flipped through her CD collection, feigning disinterest. A simple man. Beetroot farmer. His family had owned the land for three generations. He lived in the big house with his wife and two daughters and his ailing mother. Working the farm was hard work, and he never turned much of a profit, but they did okay, and they were happy. Claire leaned back in the chair, steepling her fingers and nodding as though she'd worked the farm alongside him. Until one year a massive storm hit. It rained for a week straight, flooded the ground and drowned his entire crop. Compton was a stoic man, didn't waste any time whingeing, just got back to it, replanting for the next season. But after that, nothing would grow. He had no choice but to sell off chunks of land to the bank, whittling away his family's heritage until there was nothing left but the big house and the paperbark trees. He was also a deeply religious man, and when this happened he started claiming that God had been speaking to him. Told him the land was being cleansed, that the apocalypse was coming.

Rachel accidentally on purpose knocked a stack of CDs to the floor and they clattered to the floor making Merry jump.

Claire grinned and went on. He took his daughters out of school and they all disappeared into the house. The people of Franklyn would see him occasionally, buying up cartfuls of tinned fruits and vegetables and bottled water early in the morning. None of them ever saw the rest of his family, though.

At this point, Claire must have felt the story needed a bit more flavour, so she put a toothpick between her teeth, and started speaking out the side of her mouth in a ridiculous southern accent. He din't talk to no-one no more. Jus' paid for what he needed and went on his way. Eventually, when he stopped showin' too, the local poh-lice sergeant went to knock on his door.

Know what he all found inside? Compton on the kitchen floor, couple of days dead, an undercooked beet lodged in his throat. His wife and daughters and his ma were all still in their beds, but they'd been dead a whole lot longer. Close to a year, the coroner guessed. In his journal, Compton had writ about how he'd struggled with what God told him to do. He put it off for weeks, but in the end he came to know it for what it was. A mercy. Cos he was sparing them from the horrors of the apocalypse, and so, out of love, he'd strangled them and cracked their skulls open with a claw hammer.

That's when Rachel came up behind her and slipped her fingers around Merry's neck, letting out a shrill scream. Merry screamed too, leapt off the bed, and ran out of the room, followed by her sister's raucous laughter.

It turned out, though, that Compton had been right about the apocalypse. He'd just been about a decade too early.

From the shade of one of the paperbark trees she watched the little girl run up the porch steps and into the house, the creaking fly-wire door crashing closed behind her. Across the field she could only just make out the fence and the cars, and the pale figure of Mr Blake standing perfectly still as he stared at her.

She breathed in the thick, silent air for a moment, listening for the footsteps that she was sure were right behind her. When they didn't come, she looked around the room. It had been a kitchen once. The floor had a tile pattern, but it wasn't real tiles. It was warped, cracked and curling up like wet paper. Old cobwebs hung from the ceiling, heavy with dirt and sawdust. This didn't seem right. Who would live in a place like this?

As she tippy-toed further into the house, she found a room with carpet that was dry and crusty in some places, and squelchy in others. A fireplace that was filled with sticks and feathers that spilled out onto the floor. A sagging couch that wasn't any colour she could name. In one corner was a wooden staircase with a worn red rug running down its middle and lolling crooked across the floor like a dragon's tongue.

The fly-screen door creaked slowly open, and she heard the footsteps crunching across the kitchen. She froze. He was going to find her. Zoey shook her head. No, she had to hide. She ran behind the couch and crouched down. The couch smelled like the dead cat they'd found in the neighbours' pool once. Daddy said he thought it had been poisoned. He said that when animals eat poison, they get really thirsty, and desperate, and try to find water, and a lot of the time they end up drowning. It sounded horrible, and Zoey hoped she never got poisoned. The matted brown grey thing on the side of the couch, that might once have been a blanket draped over the arm, looked a bit like the cat had, too, after they pulled it from the water.

The footsteps, closer now and softened by the carpet, stopped in the middle of the room. Then someone sighed.

'I can see you,' said the girl's voice.

Zoey ducked down even lower. Please just go away, she thought. She can't really see me. She's trying to trick me.

'Look, I saw you crawling through the grass, and now you're behind the couch. I've already seen you so you can just come out. I won't hurt you.'

Zoey didn't move until the girl walked around the couch and stood next to her.

'Found you,' she said, like they'd been playing hide and seek.

Zoey looked up at her. It was the same girl from the supermarket. She was still wearing the jumper with a line of horses running across the front, and she had that strange bat with her, too, with its long black tube on top, and metal bits on one side. The girl saw Zoey looking at it. She stepped to the side and leaned it against the wall.

'No gun, okay? We can just talk.'

Gun. So that's what it was.

'That guy that was with you, was that your Dad?' the girl asked, not looking Zoey in the eye.

Zoey couldn't look at her, either. She shook her head. 'Uncle Bear.'

The girl nodded. 'Your uncle. I'm really sorry about...what happened to him...it was an accident,' she mumbled.

Zoey wasn't sure what she meant, so she just stared back.

'My name's Meredith,' the girl said, 'But people call me Merry. What's your name?'

'Zoey,' she whispered, looking at the girl's shoes. They were bright green sneakers.

'Zoey,' Merry repeated. 'What are you doing out here, anyway? Where were you going?'

Zoey pointed to the middle of the room. 'Here,' she said. 'We were asposed to meet the man that lives here.'

Merry looked confused. 'Here? This place has been abandoned for ages. Nobody's been here for as long as I can remember.'

Zoey almost burst into tears. Through her pocket, she touched the piece of paper that Bear had given her to give to the man. The man that was going to protect her. She tried hard to understand. He wouldn't send her to an empty house. So...this must be the wrong one. She would have to go back to the road and look for the big white tyre he'd told her about.

'I need to go,' Zoey said.

'You can't go out there on your own,' Merry exclaimed. 'Are you crazy?'

'No, I'm Zoey,' she said automatically, then looked away, embarrassed. It was a game she used to play with Daddy. Are you hungry? No, I'm Daddy. Aren't you tired? No, I'm Zoey.

The girl laughed a little. She had a friendly laugh. The sort of laugh a big sister should have. It wasn't a teasing laugh. As she reached up to brush the hair out of her face, Zoey noticed some lines on her arm. They were long and red and crusty, and criss-crossed her wrist. Merry quickly pulled her sleeve back down to cover them again.

Zoey crossed her arms and hugged her elbows, thinking of the scary man with the moustache. 'Who is that man? Is he your daddy?'

'He's not my father,' Merry said quietly.

She took a deep breath and bit her thumbnail. It looked like she had forgotten Zoey was there and was fighting with someone in her head. 'None of it matters now. He always gets what he wants. He always knows...what's best,' she said, serious again now.

Her eyes kept darting out the broken window that looked over the field to the road. 'Mr Blake,' she whispered. 'He owns the grocery store in town,' she whispered, answering questions Zoey hadn't asked. 'We used to go in there all the time. Before. He'd always help Mum carry her bags to the car, and ask my sisters and I how we were doing in school, and give us sweets. He seemed innocent enough then...'

She walked over and sat down on the couch. It groaned, and something inside it pinged. 'When everyone got sick, I lost my Mum, and Dana, and Kate. Only Claire and I got better. We thought we were the only two people left in the world...until some of the people that were supposed to be dead started coming back. God, we were so relieved when we found Mr Blake. He saved us...'

Zoey saw the tears in Merry's eyes spill down her cheeks. 'He made us help him get all the bodies together, and he drove them away...to burn. He said we had to do it, to get rid of the sickness, to warn people off, so that we could start a new life. So we did it, because he kept us safe.'

Merry frowned to herself. 'He made me call him father. It kind of made me feel better at first. Like he wanted us to be family. But he wanted more than that...'

She scratched at her wrist through her sleeve, and Zoey caught another glimpse of the angry red stripes. 'He said that we have a responsibility to...to...He's...not a nice man. Claire said we should run away. We tried...he caught us...and Claire tried to fight him...she said she'd never let him hurt me...but she didn't know how dangerous he is...how powerful he is...and the next day, she was gone...He said she ran away.'

Merry put her fist to her mouth, bit her fingers and screamed. Zoey took a step back.

'Goddammit, Claire! She didn't know...that we need him. That he was right, about everything. He's not a nice man, but there's nothing nice left in the world.' She looked Zoey in the eye. Her eyes were puffy and her nose was streaming. 'Every girl needs a father. Someone to protect her. Especially now. That's why I have to take you back to him, Zoey.'

Zoey didn't understand half of what Merry was saying, but she understood enough. She would not live with that man. She'd known from the moment she saw him driving past in the green car that he was a bad man.

'No!' she said. She dashed to the wall, grabbed the gun with both hands, heaved it over the windowsill, through the broken window onto the porch outside, and ran for the stairs.

'Zoey! Don't!'

She ran up the stairs as fast as she could, holding onto the bannister to pull herself along, but Merry was much bigger than her, and she caught her as she was pushing open the door at the top of the stairs.

'Don't do that!' Merry shouted at her, wrenching her arm

upwards. 'Don't ever run again. We have to do what he wants. Don't you understand? I'm trying to help...'

Zoey squirmed, trying to twist free. Then she saw what was in the room in front of her. Five sleeping bags on the floor; some clothes; brown glass bottles and cans; a broken laptop computer and some DVDs. There were two people lying on the floor. Two people with no skin, and parts of them inside out.

Two on the floor.

The other three were standing.

Watching Zoey and Merry with their heads tilted to the side, and their red teeth clicking.

Zoey staggered back into Merry's legs, away from the three laughers. Their skin was grey and bruised all over, and it looked like they'd all chewed off their lips and tongues. Their heads never stopped moving, twitching and jerking like there were mosquitos buzzing around them, but their red, bleeding eyes never left Zoey. All three had dark red stains on their hands, arms, necks and chests.

The one in the middle, who was wearing a dark blue beanie, opened his mouth wide, and she heard the bones in his jaw cracking. His bare stomach swelled and flattened, and a loud, gasping laugh came out of him. The girl to his side screamed with excitement and snapped her teeth together. Her shoulders gave little jerks, and her spine twisted strangely as she turned her body to face them. The third one, a boy with a tummy even bigger than Uncle Bear's, took a few steps forward, his bare feet thudding on the wood floor.

'Oh no,' Merry whispered. 'No, no, no, oh my God, oh my God, no...'

Then everyone moved at once. Merry dashed for the stairs, and Zoey found herself tangled in her legs as they spilled down, spinning around and bumping into the walls. The laughers were right behind her. They hit the top of the stairs and tipped forward headfirst, snapping and clawing at the air as they tumbled. She heard bones crunch and bodies thump against wood. A cold hand was in her hair, hard fingers brushing her ear. Then a foot hit her in the back, thick toenails scraped her neck, and she slid down the rest of the stairs on her bottom.

Merry was already by the door to the kitchen.

'Come on, kid, run!'

Zoey stood up, tripped on the rug, and landed on her knees. She scrambled, running on hands and feet for a moment before getting herself upright again. She could see Merry through the screen door, already outside, jumping from the deck into the grass.

There was panting breath in her ear, dry feet scratching carpet, heavy footsteps drowning out her own. Zoey didn't slow down as she reached the screen door. The fly wire had been cut, and she dove through like Cujo through his doggy door. Then the door crashed and rattled as the laughers hit it. She heard it crack off its hinges and hit the deck, where it bounced under their rushing feet. Each step seemed to force a wheezing laugh through their throats.

'Haaah...aaaahhh...haah...aaahhhhhh.'

Zoey tripped again going down the porch stairs, but her feet must have known what would happen if she fell, so they kept moving. Someone grabbed her hand and pulled. She looked up into Merry's frightened eyes.

'Faster,' she shouted, yanking Zoey along. 'Don't stop.'

She seemed to fly across the field, dragged along by Merry, her feet only finding the ground sometimes, her head bouncing, her body swaying. One second she saw trees, dark green leaves with pinpricks of white sunlight. Then the sky, and a cloud shaped like a turtle. Then an open mouth, with long, black-rimmed teeth and gums that looked like ground sausage. Then a flash of grass. Then the sky again.

Merry was calling out to someone. Zoey could see the fence and cars, the dark green car with Uncle Bear still inside, and a smaller white one next to it. The man with the moustache was there, too, with a long gun like Merry's pressed up against his shoulder.

'Move!' he shouted, pointing the gun at them.

There was a loud bang, then a sound like tearing off a slice of watermelon, and one of the laughers fell heavily behind them. Merry let go of Zoey's hand, and Zoey slid to the ground. Dust was in her eyes, but she found the fence and rolled under it as Merry jumped over and landed next to her.

'The keys are in the ignition,' moustache man, Mr Blake, yelled. 'Start it up!' He pulled a lever on the gun and something flew out of the top, then he pointed the gun back at the laughers.

Merry took her hand again and they ran to the white car. Zoey was flung into the passenger seat and Merry piled in behind her, quickly slamming the door again. There was another bang, but when she looked through the back window, the laugher with the beanie, and the girl were both still coming. When they hit the fence, the old nails squeaked in the dry wood, and the top rail fell off at one end.

Mr Blake backed away, pulling the lever on the gun again as the laughers pressed against the fence. The girl leaned forward, reaching, and see-sawed over the fence, landing on her face. As she fell, the gun went off again, and Beanie fell back with a big red hole in his tummy. Mr Blake turned his back on them and ran for the car. He pulled the lever one last time, and another small metal thing flipped out and pinged off the car window.

As he reached for the handle, Merry dove across into the driver's seat and pressed the lock on the door. Ker-Clunk. Mr Blake stared at Merry and Zoey through the glass, and they stared back. At first he didn't seem able to move. He didn't blink. He just stared. Zoey felt small and cold under his eyes. Then he raised the gun to the window, pointing it at Merry. A frown twitched through his eyebrows, and he lowered the gun.

The laughers' footsteps crunched on the gravel as they ran. Beanie was on his feet again and had made it over the fence, too. Mr Blake spun and brought up his gun, firing off a shot that hit the girl in the neck. She twirled like a ballerina and slammed into the rear door, leaving a red streak on the glass as she disappeared from view. Beanie tripped over her and crashed into Mr Blake, and the two of them disappeared as well.

Zoey covered her ears, but she could still hear the screaming and the gasping, even when Merry started the car's engine. She pulled a lever and jumped on one of the pedals, and the car jerked backwards. It seemed to catch on something, lifted up in the air, then bounced back down. This time the sound was more like a whole watermelon falling onto cement.

Once it was over the bump, the car picked up speed. Trees hurtled past them the wrong way as they flew backwards, the sound of the engine getting higher and higher in her ears. Zoey pulled on the seatbelt, but when it wouldn't come out all the way, she just curled up and held on as tightly as she could. Merry moved her foot, and Zoey slammed against the seat as the tyres skidded, crunching gravel, and the car swayed from side to side.

They had stopped, but the world was still moving, like when

she'd get off the round-a-bout after spinning too fast. She thought she might be sick. The car jumped again and Zoey was pressed against the passenger door as it swung around and started moving, forwards this time. When the world finally stopped spinning, and the car stopped throwing her around, she realised something. Merry was taking her back to the town.

Merry spun the wheel and idled in the middle of the road, trembling. She'd stared down the barrel of the gun, and rather than try to hide, she'd leaned closer to the window so he couldn't miss. In that instant she'd realised that all his power, all his control, was an illusion. In that moment, free of doubt, free of fear, he'd had nothing left with which to hurt her. Do it, the voices had screamed. Do it! The last thing she saw on his face was not anger, not fear or betrayal, but defeat. Fragility. Then it was all over so quickly.

When she'd opened the footlocker in Blake's room and thumbed through the contents, the truth had been staring up at her. Wallets, purses, jewellery, keys—all trophies he'd taken from the grinners he'd captured or killed. And amongst them, two matching seahorse necklaces, their chains tangled with so many others. Kate and Dana.

Blake had been dragged by the car and part of his scalp was left on the road. One leg shattered below the knee. His fingers still twitched, grasping for the rifle that lay well out of reach, while

Darren sat atop him, a severed ear between his grinning teeth. Rachel lay still a short distance away, parts of the back of her skull visible through her flattened face.

What happens now? She looked at Zoey. The little girl huddled in the passenger seat, clutching the seatbelt. Thankfully, she was too short to see over the dashboard to the carnage in the road.

Claire's voice from the back seat: 'Turn the car around, stupid. There's nothing for you here.'

'Yes, you're right,' she whispered. She moved the gear lever to D, then cranking the wheel as far around as it would go, stepped gently on the accelerator and began the long drive back home.

Brave little Merry, finally cut the cord   finally lifted the blindfold   finally   but did you find freedom?

This child beside you that you thought was your saviour Saviour?   She's now your burden to carry   Better if you'd both died in that house   quicker   kinder

'We'll find others.'

Others?   Others to shoulder your burden?   Others to show you the way?   Others to hurt you?   Others to violate you?   Others to betray?   Others to sacrifice themselves for you?

'Claire, help me. Make them stop.'

She glanced in the rearview mirror, but the back seat was empty.

236

Even though she'd been spun all around, and everything looked the same, something in her chest told her she was going the wrong way, moving further away from where she needed to be. She looked up at Merry. Neither of them had said anything since it had all happened, but Merry was muttering to herself and every now and then she would shake her head a little. Her frizzy yellow hair streamed around her head and out the open window.

Zoey looked out her own window, deciding to watch the clouds rolling slowly along behind the whizzing trees. She thought about going back to the town. She thought about the supermarket, and the shelves stacked with food. Her stomach grumbled. Mr Blake wouldn't be there anymore.

She thought about Merry dragging her through the field, the look of worry in her eyes, the fierce strength in her hand.

Then she thought about Uncle Bear. Remembered sitting in front of him on the bike, his big hairy arm holding her safely in place. She smiled, thinking about him playing the gum leaf, and shaking his hips around to make her laugh. She thought about all the stories he'd told her, and the way he used to do a different voice for each character. She thought about him tucking her into bed at night and realised that he would never do that again. Tears came to her eyes, and she turned her head further to the side so she was staring right at the door. She pretended he was driving the car now, instead of Merry. He'd be telling her stories about her mother when she was a little girl, and the tricks he used to play on his brother. They'd stop for a while, because Uncle Bear would complain about his 'saddle sores', and they'd sit under the shade of a tree. She'd lay her head on his tummy, and say, 'You're my favourite pillow, Uncle Bear.' And he'd laugh and say, 'And you're my favourite blanket, little miss.' And then he'd hug her tight.

Zoey thought about the note in her pocket, and the promise she'd made to him.

She took a deep breath and let it out slowly, shakily. She turned, and was surprised when it was Merry there, not Uncle Bear.

'I need to do a wee,' she said.

Merry flicked her eyes to Zoey, then back to the road. 'Can't you hold it?'

'No, I need to do it now.'

Merry sighed. 'Okay. But you need to be quick. You know how to do it by yourself, right?'

Zoey nodded.

Merry pulled the car over to the side of the road, coming to a very sudden and shuddery stop. Zoey couldn't open the door by herself, so she had to wait for Merry to walk around and do it for her.

'Look, you're not going to try and run away, are you? I'll catch you in about two seconds if you do.'

Zoey shook her head.

She walked over to the side of the road. The fence here was different. It was much lower than the other fence, and made of metal, and it curved around with the bend in the road. It had some sparkly white dots on it. On the other side was a hill, and at the bottom, a stream that was mostly dry, cracked mud, and a little water.

As she pulled down her pants and pretended to wee, she watched Merry. She was standing by the front of the car with her hands on the bonnet, muttering to herself. Her long hair hung down, covering her face. She tried to brush it back behind her ear a few times, but it kept tumbling forward again. Then she slammed her palm on the bonnet, grabbed a fistful of hair, and hit herself in the head with it several times. Her head snapped up and she glared at Zoey for a second, then she turned away and started pacing, holding her tummy.

Zoey stood and pulled up her pants. Merry didn't notice as she scrambled over the little fence, banging her knee on the top, and slid down the hill. Then she started walking back the way they'd come.

The mud was dry and powdery along the side, but still goopy in the middle. As she hurried along, she tried not to trip over the big rocks and sticks that were buried in it.

'Are you about done yet?' She heard Merry's voice, quite far away. Then, 'Hey!'

Zoey started running.

'What the hell?' Merry called.

Zoey saw something in the side of the hill, with a trickle of water coming out of it that joined up with the stream. A concrete pipe. She squished through the mud and looked in. It wasn't much bigger around than a basketball, and very dark. It smelled like a toilet.

Stones came spilling down the hill behind her as Merry started climbing down, so Zoey stuck her head in the pipe and wriggled her way in. It was very tight. She banged her shoulders on the edge, had to draw them right in to fit. At first it was very hard to move at all. She squirmed, and had a moment of panic when she thought she was stuck, but then her shoe found the inside of the pipe and she gave a push, sliding further into the darkness.

'Zoey!' Merry's voice was right there, echoing all around her. 'Why?…What do you think you're doing?'

A hand closed around her ankle and pulled.

'Come on, come out. I'm serious. It's going to get dark soon.'

Zoey thrashed her feet, kicking as hard as she could, pushing herself further in.

'Oww,' Merry cried. 'That freakin' hurt! You little…ahh, sugar, I think you broke my finger!'

Zoey just lay still.

'Ugh, fine! Stay there. See if I care. Enjoy being eaten.'

Merry's footsteps went away. Then, after a while, they came back.

'Please, Zoey. Come out. I'm sorry about your uncle, I really am. It was an accident. If I could go back and change it, I would.'

Neither of them spoke for a while, then Zoey thought she could hear Merry crying. Now and then a little sniff would come down the tunnel behind her.

'Please…please come out…Don't leave me alone…Zoey…'

Zoey closed her eyes. She felt bad about ignoring her, but she couldn't go with Merry. She'd been wrong about her. She wasn't like a big sister at all. She wasn't family. There was something…frightening about her. She didn't feel safe with

240

Merry. Uncle Bear had been the last of her family, and now he was gone. I'm a wombat, she thought. Wombats live by themselves. They stay safe underground, and they don't come out until it's dark.

Eventually, the crying stopped, and she heard Merry climbing back up the hill to the road. Then the car started in the distance, and it went away, too.

Still, she didn't move. As she lay in the dark, her body ached. Her shoulders and back were sore from being so squished. Her knee hurt from where she bumped it climbing over the barrier. Her elbow still hurt from when Merry had dragged her through the field. Her head was hurting too, for some reason. She might have banged it when she was trying to get Merry to let go of her ankle.

She closed her eyes and waited. The sounds of the world behind her seemed so very far away, yet every tiny movement she made was deafening. She tried passing the time with singing. Even when she whispered the words, they seemed to come back to her, as if sung through the darkness by another Zoey at the other end of the tunnel.

'Ring around the rosie...the rosie,
A pocket full of posies...posies,
Ashes. Ashes. Ashes...
We all...
fall...
down...'

It was past dark by the time she arrived back. The motorcycle, still parked by the kerb near the front entrance, waited for its rider's return. Merry took the brightly coloured backpack from the handlebars and opened it. It was mostly clothes crammed inside. A plastic toy phone with oversized buttons. A handful of gumleaves stuffed in one of the pouches. A scrap of fleecy material that looked like it had come from a stuffed animal. A little girl's treasures. What was she supposed to do with them?

Merry glanced up and down the dark street, looking for an answer, but the only reply was the listless wind and the gruff growl of a brush-tailed possum. Of course, it didn't matter what she did with them. There were thousands more abandoned treasures in the houses surrounding her. She listened to the voices in her head. For perhaps an hour she listened, a slight smile on her lips as they whispered their plans. She nodded slowly. All sound and silence became one—a fierce buzzing, a storm of insects, of wasps swarming.

Like slipping into a warm bath, she gave up her control and her guilt and her fear, and let them flood her body with their soothing anaesthetic, smiling even as her vision turned white.

When she regained control, she found herself in an unfamiliar room. Her hand was bleeding, but there was no pain. She swayed and staggered. Glass crunch under her feet. Turning, she saw the door, its glass pane smashed, and realised she was in Mr Blake's office. The office he always kept locked, and which Claire had tried to break into their first night in the place. A row of filing cabinets stood against one wall. The window that overlooked the alley was wide open. The desk was sparse and neatly organised and the pinboard beside it mostly bare, except—was that...?

Merry stepped around the desk to get a closer look. Her own smiling face stared back from the photo pinned there. It was a photograph of her with her three sisters, taken last Christmas. He must have taken it from the frame beside Mum's bed. Somehow she couldn't even muster the energy to be disgusted.

She barely recognised herself. Her cheeks twitched up as she tried to mirror the expression in the photo. Smiles so unfamiliar now. She pulled out the pin and held the picture in her hand. Claire, with her half-smirk, the best Mum could ever get from her in a family photo. Kate and Dana beaming, each missing their two bottom teeth. She frowned as she slid it into her pocket, then looked down at the desk. A black ledger lay open, filled with room numbers, dates, and detailed notes written in tiny, neat handwriting. Something that might have come from a motel front desk, except that inside the cover was stapled the business card from an out-of-town self storage business.

There was little of interest in the filing cabinets—invoices, receipts, letters to and from distributors—the floor was soon littered with white and yellow pages as she discarded handfuls at a time. Then her attention fell on the desk drawer. It was locked. The key was probably still in his pocket. She searched the room for a spare for a few minutes until a furious impatience took hold of her. Snatching up a long pair of scissors, she jammed them into the space around the drawer and prised and kicked at it until the cheap metal bolt finally relented and the drawer flew open.

Annabelle greeted her again from the top of the pile of Polaroids. She flipped quickly through the rest. Most were of girls and young women. None seemed to be aware that they were being photographed. A few had been taken through windows and showed women in various states of undress. She paused a little longer when she recognised her mother's bedroom where her mother, back turned and naked from the waist up, searched for something in the closet. She let the pictures tumble from her hands.

At the back of the drawer, she found a letter. It was old, with the limpness of something many times read, and had worn through to nothing along some of the creases. In delicate rounded cursive, she read:

My dear Charlie,

Mum says I'm not supposed to talk to you anymore after what happened. I understand why you did it, and I don't think you were really going to hurt Neil, but you really scared me, you know that? You can't go breaking into people's cars and threatening them with a knife. Please promise me you'll leave him alone now? He deserved it, but I don't want you to get in any more trouble.

I've thought a lot about what you said. I've spent so many hours crying and wishing things could've been different. But Neil's the father, Charlie, not you, and I couldn't live with myself if I let you tell people you were. I can't let my stupid decisions drag you down, too. Thank you, though, for being the only person thinking of me in all this. My parents are more worried about their reputations. They worked so hard on their perfect life, and then their perfect daughter does and gets pregnant at sixteen. Sucks to be them. And Neil...well, you know how he reacted. He's couldn't get away from me fast enough. I don't know why I expected any different.

And there's another thing I need to tell you. We're moving away. Dad has a job lined up now, so we'll be gone by the end of the month. I'm not allowed to say where we're going. I think it's best for you, too. You're so smart, Charlie. You're going to go to uni and have a brilliant career, and you're going to do something great. I just know it.

Please take care of yourself.

I know we'll meet again some day.

Love,

Annabelle.

Merry lifted her eyes and looked slowly around the room as the air began to fill with a sharp buzzing sound.

Merry. Merry. Let us in. You know only we can do what needs to be done now. Let us end it. Oh. We would enjoy it so. Merry

She closed her eyes.

'Okay.'

The front windows of Campbell's Foodland blew out with a loud boom. Merry gaped at the building ablaze in the night. Her clothes reeked of petrol and she took a few steps back as the heat from the fire swelled.

The flames will take everything he has built, they said. Nothing but fire can cleanse this place. Watch it burn, Merry. It burns for you.

She turned away as another large explosion tore through the inside of the building, shaking the very air around her. On the ground by her feet she saw they had left her a duffel bag out of which protruded the barrel of a rifle, and, strangely, Zoey's bright pink backpack. She tilted her head to one side, listening to the laughter that might have been in her mind, or might have come from her own throat, then picked up the bags and walked slowly away.

The flames were just a faint glow in the distance when the first grinner found her. She heard him moving through the undergrowth alongside the train tracks, short uneven footsteps, with the occasional breathy gasp. A few rapid wheezes of delight as he saw her and staggered quickly out into the moonlight.

Merry. Oh, Merry. We've been patient for so long. Let us—

Pain tore her from the safety of her mind and back to the present where her body was moving of its own accord. Decaying teeth bit into her forearm, jarring the nerves as they ripped through her muscles and scraped the bone. Merry screamed and thrust her free hand against the grinner's face, pushing it away as it shook from side to side, trying to tear the flesh from her arm. Her thumb gouged at its eye. A finger slipped across bare, bloodied teeth into its gaping mouth, and the jaws quickly clamped down and yanked away, detaching the small bone of her right little finger and severing the elastic skin as easily as one might pull apart a chicken wing.

Her left hand swung out, and a fragment of brick she didn't even realise she was holding cracked against the grinner's temple, sending it snapping back and then up again as though on a tight spring. She struck again and again until its face was a red mess. Its legs wobbled and finally gave out and it slumped forward into the dirt, Merry's little finger still held tight between its teeth like a grisly cigarette.

A sob escaped her as she stared in bewilderment at her four-fingered hand and the open wound on her left arm.

'Aaah,' she cried.

Shhhhh.   Pain is nothing.   Not to you.   This pain is a comfort.   Each wound should be worn with pride.   Trusssst us.   No more fear.   No more fear.   We will take it all back for you.

April 26

Zoey woke to the strange music of the night. Crickets close by and in the distance tried to out-sing each other, while a frog clicked and croaked, keeping time. Something she didn't recognise chimed in now and then. Eep...eep...eep. From somewhere ahead of her, down the dark tunnel, came the gentle trickle of water.

She tried to wriggle her way backwards and quickly found that getting out was much more difficult than getting in. Her arms were pressed against her side, making it impossible to grab hold of anything and push. Something brushed against her hand. Something hard and bumpy and moving. A snake, she realised. She heard the hiss of its scales on the cement as it went away to find somewhere else to sleep.

Everything felt tingly, even in her head. She knew she should be scared, but all she could think about was how strange it was that all the world seemed so dead and empty during the day, and so alive at night. She kept wriggling, ignoring the scrapes she got on her knuckles, and the bumps on her ankles. It was a long time before her shoes found the edge of the pipe. Until then, she hadn't even been sure she was moving at all.

Eventually, she squirmed free of the pipe, tried to stand, stumbled, and fell back into the mud. The crickets that had been chirping around her were suddenly silent. Her elbows and knees were stiff and painful, so she lay on her back, staring up at the stars, breathing in air that smelled of damp grass and burnt honey. After a while, the crickets started up again. When she felt better, she stood up and started walking.

The moon was bright that night, and she had no trouble staying on the road. Her feet crunched loudly on the gravel. Most of the time, she looked up so that the sky was the only thing she could see. It made her feel tiny, and like a giant at the same time. One moment she was nothing, then she was everything.

Something rustled through the bushes in the darkness. Zoey stopped and looked. A large dark shape swung out into view and stood up on its hind legs. Two twinkling black eyes watched her for a moment, before the kangaroo moved on. She shivered and folded her arms to her chest as a gust of wind came up behind her, rustling invisible trees and bushes. She kept on walking.

Crunch, crunch, crunch.

Zoey opened and closed her mouth in time to her footsteps, imagining she was chewing a mouthful of Froot Loops.

Crunch, crunch, crunch.

'This is the story of the bunny and the bear,' Zoey said to nobody as she walked. 'Are you ready? Once upon the time,' she started, watching her feet now, 'There was a little bunny that wanted to go on an adventure. But she got lost in a scary forest, and then she got stuck in a tree. A bear came along, and he looked very scary, and the bunny said "please don't eat me, bear", but he was a friendly bear, and he res...he rec...' She paused, scratching her nose as she looked for the word. 'He got her from the tree, and said, "come on, bunny, you can ride on my back. I will give you a piggyback, but I'm a bear so it's a bear-y-back."' She had to tuck her chin into her chest to do the bear's voice.

Crunch, crunch, crunch.

She went over the story in her mind. Uncle Bear would have liked that joke, she thought, nodding. 'They came to big river, but the bear was so tall enough that he jumped all the way across in one jump. And when they came to a dark cave, the bear just laughed and went in and came out the other side.

'But then they saw a tiger. He was sitting on the path and wouldn't let them go past. And the tiger said, "This is my forest. You have to just leave!"'

An owl flew over her head, making her jump, and landed silently in a tree where it disappeared into the shadows. Zoey was breathing hard and lowered her voice to a whisper.

'The bear...um...the tiger...They started fighting, and the bunny fell off the bear's back. Then there was a storm, with lightning, and thunder, and the lightning hit one of the trees, and it fell on the bear and the lion...I mean the tiger. And they got stucked. And the bunny was all alone again...'

Zoey stopped. Ahead of her, she saw the green car, still parked against the fence.

'...And the bunny was stuck in the dark forest...'

There was a dark shape in the driver's seat, and two more lying in the road nearby. She swallowed.

'...forever...'

She watched the shapes for a while. None of them moved. None of them laughed or clicked. Her eyes never left the bodies in the road as she tiptoed past, but she tried very hard not to look at the car. Crunch...crunch...crunch. She realised she was walking backwards, watching and waiting for one of them to get up, until long after the car and the bodies had faded back into the darkness.

When she turned around, she saw him, standing in the middle of the road with his back to her, swaying slightly. She stopped, close enough to hear his rattling breaths. His skin was white in the moonlight. His hair only covered half of his head, and the rest was smooth, glistening red and white. His ears were gone, and one of his legs was twisted and flattened, and something was poking out just below his knee. She couldn't see if his moustache was still there.

His head bobbled around, and his arms and fingers twitched, like he was was dreaming about playing the piano. Now and then, he would take a few shuffling steps down the road and stop again.

Zoey couldn't move. She could hear a thump thump sound coming from nearby. It was thumping so loudly she was sure he'd be able to hear it too. She glanced back over her shoulder. Should she go back? She could go back to the car. Crawl up into Uncle Bear's lap and stay there until she fell asleep too. Fell asleep forever. It sounded much better than going on. Facing Mr Blake again, trying to find the house that she couldn't even believe was real.

Something moved in the bushes beside her, and Zoey almost jumped out of her shoes. Mr Blake's head whipped around and his white eyes found her. A kangaroo crossed the road between them. It moved slowly, reaching forward with its front paws, then swinging its long back legs over. It didn't seem to mind either of them.

With his twisted leg, Mr Blake struggled to turn his body to face them. He lunged and fell on his face, gasping and clawing at the ground. The kangaroo watched him for a moment, its ears twitching, then it turned, looked at Zoey, and hopped across to the other side of the road in three big bounds.

Zoey ran as fast as she could. Past the reaching, grasping hands of Mr Blake, she flew through the darkness.

She lost count of how many times she tripped, how many times the stinging gravel bit into her knees and palms. Each time she was sure he was right behind her, breathing down her neck, grabbing at her ankles. Was it her steps she could hear, pounding on the road, or his? She didn't know, so she just kept running.

The next time Zoey tripped, she didn't get up. She'd been running for so long. Her throat was burning, and the air didn't seem able to go in or out. She could feel her heart thumping, and after each thump her knees would cry with pain. When she tried to move, a sharp needle in her side pinned her to the ground. She clung to something, a big white rock by the side of the road, and lay her head on it. It was softer than a rock should be. Rubbery...

Through the darkness, the shuffling footsteps, the panting laughs, the piercing clicks drew nearer...

Zoey closed her eyes and tried to sleep. Sleep, she thought. Sleep and wake up somewhere else. Her finger traced the large, square-edged bumps on the rock. She picked at the crumbling cracks. Such a strange shape for a rock. It didn't feel like a rock at all.

'...here's where I need you to be really brave, little one.'

'I can do it, Uncle Bear.'

'I know you can...'

...

'When you come to the white tyre...big ol' tyre off a tractor, half buried in the ground, and painted white...when you see that big ol' white tyre, right next to it is a narrow road...turn down that road...It goes off into the trees...jus keep on that road and you'll see it...the house I told you about...It's the only one there...You got all that, sweetheart'?

The tyre was real. Zoey opened her eyes. Mr Blake was there. Close enough for her to see each of his crooked, stained teeth, and the hunger in his wide eyes. Close enough for her to see the cold, white clouds of his breath.

She cried as she climbed to her feet. Her legs didn't want to straighten or bend, but she made them do both as she staggered around the big tyre and down the dirt road. She couldn't run anymore. Tiny, shuffling steps were the best she could manage, but it was enough.

Mr Blake kept after her, though. His teeth chattered with excitement, and his breaths were loud and short. Zoey didn't dare look back. She knew he was there. Right behind her. She only had to trip once more, and he would have her.

'Uncle Bear,' she cried. Her voice was dry and chalky. 'Mummy. Daddy. Merry...' She cried for them all, over and over. She cried for anyone who could come and take her away from there. Because she couldn't do it on her own. She couldn't be brave, after all. 'Uncle Bear, Mummy, Daddy, Merry, Uncle Bear...' Clouds covered the moon and the stars, and the grey world turned black. They were all gone now. Everything was gone. Her arms swung wildly, trying to brush away the darkness, but beyond it was just more of the same. Then her foot caught on something, and she tripped.

As she hit the ground, the world lit up, and she was blinded by a white light. Brighter than the sun. All around, she could hear ringing bells and rattling cans. Mr Blake grunted as he fell behind her. His dry hands pulled at her ankles, dragging her back until he was on top of her. Spit dripped from his mouth onto her neck, and she could smell his breath. Like the bin after Mummy thew out all the old, furry food from the fridge.

With the last of her strength, Zoey screamed.

Through the ringing, clattering noise, she heard a swishing sound, followed by a thud. Then Mr Blake's weight fell on her, and his head buried in her neck.

She looked towards the light. Gradually, the sounds faded, and her fear faded with them. She knew this was the end, because she could see Uncle Bear walking towards her out of the light. Most of her body was numb, but she felt a shiver running from her shoulders, up her neck, and into her ears. She was crying, but it was happy crying.

Uncle Bear knelt down next to her and took her hand, and she smiled up at him. He had come back to her. He had come to take her away.

April 29

Heat throbbed through her hand
　Pain in the bone.　Her left arm not so bad, but her finger...
　fire spreading through her veins.　The t-shirt she'd wrapped around the wound was stained red, crusty.
　You will survive this as you've survived everything else
　We did not say there won't be pain
　There will
　But we will feel it with you
　We will stay with you forever
　Stupid, she thought. All she had in her bag were a few boxes of granola bars. A change of clothes. The map from Mr Blake's wall. All that food. Medicine. The stockpiles of weapons and fuel. All gone.
　You know it had to be done
　You wanted it gone. All gone
　The stars seemed to squirm and wriggle across the sky
　White ants crawling across a black sheet
　Faintly she heard the rustle of leaves behind her

Movement in the air   Click. click. click.   Bats navigating the night

The powdery wingbeats of the moths they hunted.

Possums in the trees

Insects picking through the craggy channels of the ironbark tree at her back

Merry leaned forward. Scratched furiously at her scalp which seemed to crawl with lice   Brushed her hair over her face. Drew a curtain on the world.

sleep

Dawn. She rose from her dreamless sleep. Picked ants from her bloodied bandage as she relieved herself by the tree. The grass around her was white   a delicate blanket of dew had settled in the night   her sneakers carved dirty tracks through it. Her clothes felt damp and heavy.

Her hand   oh God her hand   throbbing with each movement   she held it against her chest

One-handed, wincing, she extracted the map from her bag and spread it on the road.   How far had she come ?   how many days now?   what?   shadows in he corners of her eyes.   nausea creeping in   fight it   her mind would not cooperate   days slid out of alignment   the voices told her to forget   frosted the window to the past   You don't need to find her

You need to move on

'Shut up,' she whispered. 'Just shut up.' Her finger traced the markings on the map in short, trembling movements. The roads seemed to wiggle and criss-cross in ways that didnt make sense. But the next black spot was not far.   She could make it there by noon. Merry repacked the bag and carefully slid her arm through the strap, to avoid triggering another explosion of pain in her hand.

Her sneakers crunched on the dirt road

Crunch   crunch   crunch

The road was mostly deserted. Sometimes a car in the ditch— abandoned.   Sometimes a dead dog or kangaroo   eviscerated and reconstructed into an abstract form.   but mostly   nothing. She walked   how long?   until the pink silk between the morning clouds had slipped away and the sun shrank to a small white spot burning behind her right ear.

A sign appeared beside her.

Jamestown.

She licked her lips   felt them cracked and bleeding   her stomach growled

There were more empty cars here   placed deliberately to block the road   Mr Blake's handiwork. As were the crudely painted   warnings on every outward-facing sign. 'Go Away' 'Trespassers Will Be Shot!' 'Welcome to Jamestown' had become 'Fuck Off and Die!'

She sidled between the cars, heading for the centre of town litter blew through the streets   in each store window out of the corners of her eyes she saw people   faces   pale   blank watching her   but always gone when she turned to look

Her eyes flickered closed then open   the sensation of falling a voice calling   her own voice muttering   calling out to the ghosts of the town   would they let her pass through in peace?

As she was passing the pub on the corner, she saw someone. standing by the large front windows   shaded by the second storey balcony   his back to her   his head lolled to one side resting on the glass   even from behind she could see his jaw moving ceaselessly.

Calmly, she lowered her bag to the ground and pulled out the rifle. checked it was loaded checked the safety held her injured hand across her body rested the barrel on her forearm maneuvered it in such as way as to dull the roar of pain in her hand.

Merry squinted down the sights, watching the grinner

Merry, let us do this. It's why we're here. It's why you can't ever let us go. Merry—

She squeezed the trigger, shocking the voices into silence as the crack echoed off the surrounding buildings.

The grinner's head snapped forward, slamming into the window and shattering the pane. As it slumped to the ground, large shards of glass fell from the gaping hole and cascaded over the body.

Vibrations roared up and down her arm like lights on a carnival ride. Merry swayed, but kept the rifle trained on the prone figure for several minutes, listening to her breath, before returning the rifle to her bag.

Gradually, the buzz of distant voices crept back in. A swarm it was of wasps. As she passed the body, the buzzing grew she tried to ignore the wasps that teemed over the grinner. They're not real wriggling free of the bloody bullet hole in its head. Dozens of them their tiny mandibles chattering at her. Laughing

There was no movement except the birds and the wasps that crawled forth from every drain every car's exhaust pipe every crack in the footpath. She flinched away as they crawled towards her slapped herself in the side of the head.

'Stupid. They're not real. They can't hurt you.'

But her heart thudded against her chest ready to burst. Something prickled her wrist a wasp crawled out of her sleeve flicked its wings at her

We don't want to hurt you, Merry

But you must know by now.

We CAN

'Leave me alone!' She waved her hand frantically, staggered into the street. She could feel them under her clothes now. In her hair. Merry closed her eyes, willing them away. She had to have some control left.

They're not real they're not real you're losing your mind

Tiny stingers gouged into her skin her hand her neck her back her legs while in her head the voices laughed. She hugged her arms around herself and screamed a scream to wake the dead. a scream distorted and all things at once now a frightened child now an enraged animal now a blast of thunder from above now a bell shrill ringing now Claire's voice.

The scream brought her to her knees where she slumped, shuddering in the street. How long? Maybe an hour? Maybe just a second. It was the smell that roused her at last. Faint at first quickly overpowering sour burnt diseased.

There in the middle of the road ahead. Little more than a stone's throw away a dark monstrous multi-limbed shape blackened at the bottom teeming with flies.

The smell of the corpses baking in the sun for weeks was horrendous. She couldn't get near it. Turned away and dug through her bag found a thick tube sock to cover her nose and mouth returned to the pile of bodies, eyes watering.

Slowly she circled, checking each face each limb each piece

of clothing for something she recognised. Some were so disfigured by decay that several times she thought she'd found her sister. She'd lean closer   peer distrustfully into their wrinkled eyes, brush the cobwebs of hair from their forehead. She couldn't trust the colour of those eyes, the shapes of those noses which had been distorted and stretched under the sun, but the teeth couldn't lie. Always the teeth were wrong. Another few circuits to make sure, but she knew. Claire wasn't here.

Merry withdrew to the edge of the street and hunched over her map. There were two more black spots. Two more piles   two more towns two more chances. But they were so far away.

Merry

She looked up. The concrete was almost white under the sun. Bright, but the world was so cold. Everything was cold but the hot coals in her hand. Her hand.   She stared at the concrete beside the pile. Something was wrong with it.   Blood.   A hand print. The dead above it on that side were splayed out a little further than the rest   as though   something had crawled out. She cocked her head   drew her shoulders in and shuffled down the street.

Merry

The wind blew through from the north carrying the scent of death with it, and so she headed west round a bend in the road across a weed filled empty lot   past a run down petrol station where the two rusty fuel pumps quietly displayed their 'empty' tags.   The wasps danced briefly over the pumps, then buzzed off up the street towards a house with a wide overgrown front garden. Some vegetables still grew   lettuces, mostly destroyed by snails but still clinging to life   limp tomato plants robbed of all their fruit, but now beginning to flower.

Merry

Something moved beyond the corner of the house down the end of the driveway. A startled cat, maybe. But no. Bigger.

Merry lowered her bag to the ground and drew out the rifle. Wasps flitted angrily through the garden trying to drive her back a few plunged their stingers into her hand but she stepped forward around the corner. There in the shadows beyond the bins hunched a figure shivering a tangle of long blonde hair a field hockey jersey.

'Oh, God...'

Run, Merry

Before it's too late. Run!

'No.' She raised the rifle as the figure slowly stood and turned to face her.

Merry choked on a sob as Claire emerged from behind the bins, her body shifting awkwardly. She felt as though she'd been winded impossible to breathe.

Claire's eyes were bloodied vacant Her throat was purple and brown with bruises and one side of her jaw was torn open swollen Her mouth moved as though trying to speak

'Claire...' The rifle swayed in her grip unbearably heavy her arms were lead. The wasps swarmed her swarmed Claire. But even their stings couldn't move her.

Merry. Let us...

Please They sounded afraid You're not strong enough

Not strong enough.

Claire staggered closer

Merry shook her head slowly. 'You're wrong.' She lowered the rifle. Flung it as far from her as she could. 'I am strong enough.'

She fell to her knees and arced her face up to the sky. 'I'm here, Claire.' A deep breath filled her lungs and tears spilled from her eyes. Claire's feet scraped through the gravel until they struck Merry's knees and then her sister was upon her.   Fingers grasping at her arms and face. Rasping breaths washing over her.

Merry

Smile

Smile and be Merry

His hand was warm and strong, just as she remembered, and he pulled her easily from beneath the heavy body, lifting her into his arms. The safest place she'd ever known.

She looked back at Mr Blake. He'd rolled partly on his side now and seemed to be bouncing up and down slightly. He was resting on a tight metal string that ran across the path, just above the ground. That must have been what she'd tripped on. It flashed at her under the bright lights with each bounce. Tiny bells tied along its length jingled softly, and somewhere further away she heard rattling cans. Mr Blake had a long stick coming out of one eye, and the stick had little orange feathers on its end. So much of what she was seeing didn't make sense to her, so she just turned away and let Uncle Bear carry her into the light.

'How on earth did you get out here?' Bear mumbled as he carried her away. His voice sounded different somehow.

They passed through the light, and a doorway appeared ahead of her, lit faintly by a flickering glow.

'Just great. This is the last thing I need,' Bear grumbled.

Zoey looked up at him, suddenly afraid again. She saw that while his eyes were the same, and his hair was the right colour, his beard wasn't as bushy as it should be. His tummy wasn't nearly as big. And he seemed taller. Over one shoulder he carried a long, curved stick. It looked a bit like Robin Hood's bow, but it had little wheels on each end, and three strings instead of one. His clothes were different, too. His black jacket and t-shirt had become a thick, red and black criss-cross shirt. What had happened to him?

She looked around again. The bright light wasn't coming from the sky, like she'd thought, but from two big spotlights sitting on the roof of the house.

He took her inside, kicked the door closed behind him, and set her on the floor.

'Your neck,' he said, kneeling down in front of her. 'Did he bite you? Are you bleeding?'

Zoey brushed her wild hair out of her face and felt her neck. It was sore to touch. He leaned close and looked at her, frowning.

'Didn't break the skin,' he said at last. 'Must've just fallen on you. Already got a nice bruise coming.'

He gave a little nod, then stood up and started walking around the room, peering out the windows while he talked to himself.

'Where there's one, there's usually more...' he muttered. 'Too late to check all the traps tonight...should I leave the lights on? Nah, the generator's low on juice already, and it might just lead 'em here...better to sit tight and listen for the bells...'

Zoey stood in the doorway, her head spinning and her legs shaking from exhaustion, and looked around. She counted five flickering candles that seemed to make more shadows than light. The walls and ceiling looked like they were made out of trees, with the bark still on them. A large wooden table sat by the nearby window, a single chair beside it, and on the opposite side of the room, a stone fireplace with chopped logs either side and a small fire. She could feel the heat from it slowly wrapping around her like a warm hug and almost fell asleep standing up.

The walls were plain apart from a dartboard, and a few books and photos above the fireplace.

At the back of the room there was a rough-looking kitchen, with wooden cabinets and a row of black pots and pans on hooks, and a block of very large knives. Behind the kitchen, a dark corridor hid the rest of the house. The smells left behind from his dinner—some sort of soup, or stew maybe?—were so good they almost made her faint.

Almost-Uncle Bear flipped a large switch by the door, and the lights outside went dark. After looking out the window for a little while longer, he set his bow down on the table and turned back to her.

'Do you talk?' he asked.

She was too scared and confused to answer, so she just looked at the floor.

He rubbed his neck with one hand. 'Great.'

She tried her best to understand what was happening. She thought all the pieces were there in her head, but somehow they weren't fitting. Like when Daddy broke Mummy's favourite vase, and the next day when he tried to glue it back together, it somehow turned into a lopsided bowl. She thought of the last thing Uncle Bear had said to her. 'When you get to the house, there'll be a man there…give him this. He'll look after you now.'

So this wasn't Uncle Bear. This was the house. This was the man she was supposed to find. Tears came to her eyes, and her shoulders shook as she cried silently. Of course, it couldn't be Uncle Bear.

'Ah, geez, look, don't do that. Come on...'

She took the folded piece of paper from her pocket and looked at it through blurry eyes. Until now, she'd been too afraid to even see what it was. As she wiped the tears onto the back of her arm, she saw it was the photo Uncle Bear had shown her when they first met. There he was. And Mummy, too. Both smiling at her. Between them, with his face hidden under the white crease down the middle, was another man. She looked up at Not-Uncle Bear and handed him the photo.

His eyes widened as he looked at it, and he glanced back to her. 'How...?'

He turned it over and started reading the writing on the back. Zoey watched his face. Not-Uncle Bear closed his eyes and let out a deep sigh. Tears squeezed out and streaked down his cheeks where they disappeared into his beard. He opened his eyes and kept reading, his face going through every expression that a face could make. He even chuckled a couple of times, and when he did Zoey was reminded of Uncle Bear more than ever. At last he looked at her again, his eyes full of the same pain that lived in her now.

'So you're Zoey,' he said.

She nodded.

He held up the photo and looked like he was going to say something, but just shook his head. His finger traced over the people in the photo. 'I don't know how I didn't see it. You look just like Lisa. I guess that makes me your Uncle Jay.'

He gave her half a smile, wiped the tears from his cheeks, ran his hand through his hair. Uncle Jay? Zoey remembered Bear talking about his brother. The older brother that gave him the bear drawing on his arm. She looked at Uncle Jay's arm. Where Uncle Bear had a teddy bear, Jay had a drawing of what looked like a kangaroo. He saw her looking at it.

'Ah yeah, this.' A smile came into his eyes as he rolled up the sleeve and stared at his arm. 'A present from my little brother. Funny story, he tried to do it with a sewing needle and a broken bic pen. But I got him back. I'll tell you about it some day.' He met Zoey's eyes for a moment. 'Look at ya, you can barely stand. You look like you've been through hell. Come on, we'd better find you somewhere to sleep.'

He led her down a short passage to a dark room at the end. She stayed in the doorway, swaying, until he lit the candle, and another plain, wooden room appeared, this one filled with an enormous bed.

'You can take my bed. I won't be sleeping tonight.' He picked up a long gun that was standing beside the bed, a smaller one from under the pillow, and a third from the closet. 'I think that's all of them...oh, wait.' He reached behind the headboard and pulled out a knife the size of her arm.

Zoey wobbled forward and put a hand on the blanket. It was cool and scratchy, but softer than anything she'd felt in a long time. She climbed onto the foot of the bed and crawled her way down to the pillows. Uncle Jay stood, back against the wall, his arms full of guns, looking as though he'd lost something. Then he took out the photo again, gave it one last look, and set it on the bedside table, propped up so she could see it.

As she lay down, her eyes closed by themselves, like she was one of those sleeping baby dolls with the long eyelashes. She didn't think she could ever open them again. She heard Uncle Jay step up beside the bed, and blow out the candle, and for a moment she thought she sensed his hand hovering over her head, about to brush the hair from her forehead. When he spoke, though, his voice came from the doorway.

'Goodnight, Zoey.'

'There you are. I've been looking all over.'

Claire brushed aside their father's hanging shirts and crouched beside Merry in the dark closet. She'd taken down her dad's favourite navy blue jumper, pulled it on, and tucked her knees up inside it. At eight years old, and small for her age, it reached her toes with room to spare. She sniffed and wiped her eyes with one of the drooping sleeves.

'I don't want to go back out there,' Merry whispered, nodding towards the living room where a dozen sombre conversations rumbled through the walls. 'I know Mum said it was important, but...All these people keep apologising to me, as if saying it will make everything better, and telling me what a good man he was, but I don't know them, and I don't think they really knew him.'

'I know,' Claire said, stepping over a row of Mum's shoes and sitting opposite her. 'And the smell of Auntie Gwen's casserole was making me want to barf.'

Merry grinned weakly. 'She made me have some. It tasted like cat food.'

Claire clutched her stomach and pretended to vomit into Mum's slipper. 'I think that's her secret. She makes everyone so sick they barf up everything they just ate, then she whips out a casserole dish, catches the barf in it, and hey presto! another casserole ready to go.'

They both laughed at that, but quickly shushed each other when the hall light came on and they heard Mrs Selner's voice.

'...if there's anything I can do. I mean that. Anything at all. You know what? I've got some rhubarb that needs eating. I'll make you a crumble.'

'Oh, thank you, Norma. But there's really no need—'

'It's no trouble, dear. That's what neighbours do.' She clucked her tongue. 'I think you're just so brave. I don't know how I'd go on if something happened to my Bob. You're such a trooper, I mean that. And those girls of yours, oh the poor darlings. So brave, the lot of you.'

'Yes...well...'

'Goodbye, dear. My condolences once again. Remember, anything at all I can do, just call. Anything at all.'

The front door clicked shut and they heard their mother sigh deeply. They looked at each other, saying nothing for several minutes, until they heard her head slowly back to the living room.

'It isn't fair,' Merry whispered. 'I just want him back.' She tried to breathe in her father's smell from the jumper, but it seemed to fade so quickly. What if she forgot it forever?

Claire said nothing, but nudged her with her foot.

'You're not allowed to die,' Merry said. 'Not ever, okay? Not you, or Mum, or the twins, or anyone else, okay?'

Claire played with the buckle on a pair of sandals. 'Everybody dies, Merry. In the end, everybody dies.'

* * *

Merry braced herself for the pain. Claire had pinned her down was gasping   rasping   it sounded like   crying.

'Me...rry.'

Her hands cupped Merry's cheeks, touched her forehead her hair.

'Is...it...you?' Claire's voice was barely recognisable   a dusty whisper   stepped on and crushed.

Merry opened her eyes and gazed into her sister's. They were bloodshot   frightened   looking off to one side without seeing but alive.

She couldn't understand.   Was she dead?   Were they both dead now?

'You...found me...I knew...you would.'

'Claire? How?... Are...are you real?' Merry reached out with her good hand and touched her sister's cheek. It was cool, but not at all like the grinners. Their skin was cold, detached but clingy, like the film over cold custard. Claire flinched a little, then smiled, clutching at Merry's hand.

'But how? I don't understand. He killed you. I was so sure you were dead.'

'He...tried...choked   me...thought   I   was...dead.   What a...pansy!...dumped me...in a hurry...'

As she spoke she gestured weakly with her hands, her eyes darted side to side, remembering. 'I...woke up under...dead people...crawled out...couldn't see...still can't really...just...a little...hid...in here from...the grinners...but I...didn't know where—' A coughing fit cut her off. Even her coughs sounded weak, shallow.

'Where is—' cough 'Where...is...' Claire held a shaking finger under her nose like a moustache.

'Blake?'

Claire nodded.

'Dead.'

'How?'

'I ran over him in his own car.'

'You?...' Claire sat back, resting on her hands, her unseeing eyes tilting up to the sky as she rocked slightly to one side. She rolled off Merry and lay on the ground beside her. Sighed. 'Prick...deserved it. Wish...I could've...seen it.'

Merry squeezed her eyes shut, felt tears trickling down her cheeks. A ringing filled her ears and she was suddenly terrified to open her eyes again. Terrified that Claire would be gone. That this was just another cruel joke her mind had played on her. But then she felt Claire's weight shift, heard her cough again softly. She realised she was sobbing uncontrollably, squeezing her sister's hand so tight that she could feel the blood pulsing inside it. With that touch, that moment, that sensation of life, of love, something she'd long since given up on, the doubting, paranoid, hurtful voices were reduced to nothingness, her fear of Blake, which had haunted her even after his death, abated, her memories of that awful dark room where he'd raped her, all faded to white, because in that moment, she felt whole again.

Twelve years later

Merry trod silently through the long grass, following the haphazard footprints in the mud. Even the birds didn't hear her coming, chattering happily as she passed beneath them. It was barefoot, as she was—she could tell that from the tracks—and moving apparently directionless, perhaps led through the brush by a wallaby, or a—a wombat.

Yes, there were the remains. A red and white mound covered in leaves and dirt. Blood and entrails decorated the surrounding grass and branches. White wasps crawled over the dead animal's exposed ribcage, filled the trees above her with their buzzing, whispered their judgements and threats. She slapped her head a few times and most of the wasps faded, but the whispers persisted.

...better off alone...

...kill them all...

...can't trust them...

Focus   focus   there's still meat left on the carcass, so the grinner must be... yes   still here   good morning, sunshine

The grinner was facing her, but its attention was focused on a pair of blackbirds in the branches above. The lipless smile that had once terrified her no longer seemed like the face of evil, but rather that of a simpleton. He was a fresh one, not from the original outbreak, which meant he'd be faster, stronger, even if he had the appearance of a man in his sixties.

Moving slowly, Merry took hold of the rifle that was slung over her back, lifted the strap over her head and placed the weapon gently on the ground. She'd shot three rabbits that morning, which were now tied together by the feet and hanging from her belt. She set them down beside the rifle.

As the grinner's teeth chattered open and closed, the voices in her head almost seemed to come from him. White wasps spilled from his mouth and swarmed down his chest.

We're coming for you, Merry

We watch you when you're sleeping

We could kill you whenever we choose, and there's nothing you can do to stop us

Merry slapped at her temples, and the grinner's head swivelled toward the sound.

'Gah...hah...hah...' it gasped.

Merry stood, baring her teeth in a grin of her own. The grinner threw itself towards her, kicking up clumps of leaves and grass as it ran. Merry's hand went to her belt as she leapt from the tall grass, slipping a knife out with two fingers and flipping it through the air. It sank deep into the grinner's throat, causing it to stagger and flail for a moment—enough time for Merry to drop to the ground and slide under its grasp. A second knife was already in her hand and with a quick slash she cut through the tendons at the back of its ankles. She heard two wet snaps, saw the tendons ripple under the skin, then it toppled backward, almost landing on her.

From another loop on her belt, she produced an iron spike. Once a pin that held together railway track, she'd filed it to a jagged point. Using all her strength, she drove the spike through the grinner's eye, then stamped on the flattened end to break through the back of its skull.

She savoured the violent twitches of its limbs that gradually subsided, the blood that bubbled from the hole in its eye, even the sickly tang of its blood in the air, while wasps continued to pour out of its mouth, flickering in and out of existence, moving the grinner's jaw slowly up and down.

One day you will lie where we lie
You will grin as we do
Laugh as we laugh
Bleed as we bleed

She placed one foot on the grinner's neck, reached down and yanked the spike free, wiped it on the grass and slid it back into place on her belt, breathing deeply as the sounds and smells of the bush returned to her.

Moments later, Merry became aware of another presence. Someone moving silently through the long grass, but not so silent as to escape the notice of the birds, and a hush fell over the bush. She positioned herself behind a tree, took another knife from her belt. The intruder stopped by the fallen grinner, sighed softly—that voice—she edged out of cover, knife raised and ready.

Mr Blake stood in the small clearing, a dry smile on his lips. His shirt and white pants were crisply ironed and spotless, his hair and moustache neatly combed, a sharp contrast to her scruffily shaved head, torn clothes, and skin marked with blood and countless scars.

He said nothing, but took a few slow steps forward. Her eyes widened with fear as a cloud of wasps rose up behind him, encircling him—Impossible—her mind snapped and she shouted, brandishing the knife.

'Stay away from me!'

He's found you

He's come back for you. You belong to him, don't you remember? You'll never be free

Merry growled, leaping forward.

Blake stepped back, bringing his hands up in defence. 'Mum, stop! It's me!'

Merry's legs gave out and she fell at his feet, dropping the knife. The wasps swarmed over Blake, concealing his face and clothes, trailing ribbons of flesh, morphing his features into those of a boy.

'I...I...thought...' Merry sobbed, realising what she'd almost done. 'Jasper...I'm so sorry.'

He knelt. 'They're back, aren't they, Mum?'

She nodded, unable to look at him, afraid of what she might see. Twelve years old, thin, softly spoken but incredibly bright, he was becoming so much like his father. Too much. The thought terrified her more than anything she'd faced in her life.

He must die

Let us slit his throat for you.

Kill him now. Painless. While he's still innocent

You know what his father was. What he will become—

Merry slapped at her temples.

'They...tell me to do things. Terrible things. I'm afraid...that one day...'

He took her cheeks in his hands, forcing her to look at him.

'I'm not afraid, Mum. I know you'd never hurt me.'

She stared into his eyes. Those bright, grey, beautiful eyes. Her whole world.

We're the whole world now, Meredith. You and I. I'm your saviour, your father, your lover, your only friend. Me! Your life belongs to me...

She twisted out of his hands and stood quickly. 'I have to go away for a while.'

Jasper stayed kneeling. He didn't look at her.

'Just...until I can silence them. I can beat them. I know it. And then I'll come back. I need you to look after your aunt Claire until then. Can you do that?'

He said nothing.

He hates you. He doesn't want you back. They're better off without you

Merry collected her rifle, knives and the dead rabbits while Jasper remained crouched, twirling a dead leaf between two fingers.

'Come on,' she said. 'I'll walk back with you.'

The first twelve months after she'd found Claire had been hell. It quickly became apparent that the stump of her severed finger was infected. The fever that followed meshed nightmare and reality together; by night she would wake to find all of it had been a terrible dream. She'd be back in her house listening to the twins fighting over a toy, and her mum in the kitchen making pancakes for breakfast. Then she'd wake again, on a thin foam mattress in the back of a van beside Claire, and the life she'd once had would be ripped from her all over again. Her days were haunted by visions and paranoia, giant insects crawling above her as she lay, dropping into her screaming mouth.

If it hadn't been for the stash of pharmaceuticals they'd found in one abandoned house, she would have died. At the very least the sepsis, which turned her blood to poison, ought to have killed the baby that grew inside her.

From then, things only got worse. The pregnancy almost destroyed her thirteen-year-old body, but somehow she survived that too, eventually giving birth in the back of the van, while grinners, drawn by her screams and the scent of fresh blood, pounded on the doors. She'd planned to hate the baby; to leave it on the side of the road for the grinners so that the world would be free of all traces of Mr Blake. She knew this made her a monster, yet she wished it anyway. But from the moment she pushed him into the world, and she heard his cry, she felt a primal urge stir inside her—more than an urge, a powerful need—to protect her baby no matter the cost. To protect him from the world and, if necessary, from herself.

Though Claire regained some of her vision, she was permanently weakened by her brush with death, tiring quickly and suffering frequent migraines.

The search for a safe haven took them north, away from the city and larger towns, where packs of grinners would chase them through the streets, making it impossible to stop. At last they found a place. An hour's drive from the nearest town through barren farmlands, a place abandoned and forgotten long before the outbreak. Encircled by an eight-foot fence, topped with razor wire, the Dish, as they called it, had once been a radio astronomy satellite facility, run, judging from the files and crates left behind, by a Chinese university. From the viewing platform they could see halfway to the ocean in one direction, and across the trees to the dunes of Yumbarra in the other. The dish itself was close to fifty metres in diameter, large enough to swallow the modestly sized house beside it, its once porcelain white face now darkened by mould and streaks of rust.

Home.

When they reached the gate, Jasper quickly unlocked it and stalked off ahead, climbing the steps to the Dish's control room and disappearing inside. She found Claire in their makeshift kitchen at the base of the Dish. Partly buried underground, the wide, empty room was the coolest part of the structure, and had once housed the computer servers. They'd ripped out as much of the machinery as they could and filled the space with kitchen equipment scavenged from nearby farms. As she entered, Claire turned, and Merry noticed her eyes searching the darkness for a moment before eventually settling on her.

'Didn't think you'd be back.'

Merry tossed the rabbits onto a stainless steel counter. 'I always come back.'

'You know what I mean. Your...' Claire fluttered her fingers by her temple. 'demons, or whatever. I know they're getting worse.'

Merry said nothing.

'Yeah, I figured. Make sure you say a proper goodbye to Jasper this time. I know he's a tough kid, but when you go, it's harder on him than you think.' Claire took a rolled piece of canvas and unrolled it across the counter, exposing a row of butcher's blades. Moving by touch rather than sight, she slid the heaviest knife out and positioned the first rabbit on the block in front of her.

Claire had suffered just as much as she had at the hands of Mr Blake, but her trauma took the form of nightmares. She'd never really understood Merry's demons.

'I think he hates me.'

Claire swung the blade down, decapitating the rabbit with one quick blow. She then produced a much smaller knife from the canvas roll and proceeded to make a series of precise cuts along the animal's torso and limbs.

'You nob. He doesn't hate you. Only you hate you.'

'He should. If he knew the things that go through my head...' She picked at her thumbnail that was already bitten down to a nub and bleeding. 'That's why I have to go...'

'I know. I get it. We go through this every time. Just...' Claire's bloodshot eyes searched the countertop.

'Don't worry, this will be the last time,' Merry said, quietly. It has to be 'One hundred days. That's all I need. I'll find a way to get rid of them for good. I'll come back alone...or I won't come back at all.'

Claire grimaced slightly as she peeled back the rabbit's skin. When she was done, she laid her palms flat on the counter. The blood pooling there seemed to glow red as light reflected off the metal surface beneath it. She shook her head. 'He's been asking about his father again, you know. What am I supposed to tell him if...'

Merry placed a hand on her sister's. 'He can never know. If I'm not back...just make something up. Anything. But he can never know what his father was.'

Claire nodded. 'A hundred days, then.'

Merry looked back only once. She could just make out the silhouette of Jasper, perched on the roof near the top of the dish.

Wringing her hands, she turned sharply away. The note she'd

left on his pillow was a poor goodbye, but she knew that if she had to look into his eyes again, her resolve would crack. She had to stay strong—for him, and so she fought the urge to look back again.

The knives and metal spikes clinked together softly as she walked. In her pocket, the Polaroid picture she carried weighed more heavily on her than the rifle and the fifteen kilograms of supplies on her back. She stroked one of the worn edges through her pocket.

Annabelle appeared and fell in step beside her. 'What are you hoping to find? You burnt it all to the ground. What's left for you there.'

When Merry ignored her, Annabelle gave a little laugh. 'Oh, Merry. You're crazier than even you realise.'

You'll never get rid of us

You'll never see them again

Merry stopped and squeezed her eyes shut, covered her ears until the sound of blood rushing through her veins drowned out everything else. When she opened her eyes, she was alone on the sandy, abandoned road.

'There has to be a way.'

As the sun set and the shadows lengthened and moved to block her path, Merry shifted the weight of her backpack and walked forward to meet them.

Zoey opened her eyes and blinked away the nightmares. Sunlight snuck around the simple cloth curtains, turning the wooden ceiling a golden brown. The world outside was already awake. Magpies sang their warbling songs despite the heckling squawks of the galahs and cockatoos. Above them all, she heard laughter— a lone kookaburra sharing a joke with anyone that would listen. In the distance, there was the familiar rumble of galloping hooves and nickering of the horses.

She sat up and stretched. 'Mornin', everyone,' she said, turning to the photo of her mum and uncles beside the bed. Behind it were three small wooden animals: a rabbit, a kangaroo, and a bear. Jay had carved them for her in the weeks after she'd arrived. She didn't remember much about that time, but he told her that it had been a full month before she'd even said a word to him. 'And look at you now,' he'd joke, 'I can't get you to shut up.'

As she swung her legs out from under the covers onto the cold floor, she noticed something. A package by the door, wrapped in brown paper, about as tall as her leg.

'No way,' she cried, flinging the covers aside and skipping across the room to it.

A loop of twine around the middle held a little card.

Happy 15th Birthday, Zoey!

You'll find the arrows by the river. Meet me there for practice after chores.

Jay.

She tore off the paper and held up the beautifully carved bow. It was perfectly symmetrical, bending in a smooth arc that curved back on itself slightly at either end. She held it up to her face and breathed it in. It had the sweet smell of newly treated wood. The pale wood of the bow was accented with a dark walnut grip.

The string, which was only secured at one end, was some sort of dark grey, plasticky fibre.

'Uncle Jay, you're the best!' she said to the empty room.

Her eyes wandered back to the photo beside the bed, and she felt a sudden need to hold it again. To thank Uncle Bear for his gift, too. She crossed the room, still holding her bow, and picked up the photo. It was yellowed now, and fading after years of facing the morning sun, but her Uncle Bear was still there. The image in the photograph, probably taken ten years before she'd met him, had replaced the version from her memory. She wished she could remember more from their short time together, but she remembered he'd saved her more than once.

The writing on the back was cramped and barely decipherable, overlapping in places, but she'd read it so many times now that it was imprinted on her memory.

Jay (I hope to God it's you reading this),

The little girl's name is Zoey. Lisa's daughter. By time you get this I'll be dead. There's a bullet in my gut that'll finish me soon. I know it's too late cos I can hardly feel it anymore. Now quit your blubbering and man up brother! It's up to you to take care of her now. She's tough. Tougher than me. Tough enough to make it through this, but that don't mean she won't need your help. I know you can teach her what she needs to survive this goddam world.

So if you let anything happen to her, I swear to God I'll come back and haunt the crap outta you!

I was gonna get her a horse and teach her to ride. I know that jackass neighbour of yours O'Neil had a few. See if any of 'em are still alive and haven't bolted. Light brown, if you can, to match her hair. This little girl deserves everything you can give her. She's an angel and that's the honest truth.

Tell her I'm sorry for leaving her. And promise me you'll tell her about me and Lisa sometimes. Don't let her forget us.

One more thing before I run out of space. You'll find me in a green Toyota Corona on the road to Jamestown. If I've turned you know what to do.

Love you, bro. Hope you can forgive me for all the grief I've given you over the years. I'll owe you one next time we meet (but I don't think I'll be able to pay you back that fifty bucks...)

Bear.

The smudges of blood around the edges had turned brown and flaky with age, but some of his fingerprints survived. She touched them lightly with her own fingertips, then folded the photo and slipped it into her pocket. Even after all these years, he still went everywhere with her.

They had found him just where he'd said. Uncle Jay made Zoey wait in the truck while he wrapped his brother in a sheet, but when they got back, she'd helped him bury her Bear under the gum trees at the back of the house. Sometimes she'd pluck a leaf from one of those trees, and sit in their shade, and try to play something for him, or simply talk or read him her latest poem.

Zoey stood up, strapped her hunting knife to her belt—Jay made her promise she'd never leave the house without it—and started on her chores. She weeded the vegetable garden, picked tomatoes, apples and lemons, rotated the trays in the smoke-house where they dried fruits. She threw down some feed for the chickens and checked the traps surrounding the house. There was a rabbit in one, which she quickly skinned, gutted, cleaned, and took back to the kitchen where she hung it up in the cold box under the floor for dinner.

It was midday before she'd finished bringing in the last of the firewood Uncle Jay had chopped that morning. Sweat was beading on her temples and her arms were burning with exhaustion, but with the day's chores finished at last, she was free. She grabbed her new bow from the table, and a couple of apples from the bowl, and headed outside.

In the fenced clearing at the back of the house, she found Pony waiting for her with his head stretched over the railing, nodding at her impatiently. She had to smile every time she said his name. Pony. That's what happens when you let a four-year-old name her own horse.

She fed him one apple, and bit into the other. Then she saddled her horse, climbed onto the fence, and vaulted onto his back. He snorted and tossed his head as she landed, but she knew it didn't hurt him. Still, she whispered an apology in his ear and stroked the coarse hair on his neck to calm him.

Together they turned and crossed the clearing at a canter. She leaned forward and pushed herself up with her legs, driving him into a gallop, eager to feel the wind in her hair. The sounds of Pony's heavy breaths and thundering hooves filled her ears, and she scrunched her eyes closed for a moment as she flew across the grass.

As she swayed and bounced on Pony's back, and the wind rushed past her ears, she saw the stars from that night in her memory. She saw Uncle Bear's face, the pain and determination set in his eyes as he carried her small, sleeping body from the car that night. She saw the full extent of his sacrifice now. His final gift to her that she could never repay. The image of him came to her nearly every night when she closed her eyes, sometimes leaving her so racked with sorrow and guilt that she would cry into her pillow until she couldn't breathe. She almost preferred the nights when instead she'd see the lipless grin of Mr Blake as he climbed out of the darkness towards her, and she'd scream for her Uncle Jay.

Tears spilled from her eyes and were immediately whipped away by the wind. She opened her eyes again and spoke the words of a dead poet from one of Jay's books. Starting in a broken whisper, her voice grew stronger with each line, until she was all but screaming.

'There are folk long dead, and our hearts would sicken—
We would grieve for them with a bitter pain,
If the past could live and the dead could quicken,
We then might turn to that life again.
But on lonely nights we would hear them calling,
We should hear their steps on the pathways falling,
We should loathe the life with a hate appalling
In our lonely rides by the ridge and plain.
In the silent fields is a scent of clover,

And the distant roar of the town is dead,
And I hear once more now the storm is over,
Now the past is buried, now the tears are shed.
We all ride alone, by our instincts guided,
And for no man or child is fate decided.
No griefs appointed, nor joys contrived.
Just a mighty power, with one purpose — Survive.'

The End

About the author

J P Townley lives with his wife and two daughters on a remote mountaintop in South Australia — a location chosen not only for its remarkable beauty and friendly community, but also its survivability in the event of a zombie outbreak.

The Girls Left Behind is his debut horror novel.

jptownleyauthor.com

Notes and Acknowledgements

The 'dead poet' mentioned in the final passage of this book is, of course, the great Australian poet, Banjo Patterson, and the poem Zoey recites is based on his *Black Swans*. Zoey has re-written the final verse to better fit this story—I hope Banjo fans see this as the tribute it's intended to be and not as a sacrilege.

This book would not have been possible without the incredible support and encouragement of my wife, Shae—my first reader, idea-bouncer and muse.

Nor could I have written this without my daughters, Ember and Jade. Their arrival triggered in me not only a profound sense of love and joy, but also a primal fear, the exploration of which led me to this story. They also inspired more than one of Zoey's best lines, so to anyone who thinks Zoey's speech or actions are too advanced for her age: I have video evidence to back me up.

To the thousands of beta readers who discovered the early versions of Zoey and Merry's stories on Wattpad—you have my endless gratitude. Your comments of encouragement and belief in this story's potential helped me push through more than one difficult chapter. Without you, this book may never have found its ending.

Also thanks to my writer and reader friends for their invaluable feedback and inspiration. The Melbourne Sci-Fi and Fantasy Writer's group (especially Kat Clay and Tracy M Joyce), my Wattpadres (especially Vic James and Tim Johnson), Ian Harrison and the Australasian Horror Writers Association.

Last, but certainly not least, thanks to my parents, Phil and Faye Townley, for their unfailing support and for instilling in me a love of books and the magic of stories.

Notes and Acknowledgements

www.ingramcontent.com/pod-product-compliance
Lightning Source LLC
Chambersburg PA
CBHW010259100726
47904CB00011B/2670